John R. Gordon lives and works in London. His previous novels are *Black Butterflies* and *Skin Deep*, both published by Gay Men's Press. In 1992 he wrote and directed the play *Wheels Of Steel* at the Gate Theatre, and in 1997 he received a New London Writers' Award. He also paints, cartoons and writes afrocentric erotica under a variety of pseudonyms in his spare time, and he is a student of Vodou.

To Matt,
a copy of my latest,

WARRIORS & OUTLAWS

John R. Gordon

[signature]

– which I hope
you'll enjoy!

John 01

GAY MEN'S PRESS

First published 2001 by Millivres Ltd,
part of the Millivres Prowler Group,
Worldwide House, 116-134 Bayham St, London NW1 0BA

World Copyright © 2001 John R. Gordon

John R. Gordon has asserted his right to be identified as the author of this work
in accordance with the Copyright, Designs and Patents Act 1988

A CIP catalogue record for this book is available
from the British Library

ISBN 1 902852 26 5

Distributed in Europe by Central Books,
99 Wallis Rd, London E9 5LN

Distributed in North America by Consortium,
1045 Westgate Drive, St.Paul, MN 55114-1065

Distributed in Australia by Bulldog Books,
P O Box 300, Beaconsfield, NSW 2014

Printed and bound in the EU by WSOY, Juva, Finland

To my mother Isabel, to Rikki, Graeme and Andy: Thank you. I couldn't have done it without you.

'Best advice I ever got was from an old friend of mine, a black friend, who said you have got to go the way your blood beats. If you don't live the only life you have, you won't have some other life, you won't live any life at all. That's the only advice you can give anybody. And it's not advice, it's an observation.
                                                    – *James Baldwin*

FLOYD

I heave so violently I can taste blood in my mouth, man. The iron bitterness makes me heave again and a shudder runs the length of me body. Christ Christ *Christ*. For a second I'm blind but it's only the night. I want to just stay here for a minute hiding in the dark but I can still hear the sirens wailing behind me so I drag myself up off me hands and knees and run but again I just want to get away but I feel like even if I'm not caught now the dead body will be pulled towards me like my shadow as the sun goes up. Until it's right there under me feet and when I close me eyes inside me too.

In the streets and alleys on the way back home the bitter smell of blood and bile clings to me like sin.

I get home and the baby's crying. Christ, where's Astrid, that's what I want to know, man. Bitch probably still out clubbing. No, she ain't a bitch. She's alright.

She's better than I am, fuck knows. Yeah. And deserves better. But that's part of it, you know? Part of the reason why I got to be someone. For Astrid. For Jazz. And for Zarjazz.

I go upstairs, treading quiet, into Zarjazz's little room. Pink elephants and blue mice are all over the walls like we wanted the kid to turn out a acid-head, you know what I'm sayin'? He's lying there in his cot, just sniffling now. He stops and watches me when I come in the room. I squat down on me haunches, watching him, thinking, *Shit, I did it for you, Zarjazz. So you'd be proud of your old man. So you could look up to me.* But even as I'm thinking that I know it's lies, man.

I did it for Jazz.

I want to pick up me baby boy, hold him close and whisper all me secrets to him. Like, all one man's secrets to another, father-son secrets. Only I can't touch him.

The dead body is drawing towards me like a zombie. So I stay there, squatting, watching my son float away from me, feeling the sweat run down the sides of me body and the dryness in me mouth, the taste of ash and burnt rubber, waiting.

Jazz gone crazy.

JOHNNY

The moment me did see the suit me understand it all,
yunno? It was like, this black leather ting, black leather jacket,
black leather trousers, like Jazz fancy himself Shaft or Superfly
or Bobby Seale shit. All that Black Power bullshit him chat,
man. Me did let him run him mout, right, cos me did know it
was just wank, just a excuse for some action, and is action turn
Ah on. But Jazz not a straightforward man, so him can't just go
out for what him want the way most blokes them can, money,
women or action.

Me go strictly for the ride, you know what I'm sayin'?
And if that make me striking a blow against the Shitstem or
Babylon or shit then so much the better, man. Cos one ting Jazz
say that me agree wit is, shit like that don't separate: the White
man system don't fit the Black man and so him can't keep the
law and be true to the ancestors and the Motherland, you know?
So him shoulda break it wit *wildness*, man. Wit voilence. And
wit style.

So me did see it coming, the shit with the sawn-off.

Only, Ah wish it had been me, guy, you know what I'm
sayin'? I-man finger on the trigger. Cos Jazz na have the right to
make that decision on him own. He should have told the rest a
we, so we could have make we own choice on the matter. And
my choice would've been to take a piece also.

Maybe it would've been me pull the trigger, yunno?

Ah know me na feel nothing when the pig went down
except the pressure of blood in me ears, like the blood that's
been pounding alla me life, or maybe like Jazz would say, the
blood that's been spilled these last four hundred years all rising
up like the Red Sea in one movement and focus down the barrel
of a sawn-off shotgun.

Even me does get took in by him bullshit sometimes.

Him have the dollars. Shit.

Some Mad Professor dub fill the space in me chest as Ah
skank to de riddim, de bredren and sistren around me moving

to the sound too. We all in a dream, man. A dream a Afrika. Ras Ellroy pass me a spliff and me draw deep, let meself float through the riddim. Everyting alright now, everyting falling to one level.

Escaping to the Asylum of Dub.

S'weird, man: me na see the pig at all, you know? Just the gun, just the recoil when it jerk back, fucking the night. The other heroes, Jazz as well, them did froze when him fall, but Ah did know we must get outta there directly cos the pig had already radioed for support. So me start to climb the fence. That jolt the others out of it and them start climbing too. On the other side we all split up. Me na reckon no-one get caught.

Man, me did tink when me away from there, me need a smoke.

CARL

I let the white funfur bolero-jacket fall to the black varnished floor, peel off my white latex bra-top and drop it on the white silk bedsheets. I'm wreathed by the smell of sweat and cigarettes but I'm clean: it's other men's sweat, not mine. And I didn't touch none of them. I pull off my silver platform trainers and socks, unzip my white vinyl short-shorts and step out of them. Then I go to run a bath, tip in some bath oil and bubble-bath.

I look at myself in the mirror and a night in clubland hasn't done me any favours: my soft features submerged in a puffy bowl-face (*why* did I shave off my eyebrows? – oh, for a clean, smooth foundation for a million magazine-spread styles and looks of course, for the wild fun of it), pretty features on a good day, though I think my lips are too big. (So why do I paint them scarlet and sprinkle them with glitter and outline them in black? *Defiance*, girl.) At least my skin is good: smooth and brown and perfect. I'm wearing just a pair of sheer white lace briefs, working for all elegant lines, all hair anywhere shaved away leaving skin like velvet, the dirt of masculinity decisively depilated.

But don't get me wrong. I love my dick. And I love using it.

It's not until I turn the bath off that I hear the knocking and shouting out in the corridor. It's at the flat next door, the one the black geezer with the homophobic (of course) raggamuffin friends lives in. It's two a.m. I hear someone busting his larynx shouting:

'Jazz, Jazz, man! *Jazz !*'

Which is the name of the geezer who lives there. They're all arseholes, his friends. The sort of men who think you're not black if you're not a bitch-raping-minded dickhead. One time one of them grabbed my arm in the corridor, a peel-head boy with a Africa map shaved into the back of his skull, pushed me up against the wall and called me a filthy battyboy. I looked at him bold-face, waiting for him to hit me. But then the other one, Jazz, comes out and gives him a look and he lets me go, like Jazz don't go for queerbashing, like this other guy thought he might lose face by it. Jazz gives me this look, like he thought I'd think he was my hero or something. I just turned away and slammed the door.

I was shuddering.

With white, dry rage.

He's good-looking though, Jazz. Straight-looking, with a flat-top fade with a bit of orange in it, but with good dark, smooth skin and these coal-black pretty eyes. I don't normally check for straight boys, you know? But he's hot enough to make me open a window into my currently overburdened evening schedule. Just.

I creep over to my front door, moving like a cat on the balls of my feet, and inch it open. The one who shoved me up against the wall is standing outside Jazz's door. He's good-looking too, in a thuggish sort of way. If you're a masochist. He's wearing black 501s, black Cats and a black parachute-silk bomber-jacket. His clothes look all scruffy and his shaved head is white and streaked with plaster-dust and sweat. He turns and looks at me and his eyes are red and staring.

'Fuck off, battyboy!' His voice is hoarse and cracked. I'm about to shut the door because who needs it, but he catches me with a whisper: 'Wait, man, wait.' So I don't close the door. I wait.

'The guy who lives here, man. You seen him?'

'When?' I ask.

'*Tonight*, man. Tonight.'

'No.'

He gives me the sort of look you'd expect to see on the face of a drowning man.

'Where is he, man?' he asks, but he's not speaking to me: I'm not there anymore to him.

He turns at the top of the stairs and looks back past me to Jazz's flat beyond, then turns away again and hurries down the stairs.

One time I fantasised about Jazz. He was begging to give me head and I was saying, *Only if you take this big dildo up your arse*, and I came before I imagined it going more than a few inches in.

But the funny thing is, I won't be able to sleep until I know he's got back. His sexual energy charges something in the wall of the flat, changes things so I can sleep. Strange currents passing through the pores in the concrete.

Maybe I'm just letting myself go a little crazy, girlfriend. I touch myself through the stretched lace and catch my breath.

Where is he?

JAZZ

Non-violence has never been an option to reject.

ERROL

All my life I didn't know what I wanted to do, you know what I'm sayin'? And then I thought I did, for like the first time ever. I thought I'd found the answer. But I was wrong, man. Totally. And now I'm in a fucked-up situation.

What you on about, Errol, man? Judy says, handing me her cigarette as we lay in her bed. I look at the butt, stain by her plum lipstick, draw on it.

Pull the covers up, wouldja, I say, squeezing her waist. I kiss her so I won't have to talk no more, but her mouth tastes stale. Like flowers in a vase when they rot, that after-fuck feeling. But I kiss her again, maybe cos I feel bad cos I wasn't even looking at her while I was doing it, and I saw her using her fingers after. Or maybe cos of what happened tonight: ripped cloth and skin like flowers too. Sort of. Sick flowers.

We screw again even though I don't think neither of us particularly want to, you know? She's Jazz's girl but right now that don't matter to neither of us cos he ain't here and we are and the flesh has its own shit, its own laws. The cock and cunt of it. And anyway Jazz ain't just somewhere else: he's gone onto another level. Up or down. Permanently. And Judy, she was always left behind in this life anyway, you know what I'm sayin'? Left on the dead level. So it's all over for her. And I'm here with her, so maybe it's all over for me too.

Afterwards she goes to sleep and I lie there staring at the ceiling, thinking, really thinking, for maybe the first time in me life.

JUDY

So I pretended, alright? Made out it was like Jazz on top of me, thinking of the shot pig, the gun going off, like saying *So he does fuck after all.* Like maybe he's fucking that white bitch right now. Maybe he's doing it normal, not making her do shameful shit like sucking him off *and the taste of it makes me wanna heave it's like that cheese, like swimming-pools. I let it slip out me mouth down the length of your prick, push it out on my tongue like when you're hawking snot and blow it in a hanky. But you don't notice shit like that, Jazz.*

Yeah, maybe you're doing it normal. But I doubt it.

The second time's no better than the first but it seems like something. Somehow.

Afterwards I can't sleep.

Somewhere out there, Jazz with a gun. I'm wet with sweat under the duvet, mine and Errol's and Jazz's. Furtive like, I touch one of me nipples, slip a hand downstairs, feel the stickiness of Errol's sweat and come coming out, dripping like the slow clock beside the bed, each second lasting a minute and I ain't felt a minute yet.

Somewhere out there, Jazz with a gun. For a second it's like I'm the city, my body the blackness of the streets he's walking, the hotel he might be hiding in, my womb the shelter in which he might be laying.

14

Errol farts. I'm pulled back into this little room, my little life. I smell the eggs-and-bacon and despise him.

ERROL

We was all hyper, man, we was all high. This was it, man, the real thing. We was all dressed in black which was both a practical thing and a political statement, a homage. Yeah, well, and phat also. But those ain't separate things, man. They're all part of a unity.

It's like Jazz says, yeah: why Black people stylish, and also why so many Black men into like, bodybuilding, and martial arts, is cos the slaves had nothing, right? *Could have* nothing. I mean, you didn't even have your body, you didn't even have your *balls*, man. But to the extent you had one thing, it was your body, right? And that, like, legacy, is that if you're Black you look for power through your body. Like kung fu. Like athletics. Like pumping iron. Like *dance*. Cos your style ain't going to be in your race-horses or your collection of Georgian silver or your collection of Fine Art, it's going to be the glide in your stride, right? And it ain't going to be the silken robes woven from ten thousand silkworms and embroidered by a thousand peasant women for fifty years, it's gonna be the angle you tilt your hat. The gold you can wear on your fingers, round your neck and in your mouth. And that's any hat, you know? Like the gloves they Black Power saluted with at that Olympics was just any gloves, but their style made them not just any gloves. So we was all dressed in black.

See, I wouldn't say I knew anything about politics or shit, not till I got to know Jazz. He read a lot. I mean, he didn't look like no bookworm or nothing, he just looked like one a the lads, but he knew how important books was when we didn't think they was shit. You know? At first I wouldn't ask what the books was about, and he was still quiet about things which weren't just like a laugh and shit back then. But then one day when Johnny and Floyd weren't there we got talking, I mean like about deep shit. Man, that day my life change, you know? And I realised how deep Jazz was: he had Knowledge, you know what I'm sayin'? And like the song says, Knowledge is King. He

15

was younger than all the rest of us, except for Floyd, and he'd done less, had less street knowledge. But we taught him that, yeah. And he taught us capital-K knowledge.

It was like he grew when we chatted shit, got taller. He impressed us all. Specially Floyd. We useda rib 'em about it sometimes, being queer on each other and shit. Floyd and Judy, they both useda practically worship the man. I mean, I have *respect* for the brother, but I don't feel about him like they do. Or like Floyd does; Judy, I don't know about her no more, I think she's changing. Cos of Caroline maybe. But to Floyd, Jazz's like God or Allah or the spirit of Afrika or Blackness or something else Black and ultimate.

Me, I know better: I know he's just this geezer reads a lot. Or I thought I knew better. Until last night.

Maybe Floyd's right after all, man. But then again, none of us really know, you know? Not the full story.

When things started out we was just a bunch of kids hanging out together, having a laugh, but Jazz brought something different to us, something not more serious, cos we was plenty serious, but like more grand, making us like more important people. Like, people who could do something. Me and Johnny and Floyd and Jazz. The Fantastic Four.

Back then Jazz was the quiet one, man. We'd go whistling at the ladies, joking with 'em, chatting and shit. Jazz was too shy for that. But he'd smile like he was in on it, you know what I'm sayin'? He was with us. And he proved it later on as well: he had more bottle than the rest of us put together, man; giving it to the pigs and shit, not taking nothing from no-one.

More bottle and more craziness as well, man. Not like horror-movie craziness though; the craziness of the streets, yeah. The system and all that bullshit. And something else, man, something deeper down, much deeper down inside. Like his shit with Judy and Caroline.

With them he went too far, man. Like, I don't reckon a man should let his woman walk all over him, you know? A man needs respect from his women, right? But something's going on in there that shouldn't be, man. Something rank.

Judy rolls over in her sleep. Her warm arm flops over my belly. It feels heavier than it ought to, like a dead weight. *I should've gone home*, I'm thinking. *I ought to be sleeping on me own.* Man, how come things mess up so bad? I ain't never even *seen* a sawn-off before, 'cept on CrimeWatch. Ain't never done no-one.

Christ, I must be soft after all, right?

See, when the gun went off it all fucked up, man. But still I was proud of Jazz, you know? But afraid too, like I'd got sucked into his madness. Cos when he pulled out the gun, even before he pulled the trigger, everything changed, you know? What I felt was, we all became men.

Now I'm thinking, do I want to be a man?

For a second I wish Judy'd wake up cos I wanna talk. Or something. But we probably just screw again and that just makes me feel emptier every time. And Judy, it don't make her no fuller. So I let her sleep. And I just lie there, dead still, wondering where the fuck are Jazz and Johnny and Floyd?

JAZZ

Franz Fanon said that the thieves and the prostitutes, the pimps even, the glittering birds and beetles whose function it is to service the rotting teeth and sagging belly of the White system, they too can lead the revolutionary struggle. Under the neon in the arteries of the night-time streets, in the dark, warm places hidden by folds of the city's skin, an army waits.

My city. A glass and concrete battleground where there are no soldiers, only spies, where the violence that is necessary because it is the violence of one set of needs against another exclusive set, is hidden under the skin. Occasionally, welts and blisters appear.

Always moving, the city is never at peace. The cars below me glitter like the barrels of a gun. The struggle is perpetual. Using whatever means are necessary.

Malcolm X said, 'I am not concerned with the dream, I am concerned with the nightmare.'

FLOYD

We was this gang but we didn't have no name or nothing.

Well, Errol called us the Fantastic Four but that was just kids' stuff, embarrassing. *He* gave us a name: The Panther Posse. A name from *history*, man. Yeah. We was down with Malcolm before you ever heard of Spike Lee, man, before you even heard of Public Enemy, you know what I'm sayin'? He gave us that. Man, he knew so much it was like he'd lived before. He was radiant with knowledge: A Beautiful Black Brother.

We didn't have no leader, no master planner, not even Jazz at first, but before he showed himself, if there was anyone it was Johnny. Cos a that there was always this bad feeling between them, which was sometimes a heavy thing. Cos Jazz kept it all in the streets when Johnny want to take it back to Afrika, you know what I'm sayin'?

Sometimes it was like Jazz was afraid of Afrika, man. I don't know why or nothing, cos Afrika is where we all from, right? And Jazz was always telling us, Know Your History. Which goes all the way back to the beginnings of shit, to Afrika.

Sometimes I think the reasons we was into it was not the same reasons they was for him.

Christ, I'm talking like it's all in the past, you know? But it's like, tonight something ended, you know? Like I said, man, Jazz gone over the edge, like maybe he always wanted to, and now he's out there in the streets with a sawn-off, fighting the holy war at last. I hope he ain't got caught. I hope no-one ain't got caught.

Suddenly I feel like I'm on the top floor of a burning building, too high to jump.

Zarjazz moves in his cot and starts to cry. He's got bright eyes, clever-looking. You can't look at him and think, That was an accident: only a second in that kid's life was a accident, man. The rest, that was how it was meant to turn out.

Judy wants his baby real bad, man, I can tell. She got this look, yeah, fi true. Jazz's baby. Not Caroline, man; she get a knitting-needle and flush it down the john. Not cos she a white woman, though, it ain't that. It's just, some women ain't mothers and she's one of them. Lady Trophy, Judy calls her, but Jazz beyond that, man. He don't need to be no Great Black Hunter, you know what I'm sayin'? He don't need to live in no mirror of society's value-system.

When he met Caroline Jazz was already seeing Judy, or

more like she was seeing him, cos he didn't have no interest in her, he just let her tag along sometimes, you know?

Anyway, him and Caroline met at this party we crashed down the Kings Road, like a Chelsea affair, you know? Waiters in white tuxes and a bunch of people playing different-size violins. Champagne-and-sugar-cubes-cocktails shit. We was high and we crashed it and they let us in cos they thought having some niggers in would be Socially Daring. I felt kind of like, Why are we here, man? but the others was well into it, grabbing the free drinks off the waiters, checking the girls, sneaking off to the john to smoke shit. Just about every fucking white boy in the place arx me for a little grass, a little sensi, which pissed me off, you know?

People shouldn't presume, you know what I'm sayin'? Even if we was smoking.

Anyway it's later, and I'm looking for the Posse so'se we can shoot through and catch a blues or shit and I find Jazz is chatting with this girl, and she's making big eyes at him, man. She's rich and pretty and slim and white and she's got this long, straight blonde hair and she's wearing this long white dress, like simple but I'm sure very expensive. They laugh and smile at each other and Jazz don't leave with the rest of us.

CAROLINE

I don't suppose I had ever really fancied a black boy – man – before. I mean, I have several African friends but somehow language has always stood between us. Not the vocabulary or even the syntax, but the meaning of the words themselves: words like *freedom, hope* and *country* represent a gap which can never be bridged. Which I can never bridge anyway.

I'd never really met a man who was black, rather than African.

He was good-looking in a rough sort of way, and his shaved head and his clashing, baggy clothes made him look like one of those raggamuffins, you know? Except without the gold they all seem to like, though he did have a gold front tooth – the right one – that flared when he spoke. Secret gold. I was annoyed with Rupert, and to get back at him I thought I would flirt with the boy. With Jazz. With Jason.

It was stupid of me to have assumed that he would be stupid. He was sharper than most of the Oxbridge graduates I know, and better read too. The champagne made me giddy and I forget what he was saying, the actual words he said, only that I was impressed by them. Later on he told me I kept saying, 'I respect you, Jason, I really do.' I'm afraid drink stifles my eloquence; that was all that would come out: 'I respect you.'

We got a cab back to my flat. Rupert tried to cut in, offering me a lift in his GTi, but I turned him down: The flirtation had become a glissando, and I had floated beyond his reach, how far I didn't realise then.

Jazz didn't say a word, just waited for me to prove that I wanted him. I paid the cab fare.

As I snapped on the lights in the living-room I suddenly thought, 'What the hell am I doing, bringing some black man I don't even know back to my flat and letting him in? He could be a rapist or a murderer. Anything.' I wondered if he sold drugs. But he just stood there, looking round the room, taking it all in, looking sexy in baggy red, green and yellow cords and a little black baseball cap. And that gold tooth. I realised he was waiting to be invited to sit down.

He wouldn't let me make love to him. He pushed my hand away and shook his head. Which, I admit, just made me want him all the more, and at first I thought that that was why he was doing it. So I smiled and touched his arm.

'No,' he said, without moving. I let my hand fall and stood there, unsure of what he meant. With his eyes fixed on me, he slowly unbuttoned his multi-coloured shirt and pushed it open. I watched the rise and fall of his chest, the almost imperceptible quiver of his stomach, the shadows cast by his black projecting nipples. The immediacy of the contrast of the rough texture of the corduroy with the matte smoothness of his skin made me draw a breath. It was so immediate and yet so immeasurably distant; continents and centuries away yet near enough for me to feel the radiant heat of his pulsing blood. I'd never been so aware of skin before. His, and my own. It was so strange, but it was also strangely sexy. I slid onto the floor and looked up at him where he sat. His face was in shadow. He took my chin in his hand and stared deep into my eyes, not speaking. I wasn't drunk at all by this time, but felt as if I was hallucinating. He resonated with secrets, with hidden lives, his presence, the aura of his soul filling the room, making the curtains billow and the lamp-light shiver. And then he began to talk in his soft voice, the words cadenced as if he was reciting a litany, taking me on a journey from the slavery and sexual madness of the Deep South to the present day, to the present minute, to my own mind that had just thought, *Is it true what they say?* as I pressed my hand against his thigh.

And as I put my hand between my legs and stared at his hairless chest I felt that I had gained an insight, that what I had taken to be reality and secretly and only in my farthest corners found cold and empty was after all a delusion, and that to reach him, to really connect, I would have to climb up out of the filth of all our history, scale the heights, earn the right to touch him.

My heart pounded.

What he said then, what he told me then, changed me. My days and nights that had seemed so full previously were revealed to me as empty deceit. My little pains disappeared. If I had seen this situation before I reached it, I would have been quite unable to believe it. But now, now it seems the only thing that makes sense. I've always been in search of a mountain to climb. And now I seem to have found one.

I sleep on the sofa. He sleeps on the bed. Rupert rings in the morning, asking if we're still going out together. Yes, I tell him. Everything that has been annoying me about him seems trivial now. I hang up and go and make a cup of coffee. Black. Jazz is still sleeping. I sit on the chair by the door, watching him.

JOHNNY

Me and Jason was rivals, seen? Cos him did useda come out wit one piece a bullshit pon another, yunno? And the others, them just accept it like it was Scripture or Sura or shit, but me no impress so easy, you know? Me argue. Me *dispute.* The others, them was all blind by him sometimes, man, like make too blind fi arx questions and shit. *Ah* would arx. Like, What you do for money, man? Cos him always have the dollars, yunno?

Least, almost always. When me arx him that, slap me down, him tell me it none a me business, right? Floyd and Errol see a fight coming so them throw down with Jazz, say, What's it to you, man? Like as if them did know, you know. So me get curious, man. Keep me eyes and me ears open. Me know him weren't no drug dealer cos him didn't smoke noting but a little sensi and anyway him no seem to know noting about the supply end of the scene. And it weren't no regular job, you know? Just some evenings, some days. But that didn't reveal noting, cos keeping two gyal-them sweet can take up all that time, right? Me run through all the regular shit in me mind but it don't add up to noting. So after a bit me light a spliff and forget all about it.

Till one day someting come me way.

The gyal me seeing back then, she work in a office, typing and shit, getting her arse pinch by the boss. She couldn't let go of Babylon, man, so me haffi let go a she. Anyway, at this time she was working and one of the gyal-them where she work was getting married, right? So before she gets married, she decide she a go have this like, hen party, right, and me gyal, she was invited to go along. So she does.

She had met Jazz a couple times before.

The next day she telling me about the party, just labrish and me don't listening. Then suddenly she cry out, Oh, that mate of yours, the one with the flat-top, what's his name?

Jazz, me say. Is what you want to know for?

She laugh. We had this male stripper. He was dead sexy, wore this American football costume all held together with velcro, all in pieces. I've seen some crap strippers in my time, but he was good, man. A real tease.

This ain't me cup a tea, man, and me start to tell her so, but she puts she fingers on me lips to shut me up.

There was something about him, she say. But I couldn't think what it was. Then I realised what it was. She pause, like for dramatic effect: I knew him, she say. It was Jazz.

Yeah? me say, cool on the outside, hot on the inside. Me no mention it again, man, like me forget it, you know what I'm sayin'? But from then on, if Jason want to play boss, me let him. Cos me know, when someting heavy goes down, me can put him under me thumb and squash him.

JUDY

The first time he let me do it, I didn't think that was all he was going to let me do, you know?

'I need you,' he said, and his eyes was hard and hungry. And the bastard, I needed him too, the way his eyes looked, the shape of his mouth, his lips full, but his mouth wide with despair. Like he had this hunger, like he could swallow the world.

He watches me take me top off and pull down my skirt, lying back in the chair, the pattern on the rented fabric as knotted as his life, only I don't know that then, though I get to know it like a few seconds later.

This was before he started seeing that white bitch I should say.

He unzips his fly while I'm unhooking my bra. I shiver as I slip it off and feel the weight of my breasts, made heavier by his eyes being upon them. I sit astride him on the chair, kiss him but he's like twisting his head away. And then his lips is cold against mine. He sort of stands up so I'm kneeling on the floor, stands in front of me.

Judy, him say, opening the front of his trousers. I watch 'em like a flower opening. Like a slow-motion flower, speed up like. My name like the name of the flower. And I blow him, not cos it's what I wanna do, right? but cos it's the first time he's ever needed anything I could do for him.

But his hands in my hair feel like steel clamps. And I don't like the taste. But I do it anyway.

See, this probably sounds stupid, right? but I wanted any little piece of him I could get. Cos he's filled my mind and my chest ever since I seen him walking down the street with my cousin Floyd, and Johnny and Errol, in Fila hi-tops and lycra shorts that showed off the good curve of his thighs and arse. And ever since I heard his voice, the way he talks.

He's a poet, man. A natural mystic. Yeah.

Floyd thought he was a good man too, but I never did. Good-looking, yeah, but not good. And I was seeing someone at that time, you know? So just good legs wouldn't've been enough to make me turn his way. But there was something about him, man, it was like a drug being near him. He was bad and *bad*, wicked and *wikked*. You know? Something larger'n life, something dangerous. That's why I wanted him. That's what turned me on. And that's why I weren't surprised about the gun.

It makes me feel weird though, thinking about that. Hot and cold at the same time, you know? And wondering, is he going to get caught? Is the Boy going to get caught?

Errol's fear reaches out to me through the pores of his skin, his little hairs moving against me like the legs of woodlice when you flip 'em upside-down.

It's like Jazz controlled us, you know? And now his madness has spread through us like ink dropped in water. And I'm lying here, tingling, watching the ink spread. I pull Errol to me, and he feels warm and heavy. But not real, somehow, not how Jazz would feel: a pillow, not steel.

FLOYD

Jazz got secrets, man. I mean, like on one level he's open and don't hide nothing, but on another you don't get to know nothing, yeah. Except by accident. Like this one time I was looking for him but he weren't at his gaff or nowhere. It was urgent, kind of, so I phoned Judy and asked her if she knew where he was. And she give me his old lady's address which weren't far away from where I was calling from. The shit was going down, so I went.

He don't never talked much about his family but on the other hand he ain't never said nothing bad about 'em, so I didn't feel like it was like a problem to go down there or nothing.

So I ring on the door and this big black guy, his old man I can tell from his eyes and mouth, built like a buffalo, opens it. Rightaway I know there's something weird going down, man, just from the weirdness in his face. I ask if Jazz's there and he grunts and lets me pass. He used to be in the army, Jazz told me once. Something about 'em, man, there's something real similar going on there. Like, a attitude.

But in all the other ways they're very different. Like Jazz gangsta-lean, you know? And his old man's like a power-lifter, and fat. And Jazz is good with words and his old man just grunts.

24

Jazz puts out. And his old man don't give you nothing.

I go into the front room and see the shit-weirdest thing I ever seen. I *swear*, man! Out the other side in the kitchen his old lady's ironing. She looks up at me when I come in, lips pressed together, then she looks down again. She don't look up no more the whole time I'm there, don't speak, nothing. In the front room there's a video playing, soft porn girls smiling and holding their tits, the sound turned down. Jazz's sitting on the sofa looking up at me like he was asking, Why the fuck I'd come here? And sitting next to him, which almost makes me lose it, this limp, screw-face geezer, dribbling and not looking at nothing, wearing like pyjamas and moving slightly all the time.

Jazz's twin brother.

Like a jerk I'm standing there staring. Jazz jumps up and hustles me outta the room.

Who's that? I have to ask.

Sly, he says. Just as he says his name, Sly starts wailing in the other room like some hundred-and-fifty pound baby. Christ. Jazz touches me face, grips me round the chin.

Don't tell no-one, man, he says. This is personal.

His other hand's warm on the back of me neck and me heart begins to race. He runs a finger over me lips, zipping 'em shut. I nod.

Don't worry about it, man, I say. And we go on and sort out the business which was why I went round there in the first place, some shit about some dodgy video gear. He talks like nothing ever happened. Man, was I glad to get outta that house! It was like seeing Jekyll and Hyde, you know what I'm sayin'? And the air, it was so full of static you couldn't hardly move or breathe. His dad like showed me out and as I'm leaving I realise what it is between 'em:

Hate.

After that I knew why Jazz had to be out there, man: all his past close in on him, pressuring him like champagne on a cork. And all he can do is let it send him flying away.

Watching Jazz it's obvious, man: he's flying.

JAZZ

I pack the carpet-bag carefully: *rubber torches, four, gloves, four pairs, two crowbars, the sawn-off.* I finger the gleaming silver of the barrels where the metal has been cut. It feels smooth and rough at the same time. It is just an inch or two shorter than the length of the bag. *Shells, eight.* It was surprisingly easy to buy; came to me by way of a star from long time past. We lost touch when he got sent down for doing a slashing with a cut-throat razor, some big deal over some girl. He's twenty-three now, and he has a prison smell and those prison eyes that never look you in the face. When I hooked up with him again he was back down with all the wrong people, told me he had a piece to sell.

How can I be concerned with the dream when I see my brother's nightmare? When he can meet my gaze and meet it steadily, it is only then that we will be looking at the dream.

So without will on my part I become a Nigger with a Gun.

I take the bag out in the afternoon and hide it behind some scrap metal near to where I'll be meeting the Posse later. Because Black men don't carry bags at night, the pigs say, except to conceal the tools of their trade. And we don't need another brother fulfilling their expectations. Afterwards I go home, picking up my suit from the drycleaners on the way. I have a bath and wash my hair. It feels like I'm an actor waiting to go onstage, or more like (because I'm doing my own thing) a dancer, where the music is the only thing that's chosen, all the moves are mine. Or a comedian. A truth-teller. While I'm waiting I re-read Amiri Baraka's 'A Black Mass', the tale of how Dr Yakob created the white man. *'White, white,'* the white creature bellows as it lumbers around the stage. Like the angel-like Black men and women I am horrified. For a moment I sink to an inner peace: everything disconnects.

Later I put on my black leather trousers and jacket, my homage to Huey and Bobby and Eldridge, and leave quietly. The details of the plan for the theft (or liberation of wealth, ultimately, from the greedy pockets of the insurance companies) fall neatly into order. I'm tense but not afraid. Striding between tall buildings the bag not in my hand, I feel that the streets, the back-alleys are mine and the pigs can stop me but I'm clean and

I'm clean because bags and guns will be offered up to me out of every crack in the city's skin.

The Panther Posse need the money to do publicity on a brother with a broken arm and a fractured skull wrongly accused of assaulting a police officer, we can only say by breaking his arm over the policeman's boot. Floyd knows the brother, and it was him who brought this crime to our attention. We decided we were going to help him out with legal matters, raise awareness, sort out food and necessities for the family while he couldn't work, stuff like that. The Panther Posse will be changed by this job (the re-apportioning of wealth across the colour-line that the mainstream political parties are unable to countenance, the claiming of the first few coins of Reparation for slavery and the profits made therefrom). We will be changed from a gang into a force for change.

Tonight.

The other jobs we've done, a couple of house burglaries, we did just because we were skint, and although every penny the Black man can take off the white man is a penny of debt being forcibly repaid for the wait of four hundred years, we were concerned for ourselves only. And those times I was afraid and maybe ashamed and let Johnny take the lead. But not tonight.

I pick up the bag and go to meet the others. I'm deliberately late, making sure they're all hyped up. The alley is heavy with the scent of honeysuckle and the night is warm and humid. They're all there, waiting for me.

It's when we're running back to the fence that the pig shines his light on us, starts radioing for assistance. And for a second we're standing there like slaves accepting the authority of this one man because we know him to be the tip of the vast bloated tentacle of white power, of bourgeois oppression. The fact that we're standing there dumb like that, four men standing in front of one man, losing our freedom not because of being physically bound or chained or crippled, but because we've lost it already, inside our heads, makes me blind with rage. I let the freedom well up in my mind and tear through the moribund calicifying tissues of my colonised upbringing. My eyes light up the night like searchlights and everything is made clear and stark in their glare.

I pull out the gun and pull the trigger. The barrels don't catch on the bag and nothing resists the movement. Everything interconnects and the pig is dead, just an object. Floyd stares at him as if he isn't already irretrievably lost in the past. By now we've dropped the videos and Johnny's already scissoring over the top of the fence. For a moment he looks like some Olympic athlete on the parallel bars.

On the other side we split up and run. Sirens fill the air with insanity and I'm caught in the full glare of police headlights as they sweep around the corner. I scream and my scream is swallowed by the siren and they pass by me before they think to stop. I stumble down back-alleys I can hardly see, black spots dancing before my burnt-out eyes. I drop my mobile. It clatters and shatters. I pick up the pieces because the SIM card contains numbers that can be read. I'm sodden with sweat and my mouth is bone-dry. I feel like the headlights were flashbulbs, and that my face is indelibly impressed on the retinas of the pigs who saw me. I know I ought to slow down and walk but I can't stop running until I'm doubled over with a stitch. I walk slowly then, holding my side as though I've been stabbed. Through the soft skin of my jacket I can feel the wad of money we took.

I could've got the money off Caroline, of course, even this much, she's got plenty. And she's got access to the lymph-system of capital. But she understands that nothing, but above all no money, can change hands between us, ever.

Besides, a man must make his own way in the world or he is not a man. For a Black man, this is doubly true.

JOHNNY

Is one day me can't help dissing him, you know? About being a stripper and shit. Me arx him, Man you drop your drawers for the boys *and* the girls, or me hear it was just for the boys?

I don't do weird shit, man, him say. I just do it for the girls. And I just do it for the money, alright, man? Your curiosity satisfied now, is it?

No, man, me say. Tell me, yeah, you get enough money?

Yeah, man, him say. Enough money.

But whatever him tell me, man, him still have secrets-them.

CAROLINE

It's three in the morning and my entryphone's buzzing. Rupert is lying next to me and snoring like a pig and doesn't hear it. But the humid weather has kept me awake so I do. He turns over and mumbles something, probably about Maseratis or City expense accounts, but doesn't wake up. I wrap my mother's silk dressing-gown tightly around me and go to answer the phone.

'Hello? Who is it?'

Silence. Then I hear Jazz's soft voice with its trace of an accent: 'It's me.'

I press the buzzer and let him in, glancing back at Rupert as I unlock the door, knowing he couldn't even begin to understand, knowing he would see all the wrong things, the distortions that I used to see.

He has become the receptacle into which I have poured all my shame.

Jazz climbs the stairs noiselessly but I can feel the pull of the lines of his animal magnetism so I open the door as he steps onto the landing. He is wearing a black leather jacket and leather trousers and carrying a tatty old bag.

I always forget until I see him again how good-looking he is.

I imagine licking the glassy oily side of his freshly-shaved scalp, and pushing my fingers through the short, soft crop on top.

Johnny made a pass at me once, but I blushed and pushed his hand away.

Jazz drops the bag in the middle of the room. 'Get rid of this,' he says. 'When I'm gone, take it away and bury it in one of the fields at the back of your uncle's stables.' I bend down and touch the rough, textured fabric of the bag and a little electric thrill runs through me. I realise I'll never know what's in it, except that it's secrets, but I move to open it anyway.

'Don't,' Jazz says sharply, glancing at the darkness through the half-open bedroom door in a paranoid fashion. 'Bury it just like it is. It's better you don't know, okay? And if anyone asks, anyone at all, right, just tell them I've never been here.'

I nod. 'Do you want to stay for a coffee?' I ask, seeing that he's reaching the edge of panic.

'Yeah. Yeah, thanks,' he says, meeting my eyes properly for the first time since he came in. 'Look, do you mind if I use your bathroom?'

'Go ahead. I'll put the machine on.'

We sit there drinking the coffee and while we're sitting there he tells me a story, I don't know why, a strange fairytale about a mad African magician called Doctor Yakob, and how he created the first white man. Our faces are so close that I can feel the warmth of his skin. There is a faint scent on his clothes – of honeysuckle? His black eyes are like tunnels that open out into space. The Black Gods are flying through that space even as the first white man like some bestial horror tears free and begins his trail of murder and destruction.

'The angels were all torn down and destroyed,' he says, his voice calm now. 'But in the heart of every Black man who fights is a feather from one of their wings.'

He puts the cup on the table and gets up to go. His movements are more relaxed now: The drinking of the coffee, or the telling of the story, has discharged his fear (or anger, or guilt).

'Time I was moving on,' he says.

There's something in his voice that suggests a long parting and I want to hug him, as if we were at an airport or a train station. But I don't. He lets himself out without another word and I pick up the carpet-bag and put it out of the way, next to the front door. Tired, I turn and go into the bedroom.

Rupert is sitting up in bed, staring at me. He probably wants to talk but I don't, so I turn away from him as I slip under the covers and close my eyes.

'Caroline,' he begins, his voice artificially neutral.

'Don't,' I say. 'Just go to sleep. We can talk about it tomorrow.'

It's four in the morning.

I know we won't talk about it tomorrow.

ERROL

It's only eight-thirty and I'm knackered, but I can't sleep

no more. Judy went off to work at half-seven, leaving me to lie in as long as I like. But I'm wide awake now and the sun's too bright to let me go back to sleep. Man, what a night! Just thinking about it makes me sweat. Straightaway I start to wondering if the others got out of there alright. Cos if one a them caught we all caught, I reckon. Cos the pigs know our faces from being in the streets enough lifetimes, you know what I'm sayin'?

I pick up me mobile, don't want to use it.

First up, I call Jazz, but there ain't no answer. Man, I let the fucker ring for about five minutes, yeah. No answer. So I hang up. After that I call Floyd. He answers on the first ring, guy, but sounding bleached. Straightaway I'm pleased, though, cos they wouldn'ta let him out if they had caught him. He ain't heard from Jazz neither, and he tells me he tried to get Johnny but he weren't answering for whatever reason. I tell him I'll see him around then try Johnny's number, but like Floyd says, he ain't answering. I try Jazz again, but I don't get nothing.

It's when I put the phone down I realise I'm sweating heavily, and me armpits and crotch is wet.

JAZZ

Though the streets are straight lines they act like a spiral, drawing the headlights of cars towards me as I move. The spiral moves with me and I am always at its centre. It rotates like a strobe of black and neon-yellow. My shadow twists round my feet, doubles and fades out. The money thick in my pocket like the bulge in a Black man's pants draws the gaze of malicious eyes winking in doorways and in broken bottles, intending harm, intending to sever it from me. In the hot night I feel cold.

Why did I bother with Caroline when the money in my pocket draws the boot to my face just as surely as the tools and the shotgun? Remembering some TV thriller I saw about powder-burned gloves, I take the pair I was wearing out of my pocket and force them through the slots of a drain-cover.

Now there is only the money, which I could have maybe won gambling in some club or bar backroom, and my face, but maybe we all really do look the same to them. It was only me who was caught in the headlights anyway, and I never have done time or been in that serious trouble with the pigs that both Johnny and Errol have.

But what if *they're* caught?

I go back to my flat and the pigs are in there waiting for me in plainclothes looking like two members of the Inner City Firm and they've ripped up all my stuff and they grab me with grips like vices and smash my head against the wall till there's blood in and behind my eyes and twist my arms behind my back until they dislocate and they're not asking me any questions just kicking me in the gut, then they throw me out of the window and watch me fall six storeys. I wake up strapped onto an iron-frame bed with my legs spread in a hospital with bars on the windows and the doctor says, I think he's fit to be questioned today.

I stop on a street-corner and try to shake the craziness out of my head, put the real, known fears of a young Black man in this society on one side, and the nerve-scraping paranoia on the other. The tension of the last few hours has made me feel like I've gone for days without sleep and the streets feel hard beneath the worn soles of my Cats. I look at my watch: it's gone four a.m. *Going back to the flat isn't paranoid*, I say to myself; *it's a risk, but...* But either I do that and carry on along the same line that I have chosen for myself, or I take the other line and become marked like Cain and take the form of a man who will always be hunted.

It doesn't occur to me that there are other lines.

I don't have the guts yet to be marked and take the battle out into the open, and I know anyway that I don't have the right to choose what even the best of us accept only under duress, and that if I did make that choice then I would be insane. The spiral of the city softens and blurs, and the streets are at right angles again. I am no longer the city; its battleground is no longer inside my chest. I am just a stroller in the danger zone.

I head for home. It's a forty-minute walk under a lightening sky. As night fades the events of the dark fade with it. For minutes at a time I forget the things that have happened and I know it is then that I'm at my safest because I radiate nothing of interest to anyone I pass on the road. But there's no-one about anyway, and any passing cars only glow softly like ghosts and disappear.

It's as I turn into my street that I realise there's a car crawling along behind me. My hackles rise. I keep on walking. Slowly it draws level with me. A police car. I look straight ahead. Out of the corner of my eye I see the two pigs staring at me. Just as they're passing I reach my building and turn and hurry up the stairs to the entrance lobby. There are eighty-five short-life flats in here, eighty-four chances if the pigs are just guessing. Or else I'm screwed. From out in the street I hear car doors being slammed and the crackle of a radio. The lifts aren't working, so I take the stairs, pounding up them as fast as I can, thinking *Got to get out of the stairwell before the pigs look up it, so they won't know which floor to start with or else the odds are down by eight.* Maybe they hear the sound of a fire-door closing but that's it.

But if they know who I am and where I live then I'm running for nothing because however fast I run I can't move and my freedom is gone already. My tee-shirt feels tight on my chest and the ceiling of the landing presses in on me. I fantasise that I can hear footsteps in the stairwell but then I can't tell if it's fantasy or not. The silence crowds my ears. I look at the door to my flat and it looks like the most dangerous place in the city. The locks are already perverted from their purpose of keeping thieves out and the door too is corrupted, making the flat a hiding-place for something that got in, something waiting inside.

Down the stairwell I hear a firedoor bang.

I press myself up against the door to the next-door flat but there's no shadow for me to hide in. Self-loathing floods up in me for being paralysed by fear. My childhood touches me and I remember what Mister Miracle would say: A man is only trapped when he allows himself to be trapped.

The thought makes me smile a tight smile. I turn and knock softly on the door of the next-door flat, softly but insistently, needing an answer. This Black freak lives there. I've never spoken to him really. Even though he's Black. The door opens a crack and he peeps out, wide-eyed. He doesn't say anything. Quickly I whisper, 'The pigs are after me, man. Let me in.'

He opens the door a little more and I squeeze inside.

ERROL

About the nine-millionth time I phone I get Johnny. Finally. He sounds bombed and pissed but I got to get stuff out of him, like has he seen Jazz, has he been sussed, you know?

Fuck Jazz, man, he says. Man, that bwoy one brainless fuck.

Leave it out, man, I say, cos I've heard this shit a thousand times already, you know what I'm saying? Do you know where he is, man?

No, man! Alright?

He hangs up without even asking if Floyd made it out alright. Fuck him, I think, cos, like, Johnny's a good man, that's why we waste time with him, but sometimes he thinks his arse is a lollipop and the whole world wants a lick, you know what I'm sayin'?

JAZZ

I'd never seen inside his flat before. The layout's identical to mine, but the floor and the walls are painted gloss-black. At the back of the room is a big futon-bed with white silk sheets on it. In one corner several piles of *Vogues* and magazines like that touch the ceiling like pillars, making about twenty feet of glossy, mindless consumerism. There's some books also, in a pile, loads of CDs, some records and a cheap deck. On the speakers sit bowls with water and white lilies in them. There's a 30-inch colour TV and video in a corner. A huge cracked mirror, six feet high, leans tall side uppermost against a wall. There's also a sort of dressing-table block solid with creams and lotions and make-up and shit. All over the place there's bits of clothing, a lot of it women's lacey stuff and stuff.

In the middle of it he's standing looking lonely as a star in space. I don't even know his name.

He's short, five foot six, or maybe petite would be a better word, and his hair is in baby dreads, shaved round the sides. All he's wearing is a pair of lace like women's panties and I can see every curve of his body, which is smooth and lithe and an even mocha brown, under an oversize man's white silk shirt which is hanging open and slipping off his shoulders. No woman could do it so well. There's a little gold on his lips. He's a freak, but I wish I knew his name. He watches me looking around the room.

There's a poster from Betty Blue on the wall behind him. I wish I could ask him his name. I want to say, *Don't be afraid of me*, but I don't have the right.

'Why do you hate me? You and the others?'

His voice is soft and deep and has a lisp on the s, and it cuts right into me. I remember stopping Errol from slapping him around one time, but this shy Black boy doesn't know me apart from as some thug, which is just what I must look like to him right now. I wish I'd said *Sorry, man, in this world we should all be fighting together not fighting each other.* But I didn't.

Why do you hate me?

I could say, Because you've got the white man's disease and you're his pissed-on woman, man. Because you dress like a girl like you haven't got the courage to have a dick, let alone use it. Because you live in a world of glittering trivia ignoring the battle raging around you. Because you don't have the right to do what you want when so many men can't even get a good woman, when you should be hard and something The Man cannot look down upon let alone piss and defecate upon, because you do what you fucking want and I am tied to a burning wheel knowing with every turn I will be crushed beneath its bottom and that I have humiliated myself more than I can ever be humiliated. I look into his eyes and see Black coolness dousing my white rage. For once I must tell the truth.

'I don't hate you, man,' I say.

'Looks like it.'

'What you mean, man?'

'I seen the way you looked round here.'

'I was just looking,' I say.

'You were making judgements,' he says. 'Putting me in your freak box.'

'No, man,' I say, blood flushing my face.

'Yeah, you were. And you don't have the fucking right.' Swearing sounds funny coming out of his mouth. But I'm not laughing. Then: 'Could you leave, please?'

'No, look,' I say, 'the pigs could still be out there. You want to see me slammed in a cell?'

'What did you do, then?'

For the first time I don't want to say. I feel stupid and trivial, which are the wrong words for how you feel about kill-

35

ing someone, but they block off the knowledge that you've torn the membrane and plunged through. So I say, 'This burglary, man.' But I know he doesn't believe me.

'Look,' I say, exasperated now, 'what do I have to do to convince you I don't hate you, I'm not crazy and I'm not about to mash you up? Fuck you?'

'I never let straight boys fuck me,' he says, deadpan. 'I only fuck them.'

'Look, I'm sorry, man, I – '

'You better go. Please.'

'I'm not trying to humiliate you – '

'You can't humiliate me, man. You can only shit on your own plate. Please go.'

He's frightened but he hides it well: the steel not the pillow. I'm standing near to him now. He's smelling clean with the clean scent of deodorant. The curve of his side looks made for the shape of my hand. I realise I want to touch him, I want to hold his face in my hands and kiss him. My heart's thrilling like it's going to explode.

'What's your name, man?' I ask.

'Carl. Now go.'

'Goodnight, Carl.'

During the time all this was going on I didn't hear the pigs come down the hall so I go back to my flat. I wash, change and shave, putting the money in my new clothes, then I go straight out. I hear the phone start to ring as I close the door, but I don't go back to answer it: my head is too crowded with thoughts to speak.

I head for Mama's Place, where you can get coffee and a fried- egg sandwich any time of the day or night and make small talk with the all-night ladies until the truckers come in. It turns on the poet in me, the self-taught street boy turned Bohemian wannabe, which is how I sometimes want to dress, to appear. But I need to be harder than that so I go in my Cats and a green ragga suit, a leather Afrika hat screwed onto the back of my head, fingerless black leather gloves protecting my hands.

In the cafe, for the first time in years, I think about Steven.

CARL

I have a cup of hot chocolate, like to calm me down. Before getting into bed I lean a chair under the doorhandle. Why do I always get the weirdos, I'm wondering, weirdos made dangerous by the flash of gold in their mouths and the fluid way they move. At about six I drop off to sleep, just after I hear him locking his door on the way out, and the sound of his boots squeaking down the corridor.

At ten Molly's knocking on my door.

'Hi, girlfriend,' she says, smiling. She's working her Sally Bowles look today, right down to the bowler hat on the back of her head and the saggy low stockings, which is frankly not wise.

'You look like shit,' she adds brightly.

'Thanks, girl,' I say. 'You a go haul that big ol' booty in on out the hall so folks can squeeze by?'

Molly laughs and comes in. She's like sanity after the craziness of the small hours. Rightaway she susses it's been a night of adventure, and she eyes me expectantly. I suddenly don't want to tell her about it, but I know I will in the end and I know like she knows it, so why hold back?

'Dish, girl,' she says, just in case.

'I had a visit from the Boy Next Door,' I say. 'At four in the morning.'

Molly takes my hands in hers. I know she's thinking about should she be flip or serious? She goes for serious.

'Poor baby. What happened?'

So I tell her. She's been to hell and back, eleven different foster homes, one where the mother used her for a slave and the father wanted to pimp her out, stuff like that, so I know she understands the shit of it, you know? Plus, she knows my secret shame, which is I can't help fancying them raggamuffiny types. She's always reading me for it, though. Black skinheads, she calls them, and I guess she's almost right.

'Don't waste your time there, love,' she tells me. I nod to make her happy. 'There are plenty more Adonises in the sea, black, blonde or purple. Or green. Yes?' I nod again, failing to convince her that I've sealed this naive leak in my otherwise watertight personality. 'Look,' she says, wanting to lighten the mood and give herself an edge, 'why don't I fix us a *chocolat* and then I'll make you over.'

I smile and humour her.

It was Molly who got me to go to beauty school. We met at this mixed night in this punky little club I used to hang out in. I was sixteen, she was eighteen. My friend Gareth, this tv rentboy I was working the scene with back then, pointed her out and said, 'Man, that girl has *it.*' She was short and overweight but she had this definite, like, hard-core glamour about her. I spent the whole evening wanting to talk to her but not having the nerve. Anyway, eventually she was sitting on her own so I took a deep breath and went over.

'Excuse me,' I said, 'but where did you get that look?'

She was flatter straightaway.

'It's all my own creation, love,' she said, striking a pose.

'Really?' I went. 'Girl, it's *fierce.*'

I snapped and she smiled and we was friends for *life*, darling!

She asked me about my eyeshadow and we compared eyeliner and foundation and stuff. I know it sounds real stupid to say it, but she was the first person I ever met who really loved make-up, you know?

We'd spend like just hours practising on each other and try to create exotic effects, following hot on the heels of RuPaul, Madonna, Diana and the Supermodels. We'd dress up the same and go out together, mixing femme and butch and people would wonder, was we sisters under the skin or what?

The make-up made us glamorous and it also made us different people, bolder, brighter people. That made it our war-paint.

Anyway, she was like training to be a professional make-up artist and said why didn't I do a course like the one she done?

I was surprised cos there were a lot of boys on the course.

I lived with Molly while I was doing it. Then she kicked me out over some boyfriend she started seeing. We didn't speak for months but we got over it when he turned nasty and beat her up and now we're best friends again.

It wasn't all make-up though: Molly's read more than anyone else I know. All the books I got, she gave me: *The Thief's Journal* by Jean Genet, and *Our Lady Of The Flowers* , *The Little Prince* , *Giovanni's Room* , and my favourite, *Blackbird* by Larry

Duplechan. Also loads of more trashier stuff. I hadn't hardly read no books before that, except when I was at school, and they was all crap like *My Family And Other Animals*, which I'm sure is probably a good book anyway but I didn't like it.

It wasn't something I could, like, relate to.

I sit back and Molly massages my face.

Goodnight, Carl.

Why did he want to know my name?

JAZZ

The shit with Steven happened when I was young and maybe innocent, if any Black man can ever really be innocent in a world where the knowledge of the colour of your skin is ingrained in you in your mother's eyes, and when the first time you graze your knee the flesh-coloured plaster she sticks over the graze is a bright pink that stands out like neon against your dark-brown skin.

I was eleven, twelve, maybe when it happened. It was the time of Rock Against Racism, riots and the Two-Tone thing, a moment of anger and hope, where it felt like a revolution might catch fire, and the oppressed might really rise up against the oppressors. Black *and* white.

See, I have never believed in race war. In this country, as in America, Race War = Suicide. So any fights for change or justice must involve all races. Just, I'm with Malcolm in believing that those white people who say they oppose racism must work within their own communities.

But back then there seemed to be a possibility residing in the pork-pie hats and the wraparounds. And maybe there was, who knows?

It was after all this that I started to run with Floyd, Johnny and Errol, and I've been running ever since.

There was this Rude Boy named Steven who I got to know at school. He was fourteen, fifteen, which seemed old to me. Man, he was cool. Cool and white, but that seemed a transparent thing then, invisible and unimportant. And it was Steven who threw stones at my window one throbbing August night and, when I opened it, whispered, 'Come on, man. The city's gonna burn tonight,' his face flushed, his smile wide, his eyes crazy. And he watched me as I shinned down the drainpipe and we ran through the backstreets to where the rioting was. It felt apocalyptic. And it felt as if he had reached inside me and pulled out my dreams.

Oh yes, I have been young and foolish.

And we ran and we ran and glass burst about us and rained like confetti on loveless and plastic-faced pigs and flames erupted volcanic vents of possibility Molotov change and somewhere I stumbled and Steven took my hand and we ran on like that wild and free and careless like we should have been, like we should have been allowed to be.

One night about a month after that I went round to his house after school and his folks were out. We went and got beers out of his fridge. He was still wearing his school uniform.

'I gotta get changed, man,' he said. 'Come up to me room.'

I still had cinders in my eyes, so I followed him up the narrow staircase and into his small bedroom. The walls were all covered with posters for bands like the Specials, the Clash and stuff like that.

'Cool posters.'

'Yeah.'

He stripped to his underpants. Cream Y-fronts with brown trim. I looked down at his crotch and saw he had an erection pushing against the fabric. I looked up at his face. He was watching me.

'C'mere, man,' he said. I didn't move – *either* way, you understand? – but he came towards me and kissed me on the mouth, sticking his tongue in. I wriggled around because my hard-on was getting wedged down my trouserleg. I felt strange. I unexpectedly felt I had wanted this all the time, and I felt nothing, and I felt afraid. My mind, my thoughts, ran down like the mechanism of a clock, stopped. Only my body was still moving, was consciously acting. The only will was my body's will. Sounds seemed heightened, walls threatened transparency, but I pushed him away so I could quickly strip, my heart and the stiffness of my dick choking me. He took off his underpants and knelt. I stood there while he blew me for a while, my mind a cold void, my body hot and full. Then he said, 'Do you want to blow me?'

He stood and I knelt down in front of him and took him

into my mouth. There was a sweaty taste, but it was okay. He groaned too loudly as I moved my head. Time gradually started to move forward so I got afraid again, but I didn't stop. I couldn't stop. My mouth melted on him so we were like one sinuous machine. His groans got louder and he started to chat:

'Oh, man, don't stop, oh yeah, yeah.' Then: 'Suck it, man, work those big black nigger-lips – Oh!'

And he came in my mouth, flooding it with salt and slime. Choking, I twisted away and tried to hawk it out. It dribbled in long lines from my lips, but I had already swallowed some. I felt contaminated. I stumbled to my feet.

'You cunt,' I choked, wiping my mouth with the back of my hand, staring into his flushed and unfamiliar face, the sour smell of semen filling the room, soaking into the furniture, our clothes, our skins.

'Shit, Jazz, I didn't mean it, man,' he blurted, suddenly frightened. 'I mean, I didn't mean it in a bad way, I just – '

I grabbed a length of curtain-rod that was lying in a corner and slashed him across the face with it. He stumbled back and fell to his knees in shock and surprise, bleeding. I wanted to stick it in *his* mouth and grind and twist it till he was choking on his own blood but I felt sick and dirty and more than anything else I just had to be out of there. Man –

At school the next day I acted like he didn't exist. I didn't know what else to do. And then I imagined him telling people about what we did and I got scared, so scared that when he grabbed my arm in the toilets I didn't spit in his face and run like I thought I would, I just stood there limp and let him talk. But I was so full of hate and fear and rage that I expected my skin to bubble up and split and burn the dirty hand gripping my arm.

'It was just a joke, man,' he said, his eyes desperate, mirrored, meaningless. 'Like black guys call each other nigger all the time, right, man? I didn't mean nothing by it. I mean, I like your lips, man. I – Look, I'm sorry, alright?'

I couldn't say anything.

'Alright?'

I clapped my hand on his.

'Alright,' I said tonelessly. He let go of me and a weak smile flickered across his face. He couldn't really meet my eyes.

'Later, then,' he said.

'Later,' I said.

I never spoke to him again, and he never tried to speak to me.

Now I have two women and they are good and loyal to me. I even let one of *them* give me head. And since Steven I had never even looked at another male until I moved into this flat where I'd see – Carl – from time to time. I even jerked off thinking about his bitch-boy fuck-me looks. But I didn't want him, not really; it was just a game.

But when I think about how he looked last night I know I've gone through my life just looking in the opposite direction. And the truth is, not even that. In my Blackheart heart and in my reddest hours I've sought them out, the instruments of my revenge: I've let old men, ugly old white men kneel in front of me and blow me. I've shot in their ugly mouths. For money. At least, I've always told myself it's for the money.

But this is different, a universe away from that. This one I want. For the first time ever. Without shame or pain or degradation.

It must be after ten when I leave Mama's Place. I wander around, waiting for something to happen. After a while I see a flower-shop.

I've never bought anyone flowers before.

I buy orange lilies, purple irises and tulips, scarlet ones. They probably all clash but what do I know except that I'm down by fifteen quid. I take them round to Carl's flat, stand in front of the door for what feels like half an hour without knocking and then finally stump up enough courage to bruise my knuckles.

A plump white girl with a glossy black bob and startling eye make-up answers. I feel so embarrassed, I want to shrivel away into nothing. I half-turn to go. Then I turn back and shove the bunch of flowers out as clumsily as if I was a little six-year-old boy.

'These're for Carl,' I mumble. 'To say thanks.'

She takes the flowers and closes the door.

MOLLY

I don't believe it. I take the flowers, hand them over to Carly, who was hiding behind the door, listening. He takes them awkwardly, like maybe he shouldn't.

'I'll do the stems,' I say, 'if you change the vases. And then I'll give you some dish you just won't believe!'

He looks pretty and puzzled and innocent as he empties vases and bowls down the sink, refills them with fresh water. He's always stayed a damn sight more innocent than many who've done less, as if some guardian angel watches over him. Or maybe a succession of guardian angels, of which maybe I'm one. Funny angel.

We tried to make love once and it was kind of nice but it didn't work out. We both just ended up feeling silly. Actually, since I've known him, it's more like *he's* been *my* guardian angel. Pretty angel. No-one should ever clip his wings.

'I've seen your friend before,' I say, crushing the stems of the irises with the flat of a breadknife as Carl tries on a black lycra 'Boy' dress. It hugs his body sexily, leaving most of his smooth brown thighs showing, just keeping him decent, ambivalent. He snaps the clasp of a broad leather belt shut and shoves handfuls of bangles on his wrists, wriggles into a low pair of Cuban-heeled cowboygirl boots. The belt has a large steel heart on it. And finally a paste-pearl choker seven rows high. When he's dressed this way, people can't make their minds up until long after he's passed on anything except he's sexy.

Sure, he's been spat on, had mouthfuls of vile words, had people touch him when he doesn't want to be touched, even shove him around. Which makes me so mad, I could just kill them. It's like with flowers: some people can't just let them grow. They have to snap them off at the stem, to possess them by disfiguring or destroying them. He deserves better than that.

We all do.

'Course you seen him before, girlfriend,' Carly's saying. 'He only lives next door.'

'No, I mean in clubs. *Night*-clubs. Places of ill repute.'

Carly looks around from the mirror all too interestedly. Falling for another screwed-up, hopefully not homophobic, but horribly heterosexual heartbreaker. While I, needless to say, always pick the Kinsey scale-ten fags. *C'est la vie.*

'How d'you mean, girl?' he asks me. 'Like what sort of clubs?'

'Adam dragged me along to the Black Cap one night, darling. *Drag* being the operative word.' (I pause to tease Carly, drag on my cigarette, exhale) 'Anyway, there were a bunch of male strippers happening as well as the drag, and I'm reasonably sure, no, one hundred percent sure, that one of them was your Boy Next Door, whatsisname, up there parading his wares.'

'Jazz.' He doesn't bat an eyelid. Still as a lizard, eyes golden. 'What was his act like?' he asks.

See, Carl believes you can tell if a stripper's gay or straight from the way he does his act. He reckons the more cock and crotch-orientated the routine is, the more likely it is that the man is straight, the more arse the more gay. Me? I say you can't know unless you ask them or screw them and in both circumstances they could be faking it. But I tell Carly anyway, to see what he'll come out with.

'He jumped up on the bar all crazy, dressed like a rapper kind of thing, in a red tracksuit, big unlaced trainers, loads of fake gold rings and chains, wraparound ski-shades and a red baseball cap on backwards. There was something about him, like he was stoned or high or something, but very sexy. I mean the real thing, not just the motions. The moment he was up there he was shaking his tush, working it, you know? I don't think most of the boys in the crowd, who I guess just wanted to see how big his cock was and get back to the ecstasy and the Industrial, noticed that what he was doing was more *intense* than the usual stuff. I thought...'

'What?'

'I don't know, really. Like there was something desperate going on up there.' I shrug. 'So he's jigging away and he unzips the tracksuit top, and lets it slip off onto the floor. Okay, he's got really nice arms and shoulders, that much I must admit. Not too muscley, you know? Just right. And he's wearing this tight red lycra tank-top that doesn't cover his middle which is all like, lean with washboard abs etcetera. Then he pulls off his top so his top half's bare, gets out some baby oil, pours it over his chest, rubs it in, the usual stuff.'

'Get to the meat, girl,' Carly presses me, in a less-than-quality way, I feel.

'He comes forward, working it, very up there, very arrogant in this kind of out-of-it way. Pumping everything violently. Then he gets two guys to pull at his trousers while he jerks and twitches. They've got velcro seams, so each half just rips right off. Underneath he's wearing silky orange short-shorts and his legs are good and they're so lean you can see sinews on his thighs. He puts them together and the same guys pull the shorts down, while he's pulling kind of weird, mad ecstatic faces and keeping up kind of vogueing arm-movements while they're doing it. He stepped out of the shorts. All he had left on was this shiny black latex jockstrap with a zip in the front. Then he starts grinding his butt again, running oil down between his buns, waving it all around. I thought I saw him even putting a finger up there, I'm not sure about that. Maybe it was just wishful thinking, though why I'd be wishing for that exactly I don't know. But it was weird somehow, Carly. Really weird. Anyway, then he gets some old queen to unzip the jock and pull his stuff out, tries to embarrass a few people a bit, and that's it. There's a bit of applause, and he bundles off-stage with his clothes. But I did think even then, *Girl, there's more going on here than meets the eye.* '

'What was the music?' Carly asks.

I leave a beat before answering. 'My Jamaican Guy,' I say.

JAZZ

It's always hard to be honest. Nothing we ever do is not done with mixed motives, that is, with a certain amount of dishonesty. When Caroline started to flirt with me that night at that party I believed I wanted her. Certainly she offered something I wanted. But when we were there in her flat, knowing she wanted to screw with me, I knew that I wanted something else. So I didn't have sex with her. I seized the power by not doing that. But for what I needed I needed a sexual tension there: her wanting. And I made my Blackness my outermost edifice and my innermost, most inaccessible core; my skin which she must always see and never forget, and my psyche all the secrets she would have to tease out of me. All the terror and the beauty.

45

I made her focus on my Blackness, floundering in the new-found sense of her own otherness (because in this time and at this place, the white is never the other; for even Black people are taught to see themselves as other through the distorting lens of the white gaze).

I never tried to humiliate her.

I never tried to humiliate her, and it would have been easy, she would have let me. But instead she let me be kind. But I have never needed a blonde girl on my arm to prove that all's right with my world.

Judy, I met Judy through Floyd, and it was through knowing him that I started to hang out with the others, Errol and Johnny. I liked Floyd, I like him because he's shy, but still cool. And he's cool without cutting you out. Or he never cut me out, anyway. At that time I was opening my mind to radical thoughts by men like Cleaver, Franz Fanon, Huey P. Newton, Stokely Carmichael and Amiri Baraka, and I would tell Floyd the ideas I was reading about, would practise explaining them to him to see if I really understood them clearly myself. We would talk and argue shit, which sharpened our minds, and we also made rap our culture, like a lot of the youth were and are doing. People say the youth have no respect, especially the Black youth, but if you have something worth saying and you say it well, they will respect you. That's how I got Floyd's respect, and that's how I got respect from Johnny and Errol.

Judy is Floyd's cousin or something, and she started saying she was going out with me a few weeks after I got to know her. It suited me to have her chasing me and, truth to tell, if bad things have happened in your life, it's important to have people who want to be with you, who fancy you. But I never wanted to get it on with her in any way or on any level.

One time I'd been hanging with Floyd and he'd been telling me about screwing some girl and I'd been thinking batty-man thoughts; trying to chase them out, but they kept coming back into my mind, Floyd's cock, his arse, the soft warmth of his mouth on mine. Then Judy turned up and I was feeling crazy and hard, so I got her to give me a blow-job. And all the time I imagined it was Floyd down there, or some other good-looking brother. When I came I emptied into Judy and felt hollow and dirty. I hated, I hate treating her that way but sometimes I can't help it because it's like she's a doormat, always trying to get under your feet. And sometimes you let her.

I should stop. With both of them. But I like the other guys to look at me and see the sex in me, even if they don't know how things really go down, you know?

FLOYD

It must be mid-day and I'm phoning Jazz for the five-hundredth time when suddenly he answers.

Man, where you been? I shout. We was all thinking the pigs had got you!

I had to think, man, he says. And they almost did get me.

Shit, man! I say. What you do?

Fronted it out, man. Then ran like shit. My mobile got busted

Shit, man! I pause. Look, man, we got to meet up, innit. Check we still running things, you know what I'm sayin'?

Look, he says, I think maybe the pigs saw my face. Maybe some of them would know me again. You better not be seen around me for a bit. Like, say, a couple of days for sure, okay? Just in case. But keep in touch, yeah.

Okay man, I say. Seen. And I hang up.

Me palms are wet and my hands are trembling. I wipe them on me trousers.

Shit.

JOHNNY

So Floyd dial me, tell me say Jazz alright but maybe the pigs them see him. That's the breaks, me say.

Yeah, him say. Bad breaks.

You arx bout the dollars? me arx, knowing him don't.

No, man, him say. It weren't the time. Which piss me off, right?

It never is, man, me say. We all risk we necks, ennit? Any one a we could be being worked over right now, man! Not just for tiefing some shit, you know. For icing someone. And me na see Jazz a go walk inna the pigpen like the Pale Rider, going *I did it, man, this geezer innocent.*

Halfway through what me saying motherfucker hang up, innit.

CARL

I change into sluttishly tight pink plastic lower-than-hipster shorts and a white stretchy string bra-top, pull on a pair of white vinyl platform boots. I keep on the bangles. I'm wearing only a little light make-up, a bit of lip-gloss, Molly's speciality light touch. A butch ensemble. For me. And that's the way I am, you know? Not a tv, not a drag queen, and a cross-dresser makes you think of ugly, hairy old men in hideous bras from their wife's bottom drawer, or buying crotchless knickers 'for the wife' etcetera.

No, I'm like in that Prince song: Not a woman, not a man, something beyond all that obviousness. And who knows, maybe I *would* die for you. All you need is to believe...

Jazz rises in my mind.

I've put each type of flower into a separate vase and stood them in all different corners of the room so his faint perfume is all around me.

I could just have him as a fantasy now, you know. And once I've done that, whenever I see him, the real Jazz won't be there because he'll be totally covered by the fantasy one. And then I won't have to think about him or deal with him at all. He'll be just another of the jerk-offs I pull out of the passing crowd of crotches and butts, eyes and smiles, every day and every night. But then I say that, but in a way I've already done that, played with the fantasy of him, and then the real one comes all but kicking the door down larger and darker than the fantasy, and full of surprises. Like the flowers.

Maybe I should give him something.

I've got a copy of *The Little Prince* that someone gave me that I already had. Inside it I write 'to Jazz from Carl' and then wished I didn't because it looks like some retard writing. But on the way out I drop it through his letterbox anyway.

Then I go shopping.

ERROL

Me and Floyd, we're shooting some pool at Dexie's. Boy's knocking 'em back.

Don't drink so fast, man, I say. Chill out, I say. But he ain't listening. He's starting to freak out, man. Right before me eyes.

Christ, man, he's saying. What happened, man? What the fuck *happened*?

I'm not happy with the way this conversation's headed, the place not that busy but still, you know?

Shoot some pool, man, I say, shoot it and shut it. I'm chill cos someone has to be, you know what I'm sayin'? But he won't shut it. He shouldn't have drunk nothing in the first place, you know? Like, he's me star and shit, but he's like a woman over his drinking. Like a pint and a short and whoops, man overboard, you know what I'm sayin'?

It's when he says, the gun, man, you got the gun? that I belt him. But he's so high it don't bring him down and he starts waving the cue around and shit, calling me a motherfucker and shit which I don't mind cos we all been through it, man, but for fuck's sake we got troubles enough without this kind of shit, you know what I'm sayin'?

So we end up out on our ears, man, thanks to the assistance of the ejection technicians. Floyd throws up in the gutter which shuts him up finally, thank Christ.

Sorry, man, he says, looking up at me red-eyed and with puke wet on his lips.

S'alright, man, I say. Forget it.

FLOYD

Looking out the window this morning I see the gun floating there only it's a reflection so I look behind me but there ain't no-one there and no gun. I run upstairs to where Zarjazz sleeping cos I keep on thinking, what if they take him away? And I know I gotta be ready to fight against that cos you gotta fight, man. I crack a Red Stripe. It's ten in the morning.

After finally reaching Jazz I feel like celebrating so I call Errol up and say let's shoot some pool, man. But on the way there I start to feel like the whole world's looking at me. So I have a couple shorts on the way over to steady me nerves.

Next thing I remember I'm heaving me guts into the gutter. I'm losing it, man. Like, really losing it.

CARL

I'm in the lobby waiting for the lift trying to hold onto all my excessively promiscuous purchases. Like some Hollywood Heights bimbo I've bought more than I can manage. A small M&S bag with a discount pair of gold lamé evening gloves falls to the floor.

'Can I give you a hand with those, man?'

It's Jazz's voice. I jump and drop some more bags just the moment the lift doors open.

'Thanks,' I say, all embarrassed. He picks up the bags I dropped and holds them for me, like I shouldn't be burdened with such weight. We don't speak in the lift. He lets me go out first. I turn at the front door of me flat, to stop him coming in. He's smiling at me over the shopping.

'I really do fancy you, man,' he says. My heart sinks and leaps at the same time, kind of.

'Look,' I start to say, but I don't want to talk like this in the corridor, it doesn't seem right. So I shut up and turn and let him follow me in.

'Thanks for the book,' he says. 'I read it while you were out.'

'Did you like it?'

'Yes.'

But I don't know if I believe him. Suddenly it all seems like a big mess and I feel stupid.

'Look,' I say, dumping down my bags on the bed, 'you say you fancy me, right? But I don't think you really do. I'm just a freak to you. A white man's African Queen or something.' I put my hand up to stop him interrupting. 'You fancy a fuck or something. But you don't fancy me. You've gone too far the other way, yeah. The straight and narrow.'

He's still smiling. 'You've got a beautiful voice, man,' he says. Then he adds, 'But you knew that anyway.' Which is shit cos I hate my voice, all soft and lispy, not like Bette Davis or Marlon Brando or anyone like that. Or deep, like his. For a moment I'm taken in, but then I realise: 'You haven't listened to one thing I said.'

'I was listening, man. What makes you reckon I'm so straight?'

'Look,' I say, 'you hang out with a bunch of lads, have a bunch of girlfriends, go queerbashing. I don't think you could even be my *friend*. I've taken shit from black guys like you – '

'You don't know me,' he says quickly. 'There's no-one like me.'

'So prove it,' I say.

'How?' he asks.

'When you know,' I say bold-face, 'you're almost there.'

He laughs. 'You're a hard man to convince, my brother. Fucking hard.'

'Yeah?' I can't help smiling just a tight little smile. He smiles back.

'Later, yeah, man?'

I nod the ghost of a nod.

He pulls the door shut on the way out.

I feel weird, you know? Weird but good.

JOHNNY

Me want the fucking money, man. No bullshit. Me tink bout going over there and getting it, but me keep getting this here twinge of, like, apprehension, like maybe the pigs is watching the place or shit. Like maybe someone see someting and none a we know it.

If Jason dropped the wad so him no get done by it, me a go fucking kill him, yeah.

Maybe me go pass by him yard tonight. Like, after dark. The back way.

MOLLY

'Don't trust him *ONE INCH*,' I'm shouting down the phone to Carl. 'Carly baby, they *ALL* say that. I tell you girl, it doesn't matter how good-looking he is, he's still *FUCKED UP*... I just don't want to see you used, baby. Yeah? Yeah? And then they *ALL* fucked him, remember? He needed *STITCHES. SURE* he's not like that. Girl, you've picked some psychos in your time, don't trouble to deny it. No, I am *NOT* jealous... Guys who swing follow the path of least resistance Carly, and that's straight. I *KNOW* Ruben was bi, but I was desperate and I knew it wouldn't last anyway... Yeah, well, I'm just saying, you know? If he's not going to be your knight in shining armour he's not worth the trouble... Yeah. Or your damsel in distress. Whatever. I know. One day you'll get someone fabulous... *OK. MAYBE* he's the one. All I'm saying is, *BE CAREFUL*, okay. See you soon, girlfriend. Ciao.'

I hang up. Well, who wants to lose her man to some two-bit hood from the 'hood for Chrissakes? Not *this* girl, that's for sure. *Then* who would I go shopping with?

JAZZ

For the first time in a long time, for the first time since I became radicalised and really changed and grew up, I feel stupid and ignorant. Not uncultured, not that sort of stupidity, but like I don't know myself. Floating above my head, to the back just out of sight, is a large burden of thoughts that I haven't acknowledged before. I've felt them, sure, but I knew I was right in myself, in my intellect and my actions, and I knew that with revolutionary certainty, so I never saw a need to confront them.

It's funny: being with him, you'd have thought it would make me feel more of a man, but it doesn't. I feel more like a kid, not knowing my feelings, not knowing who or what I am.

I want to talk to him, to really talk, but I can't just go round there. Funny. I could ask Judy to blow me, but I couldn't even ask him to *talk*.

On an impulse I call up Caroline, I don't know why.

'Hello?' It's Rupert's voice I suppose. I don't want to talk to him so I hang up. If she was in she'd have answered. She must be out, burying the bag maybe, taking care of details. Suddenly I'm glad she was out: I feel like that part of my life is winding itself up and I don't want to step back into it.

I try to write a poem for Carl but I've never written a poem for anyone before. I give up: things are too unresolved all over, the words slip like ghosts over the paper, unanchored by any concrete certainty.

CARL

Oh, girl, maybe I *should* make the effort, you know? If you've been fucked around, it's easy when someone fancies you to want to humiliate them because of that. But you shouldn't cos it's revenge like that that adds up to all the shit in this world, abused to abuser to abused to abuser etcetera.

I take a deep breath and go round to Jazz's with a hairdryer. He grins like a little kid when he opens the door to me. His left front tooth is a block of gold, I like it. I hold up the hairdryer flex, plug dangling.

'Have you got a spare fuse?' I ask, mumbling the words cos I'm already like really embarrassed.

'Sure, man,' he says lightly. 'Come on in. I got one somewhere.'

He holds the door open so I have to pass in under his arm. I flinch like I think he's going to grab me, but he doesn't. And he doesn't try anything like locking the door, which I always watch for on account of a friend of mine – I don't let anyone lock me in, put it like that, not unless *I* get to keep the key. He's looking at me standing there and I can tell he wants me to trust him but I can't. There's still a lot of words that have to be said. And then there's a lot of deeds that have to be proved.

I look round his flat. It's the same size as mine, maybe a bit bigger, or maybe there's just less stuff in it. It looks spartan, like the person who lives here is afraid to be sensual, afraid to enjoy touching or being touched. Afraid to live.

Thinking that draws me closer to Jazz because it's like too much, you know? Like the manliness is sort of a self-defence.

But then maybe I'm just making that up cos it's what I want to see, like the butch soldier wounded and made vulnerable who I save his life. But I don't think I'm making it up.

He's wearing red and black ragga pants and a black mesh vest that shimmers over his lean torso. There's a tall black leather baseball cap on his head, and the way he's standing with his legs spread and his arms loose makes my heart skip a beat. Perfect raggamuffin, you know? Putting out sex and anger, rage and fear. And vulnerability, like they do, like child-soldiers on the front line. They've got frightening vulnerability and frightening hate and anger, you know? And I can't forgive the hate, the words of hate, I can't forgive Buju Banton and Shabba Ranks, and I don't even want to. But I know anger. And I know fear. And how wearing your vulnerability on the outside and facing down the world can make you feel. So I'm *drawn*, you know?

Just not easily.

There's a heap of political stuff on the black Ikea bookshelves along one wall which kind of puts a chill on me, though: a lot of straight black guys, actually gay ones too, it's like they want to measure how *Black* you are. Usually it's to prove that they're of course the real thing and you of course aren't. Like, as if melanin comes or goes depending what magazines you buy. And the more of those books they have, the more likely it is that that's going to be their scene, you know?

He has five shelves, which is more than I've ever seen.

But now I'm here I might as well talk: 'You've got two girlfriends, right?'

'How did you know that?'

'I've heard both of them knocking on your door, like, here and there. Alternately.'

'Yeah, well, I'm not going out with either of them, not at the moment.' He sounds awkward.

'But you do screw with them?' I say, hard as nails.

'No,' he says. 'Well, yeah, sort of. But not often. Man, can we talk about something else? Like us, for instance?'

'Look, Jazz' – I say his name quickly, then pause – 'if you treat them like shit, how'd you treat me? Say if I did fancy you.' Which is such a dumb thing to stick on the end that he has to smile. I keep my own face hard: 'I don't need to be some closet's swinging trick, you know what I'm sayin'?'

He turns away. 'Man, you don't understand,' he says, not looking at me. When he turns back there's a glitter of pain in his eyes. Like shards of pain. I want to go and hold him and let him let go of the pain but the invisible line drawn between us stops me. He sits down on one chair, I sit down on the other.

'All my life I've been afraid,' he says quietly. 'Of being weak, of being stupid, of being a failure. And what those things mean is something you can only see reflected back at you from other people, what you are is about what other people see in you. And you have to make yourself in their eyes, you understand? So when I dropped out of school, which could've been a failure, I educated myself in ways no school could do. Out of books no school provides. And on the streets. And being Black which could've been a weakness, I made it a strength. I made myself into a warrior, with my own posse and with women who wanted me more than I wanted them.' He looks at me with dark secrets in his eyes. 'All I wanted from them, from the women, was what they signified. To the others. I tried not to hurt them. I mean, I never encouraged them, just if they came I didn't send them away. Look, look I don't want to talk about this shit, man. It's so – *humiliating.*'

'You'll survive it.'

'Yeah, man. Well, the way you dress, you should know.'

I look away from him. 'Look,' I say. 'To be true to yourself, you got to accept humiliation, yeah. This is how I want to look, and I don't compromise it for no-one. So I been spat on and stuff but I think, Who's doing the spitting? And it's always someone who wishes they had the nerve and they don't. So all they can do is hate and envy.'

'Man, I wouldn't let them touch a hair on your head.'

'If your mates was round here you'd all be laying into me. Them. And you.'

He doesn't answer because he knows I'm right. He just sits there, staring at his hands. Maybe he's almost crying. I pick up the hairdryer, get up and go over to the door, open it.

'See you around,' I say.

And then I'm out.

JAZZ

I should have told him about Steven. I should have told him about Sly. I wanted to compress my life into a tiny clear crystal and show it to him, all at once. But I couldn't. And what I was saying, I couldn't get it under control because he kept pushing me off balance. But I deserved it, man. That's the worst part. And what was I going to do, lie about Judy and Caroline? Only until he said what he said I hadn't thought about them, about what they meant, to him or to me. I thought it could all be straightforward: We fancy each other, go to bed together, take it from there. Like I said, I thought I'd made my life strong, I thought there was nothing there that needed apologies, that it all rode upwards on the great Revolutionary wheel. But now I see that there are wheels within wheels, all going the same way although they look like they're turning in every different direction.

I could've balled Carl out for his lack of ideology, for his complicity with the mechanisms of White Power and for having a colonised state of mind and arse, and deep down I still believe there's maybe a truth in that. But just now I realised that an ideology doesn't have to be articulated to be strong, and that I can't criticise him until I myself cease to be a hypocrite, you know what I'm saying?

I wish there was someone I could talk to.

For the first time in a long time I feel lonely. I put a video in the machine and let it play with the sound down. I watch the film idly for a bit, tidy up for a bit.

Then suddenly I know what to do.

CARL

The air in there got so dense I had to get out just to breathe. I think about phoning Molly but it's all got kind of personal so I don't. See, the trouble is, I think love or wanting to make love, it shouldn't stifle you, it should make you feel free. And I don't think Jazz can do that for me. Or anyone. And I could go with him, I could do that, but I don't need another one-night-stand,

and I don't need for my world to get any smaller, and going with him would be like going into a tiny cell made up of all the prejudices which crisscross my body like a lace net with unseen scars. And doing that wouldn't make me brave, it would make me fucking stupid.

But still, I could do it.

JAZZ

The horse bucks under my hand. My Filas are soaking from the pools among the tufted grass. It tries to rear but I've got hold of the bridle. It whinnies and I look round at the stables to make sure no-one's heard. Crows caw loudly and take flight, nature conspiring to gather round me in a vortex. Even the patterns the grass makes when it billows in the wind have a spiral to them, leading any stray eyes towards me.

I waited until Marcus and Colonel Maynard drove off in the Landrover. The Colonel laughed the first time I came to ride, to see a darky on a horse, rather like having a monkey playing the piano, and when I did it well as weird to him as that, and as threatening, for the moment when he realised I could ride he also realised, and though false logic the realisation was true enough, that I could fuck and probably was fucking Caroline with every jolt in the saddle.

The horse whinnies again. She's a mare. I rub her back and stroke her nose, calming her down. The wind has a wildness that runs through her and it runs through me too. I bring her head around. I've never ridden bareback before but the tackroom was padlocked and I haven't brought a crowbar with me. All I could get was this old bridle, left out in the weather. I swing up onto her back with a grunt and almost slip off. I feel her flanks trembling between my thighs and slide forward, catching the reins in one hand. I keep an eye on the house as I trot her to the drive but I don't see anyone looking out. The Bentley's not out front, so Lady Muck's not back from her shopping day yet probably, and the servants, they've seen me before, they'll just think Caroline must be around here somewhere. All there is is the crush of the horse's hooves on the gravel and the sound of her snorting breath.

'Trot on,' I say, flicking the reins. 'Trot on.'

JOHNNY

It dark by the time me reach Jazz's block. Ah been tinking all day, like, about the dosh, and how me na go take no shit over what me stick me neck out for. Matter of fact, maybe me a go pick up Floyd and Errol-them cut too, you know what I'm sayin'? Since them too chickenshit fi come get it fi themself. Sometimes me reckon it oughta been just me and Jason pulling the job, but then him a flake too, ennit.

Me knock but no-one answer.

Jazz! me shout. There ain't no reply. Jazz, you motherfucker, open the fuckin' door or me a go fuckin' bruck it down, man!

Me bawling me head off, but this place so full of shit-for-brains crack-heads, no-one even look out their fucking doorway, not even that shitty little battyboy next door. I start kicking in the door. The third kick break the hinge-them. Jazz ain't got much worth lifting, just his stack. So me take that and the video.

Me yank the door shut on the way out. Me no want no fucking junkies messing wit him stuff, man. You know what I'm sayin'?

Me just want what me owed.

CARL

I'm sitting in front of the mirror knotting white rags into my baby dreads. They make me look kind of pure and virginal. The perfect look for a evening perched on a barstool with Molly and Bernard. While I'm doing this I'm listening to a tape Auntie gave me by her Goddess of Goddesses, Miz Nina Simone, performing her classic 'Four Women'. Her eerie voice makes me shiver, makes me tingle. Then it harshens, hardens.

'Tell it, girl,' I say, moving my shoulders, clicking my fingers, living a True Drag moment. 'Tell it like it is.' Whose little boy *am* I? Yours, Miz Simone. My skin is brown too, Nina.

Her voice shrieks, falls. My brown skin prickles. *Ladies*

and Gentlemen, Miss Nina Simone. Ain't nothing for me to add, you know?

Auntie's Goddess. Auntie Goddamn after all the places she's left.

Auntie, who I was having tea with this afternoon, all refined out of porcelain cups with gold insides. Auntie is a Lady of Refinement, at least when she's not out cruising the leather scene, and she took me in, gave me a home when otherwise I'd've been working the streets cos I didn't have no money or nowhere to go. If it wasn't for Auntie I'd probably be dead already, like the rest of the boys I knew back then. Like Dexter, the most beautiful coffee-coloured boy you've ever seen, started off all sweet and mild but getting fucked up the arse by that many fat businessmen for a fucking doughnut and a Large Coke made him hard and freeze-dried his heart. He hanged himself in a police-cell cos he was only fifteen and they were going to tell his parents: his father who stubbed cigarettes out on him, and his mother who let his father do that. He was like my brother.

That's why I'm crying now.

You Must Never Forget The Injustice.

But still, I dry my eyes carefully. I don't want to smudge my eyeliner. Christ. No-one remembers Dexter. Especially not the bastards who took him up the arse. And even I forget when I can, because the lines of pain can ruin a good complexion. And suffering can make you dirty. If I could've said that to Jazz, maybe he would have really understood. I should have tried. Cos if you don't explain, why you'd expect anyone to understand?

Tonight I will dress all in white.

If you don't know Auntie, she's like this tough, skinny black drag queen. She's got style, bone-structure and ruined good looks, sucked-in cheeks, a shaved head, big lips, big eyelids, and out of drag-drag she favours leather drag. And so of course everything in Auntie's house neat and ever-so like a typical leather queen. On stage she works kind of a Grace Jones thing, not straight drag, and she sometimes mimes to 'My Jamaican Guy' in her act.

I guess Auntie's my main style guru, you know? Cos she's *committed*, she's *on* twenty-four hours a day, like I try to be. Only I skip the cigarettes and the drugs so as to avoid characterful but unnecessarily early ruination, you know? But a lot of my style is hers. She's like a DQ father-figure to me, if that makes sense. Or a mother-father figure.

I lived at her place for about two years, till I was seventeen, eighteen, keeping it clean, stuff like that, for my board and lodging. Then we had this big row over this man who she had move in, who used to beat her around till she was bloody, and she wouldn't get rid of him. So I had to leave cos I couldn't watch it, it was too like my blood parents. Also this guy would come on to me, which I never told Auntie. But me and Auntie, we're good friends now. I didn't mention Jazz, though, when I saw her today. Auntie's sweet, but she can be real bitter when other people start talking romance around her. I had a nice time though, and just when I was going she gave me this tape. Another gay rite of passage, you know? Miz Nina Simone.

My hair's finished now. I push the rags around a bit until they look nice, fluff up a couple of them. Very *Farina* (are you hip enough?). And then everything else white: lycra bra top, big loose man's silk shirt, left open, lycra mini-skirt, and black patent-leather DMs. Underneath I'm wearing one of my new purchases, a white suspender-belt and delicate lace stockings with matching panties. Rolling on the stockings, fastening them to the straps, makes me feel like every sensual film-star of the silver screen, like the spirit of sex and sensuality. I feel like this is what my legs were made for. And my cock and balls oveflowing the panties feel large and full and heavy.

I spend a few minutes making adjustments. One good thing about working with models is you get to learn how to wear clothes right. You've also got to know your fashion, how it's meant to look so you know when you've got it right. Like, how to work the accessories, stuff like that. I retouch my eyes and put a little gold on my lips, put some essentials in a clutch-bag. Now I just have to wait for Molly and Bernard to pick me up. I sit there thinking, *Hope he doesn't try it on again*. Last time he got drunk he told me he wanted to be my dirty fuck slave, doing my biddings and me chastising him etcetera. *Me!* Girl, that man's got *problems*. But he's also got a Porsche.

At about half-nine I hear a voice I don't recognise shouting my name in the street. At first I don't go and look cos I reckon it must be some other Carl. The voice shouts again, twice, three times. I go over to the window, open the curtain and peep out.

What I see is Jazz waving up at me from on top of a white horse. *A white horse.*

'Come on down, man,' he yells. 'Come for a ride.'

I sling my keys in bag and I'm *gone*, sister! I run down those stairs like to break my neck just in case it's all a dream and I'm going to wake up any second. But it's not a dream. The horse rears and champs on its bit. I forgot how big horses are. Jazz smiles down at me.

'Glad you could make it, man,' he says.

'You're crazy,' I answer back.

'All the best people are, man.'

I can feel the horse's blood or is it my own pounding between my thighs and Jazz's body shields me from the wind. I bury my face in the leather of his Tommy Hilfiger jacket. I can taste the tang of his aftershave and feel the heat of his neck. We're galloping now. My white shirt billows out behind me. People must be looking and above us in the block curtains are being pulled back. And they're seeing me galloping off on a white horse with my dark knight.

'D'you know how to steer this thing?' I shriek as we almost collide with a black cab. Car horns blare. We slew across a zebra crossing, past some railings and into Kensington Gardens. And then we're galloping through the trees. Twigs brush our heads and the horse's hooves send flurries of red and brown and golden leaves whirling up around us in glittering tornadoes. We slow to a trot by a little bridge by the lake. Jazz pulls the horse up, grips my arm and lets me slip gently down to the ground behind him, then he smoothly dismounts. He takes me in his arms and kisses me long and hard. Oh Christ I can't believe it, no-one's ever kissed me like that, even without the wild wind and white horses, no-one's ever kissed me like that.

'Did I do the right thing, man?' he asks, his voice low and husky. I wrap my arms around his neck and my mouth meets his a second time. I can hardly breathe. I feel like I'm going to faint.

'Hold me, Jazz,' I whisper. My thumping heart fills my throat, choking my voice off. He holds me tight, needing me. And even if he's crazy, like the song says, I'm going to travel with him, I'm going to travel blind, cos he's touched my perfect body with his mind.

We start to laugh, and it's out of real joy, and I feel a wild freedom rising in me and I see it rising in Jazz too, in his eyes and in the rise of his chest. I unzip the front of his jacket and hug his warm, smooth, bare waist. He runs his fingers through my dreads.

'Pretty hair,' he says. Behind us the horse has wandered off and is grazing, just like this happen every day of its life.

'Uh, where did you get it, Jazz? The horse, I mean.'

He laughs again. 'I just borrowed her off a friend who didn't need her. She'll be fine here. There's enough grass.' The horse whinneys. 'C'mon, man. Let's go home.'

We walk hand-in-hand through the park. A few people turn and stare but they're just nobodies; the others either don't give a shit or else they think I must be a girl. At the gates of the park his grip tightens and I know he's fighting not to let go of my hand. And that's how we walk through Bayswater and further down until we're back at our homeblock again. He kisses me in the lift, puts a hand on my backside.

I don't stop him.

JAZZ

So here I am with this angel on my arm, and I ask him into the flat and he says yes. But the door's been kicked in and my stack's been lifted. It could have been anyone, but I know it was Johnny, wanting his cut. Fucking psycho.

'Some of this stuff's valuable, Jazz,' Carl says, looking at my scattered CDs. Man, that lisp! Why it should turn me on the way it does I don't know, but it does. 'We could store it in my flat if you like?' he suggests. 'At least there's a lock.'

'Thanks, man,' I say. I hold the tips of his fingers in my hand, let them fall.

It doesn't take long to move the records and books and stuff and pile them up in a corner around Carly's stack of *Vogues*, but in that time I can see doubt surfacing in his eyes again. *C'mon, man,* I'm thinking, *I didn't steal a fucking horse to have you fucking freeze up on me now* , and the fact of that thought opens a little distance between us. I want to hold him but I'm paralysed.

'I need you, man,' I say.

'I need you too,' he replies. But even so there's still things to be sorted, and it's up to me to sort them. I take his hands and we kneel down together and sit facing each other, legs intertwined.

CARL

And he tells me about his family. Not with, like, self-pity, he just tells me matter-of-fact. About his twin brother who's a vegetable cos his father threw him up in the air one time and accidentally let him drop, and about how his mother would never let his father touch him, Jazz, and she shrank away from him too, leaving his childhood cold.

'It wasn't that that made me like...' He pauses, struggling to say what's virtually unsayable for him. 'I mean, it's not like they say, that isn't the reason why I go for guys, you know? That's like something else, like an insight. Like maybe what a religious experience must be like. But my dad, you had to be a man, you know what I'm saying? There wasn't any room to grow and explore yourself.'

There's an edge of hatred and self-hatred in his voice. He sighs, looks down. I catch his chin and reach and kiss his lips softly. They are big and beautiful and soft and warm. He hugs me like maybe a little boy would hug his father, if he knew who he was.

'C'mon, baby,' I say softly. 'Let's go to bed.' We slowly get to our feet and arm in arm walk over to the bed.

As I'm unzipping his leather jacket, Jazz looks at me with alarm in his eyes. He stops my hand on the zip. 'If I can't do anything, man,' he says hollowly, 'you won't despise me?'

'I won't despise you,' I say. But as I push the jacket back off his shoulders my hand brushes one of his erect nipples and he flinches. I take it away gently. But he catches it, puts my palm back against his chest.

'Sorry, man,' he whispers. 'But no-one's ever touched me the way you have, nobody's ever touched my body like that, not with – tenderness.'

His eyes glitter moonlight on dark water, shuddering in the rushing tide.

We sleep in our underwear, entwined in each other's arms. We haven't made love or nothing, but we're lovers alright. And for tonight at least, I feel closer to him than I've ever felt to anyone else, even my ex Andy, and me and him were together for two years. For a second I wonder if it's to do with that Andy was white where Jazz and me, we're a pile of warm brown limbs, but I don't think that's what it is. What it is is, Jazz is a very special man, like no-one else I've ever known.

I stare out the window at imaginary stars, cradling his head on my chest, and wonder what things'll be like in the morning. And in my mind I'm humming *Are you warm, are you real, Mona Lisa? Or just a cold and lonely, lovely work of art?*

JAZZ

When I wake up the sunlight's streaming through the gaps in the yellow satin curtains and the room is lit up a soft lambent yellow. I look with lidded eyes at Carl's face across the pillow from mine. His make-up's a little smudged but that doesn't matter, he still looks really pretty, though even with the make-up he's not pretty like a girl. And yeah, that is important to me: I've made enough false starts in this life without anyone saying to me, *You're only halfway there, man, you couldn't deal with a real man.*

And anyway I would say, 'And what *is* a real man?' You know?

I want to wake Carl up but I'm afraid to in case he kicks me out for being weird, I mean I didn't suck him off or fuck him or sixty-nine or anything. He probably thinks I'm a freak, but all I wanted to do last night was just be held, you know? Hold him and be held.

Still I feel dizzy with freedom, dazzled.

Maybe I *am* a freak.

Maybe I should just go now, take my troubles with me and leave.

But the bed's too warm to get up right now, so I'll leave it for a little while. I wrap my arms around Carl and pull him close. He wakes up then and smiles at me sleepily and I hug him again.

'I thought you might of got scared,' he says softly. 'I thought I'd wake up and you'd be gone.'

'You pleased, man?'

He smiles like, why did I bother asking. 'You weren't thinking of going nowhere, were you?' he asks.

'There's nowhere I'd rather be,' I say. And it's the truth.

'Good,' Carl says, rolling onto his back, streching his arms above his head. He's undressed in the night and lies there unselfconsciously naked. I run a finger up the groove of one of his wax-smooth hairless armpits. He wrinkles his nose. 'Don't do that, baby. It tickles.'

I look down the smooth, firm brown length of his small, lithe body to the grey silk skin around his full, soft cock and balls.

'Man, you shave it all off?' I say, half-smiling, a current tingling at the base of my balls. He nods. I shake my head to myself. 'I always wanted to do that, man. But I never had the nerve.' The admission embarrasses me. Carly's gaze embarrasses me. 'Roll over, guy,' I say. 'Let me give you a back-rub.'

Let me touch you let me be innocent.

He rolls over for me.

CARL

'So, I mean, how come you've been a stripper?' I ask Jazz. He's rubbing my back, sitting astride me with like a comic-book sense of sexiness which works very well on me. 'Mmmm?' I encourage. I can't be bothered to open my eyes. And it's like, because my eyes aren't on him, he finds it easier to talk, and surely by now he must be more relaxed also. Unlike me, with my dick digging hard into the mattress as he moulds me.

'A mate of mine, well more like a friend of a friend, he was getting this extra cash, and it turned out he was getting it by stripping,' Jazz says, working his hands down my spine. 'And he said, why didn't I give it a try? And I laughed because it was just the freakiest idea. But it stuck in my mind, so – ' His voice trails off into introspection. He kneads my sacrum.

'So anyway,' he carries on, leaping a couple of psychological ravines with a single bound. 'I worked out a bit of a routine to some music and a few months after that this mate got me a spot at a hen-night. And the rest, as they say, is history, man.'

He bends over and kisses the back of my neck.

'But I don't just do it for the money,' he says, his voice suddenly quieter as if he's letting a secret out softly. 'The money's just an excuse, a reason that lets me do it. See, I learned something when I got up there: that I liked it. I liked having people looking at me. At first I liked having women looking at me, but then I got my first gay gig – standing in for someone else, a last-minute thing – and being up there above all these queers – sorry, man.' He winces, I can tell, behind and above me. 'Habit, you know what I'm saying?' His hands keep moving on me. 'These geezers, all watching me and all waiting, waiting for something, some principle that'll always stay with me even when I'm naked, some *truth* about something primal. And it turns me on. It's a kind of power. That thing that's what they're really waiting for, that you always wait for watching a stripper, whether it's a man or a woman, that mystery, the reason why you watch that gets taken apart as the stripper takes himself apart, the mystery of sex maybe, I don't know. But in the end I always walk away with it, and that's power. That's why I do it. And man, they could rape me or whatever they liked up there, but I'd still walk away with it. Because it would still be my show.'

Jazz squeezes my shoulder-blades, works down me back again hard.

'Sometimes when I'm up there there's nothing in my mind except I want to shout at them *fuck me.* Or it's not that, it's more like I want them to want me so much they lose control, so they rape me. So I lose control. Because I've never lost control. And I'm spread across the sky and all the evil is fucked out of me. And the less they get to touch me, the nearer I am to that understanding, you know what I'm saying?'

There is such a violence in him. And he doesn't know it.

'Because it's not a real violence,' he says, almost telepathically in a sideways way. 'I don't really want to be gang-banged and have my arsehole torn out, man. I don't want pain: I'm not a sadist or a masochist. That's not what I want.

'Only, sometimes you have to burn to get something pure.'

JAZZ

See, race consciousness pervades my mind at the conscious as well as the subconscious level. Just as I feel things through my Black skin, so I structure my feelings within a Blackness of mind. In an insane and racist world where proportionally five times as many brothers as whites are locked up in insane asylums, it is the only sane thing I can do. See, either you can deny that this society is a fundamentally conflicted one, or you can face up to it. And if you face up to it, some men will call you crazy. But then you remember – the lunatics don't just run the asylum. They built it. And in its walls, its confines, they frame the very definitions of madness.

So if I talk about flowers and sunsets and the curve of a guy's eyelash, don't forget where I'm coming from: loving another guy is No Sell-out. And if I have to prove that to you, then it's you who have sold out and sunken into reaction. And you deserve violence for that. A Zen slap to shock you into enlightenment. And in order to see clearly, as I am struggling to do, you must step beyond the bounds of the conflagration and stand cool.

But there is always a tension involved in being simultaneously both here and there.

My father made me become a man, but I have not become the man my father expected.

CARL

When he holds me wrapped in his arms so I am like the bud of a rose protected by the plant's leaves, I can talk to him easily. And I feel safe cos his violence goes outwards like thorns. So I tell my own story, or bits of it, anyway:

'I was fourteen. My Mum and Dad, they were always fighting. My old man was a total bastard and my Mum was his doormat. Only to stop herself from getting trodden on, she would always try and get me in the way. That's why I left home.' I sigh, try to tell it without remembering. 'One night they were having a row. He was drunk as usual, she was too. They'd been

67

out on the town, trying to get it back together, only for the nine-millionth time it hadn't worked out. She was screaming stuff at him and I was thinking, Girl, this is where she gets hit. Cos it always went like that. She push him too far, he hits her. Then I hear her say (cos I was up on the landing, listening), she says, 'You're a fucking worm, not a man. You crawled out from under a fucking stone. You've got so little balls you couldn't even stop your own son from turning out queer!' And he's going, 'What you talking about, bitch? That's bullshit.' And she goes and gets this magazine she found in the bottom of my chest-of-drawers. It wasn't nothing extreme, just pictures of guys, but he runs up the stairs and yells, 'Is this yours, you lisping little battyboy?'

(Jazz hugs me tighter, like he would've liked to protect me even if just from the pain of the past.)

'I say yeah, and he grabs my head and hits it against the wall. And he grabs my arm and throws me down the stairs. He broke my arm.'

Jazz shudders involuntarily. It's a genuine shudder, not dramatic.

'When the cast came off I left home. I've never spoken to neither of them ever again.'

He holds my head to his hard, smooth chest. I feel like a baby being held there. His black nipples are large bullet-like protrusions almost a centimetre long. I turn my head and take one between my lips and he arches his head back with a sigh. I bite it a little and he moans.

'Don't stop,' he whispers.

JAZZ

Carl keeps on playing with my chest, biting into my nipples with his teeth and glittering nails, touching the secret me no woman – and who else was there ever really? – has ever touched, laying claim to the part of me I've only ever shown and walked away with. I'm lying there with my arms outstretched like Christ and despite my moans and groans he's still surprised when I come.

'Wow,' he says, looking down at the white line shot up

68

my belly. 'You sure liked that, baby.' I grab him round the neck, pull his face to mine and hold it there in a lock, kissing him until he's gasping for breath, until he struggles away. I feel like a kid who's just lost his cherry. He takes one ragged breath and then I'm kissing him again. I push my tongue into his mouth and reach down for his quivering hard-on. I squeeze his shaved balls then start to slowly jerk him off. Within a few seconds his body stiffens and he's moaning into my mouth and I feel warmth on my fist. Impulsively I bring my fist up to my mouth and taste a little with my extended tongue. Warm and salty. Then we kiss again so he can taste it too.

'You like to eat it?' Carl asks, his face flushed and a little shocked, which is funny because he clearly takes me for this suck-me-bend-over macho type of guy, which is not how it is at all. I mean, that's a part of it, but not the whole story, you know what I'm saying?

'I know it's not safe, not one hundred percent, but I just needed to – I've never tasted anyone else's before. So I needed to...' I peter out. Then: 'When I was a kid,' I tell him, 'I used to jerk off with my legs doubled over my chest so I'd shoot in my own mouth. I never tasted anyone else's before.' *No taste no Steven no memory no reality no nothing only here and now warm and salty overwriting nourishing necessary good.* 'But yeah, I like it.' He looks at me kind of funny. 'What's wrong, man? Shocked?'

'I was wrong about you, Jazz,' he says. 'I'm sorry.'

'Hey,' I say. 'Ain't nothing to be sorry for.' And I hug him.

CARL

Just like Jazz makes his world into black and white, I guess I make mine gay and straight. And the more you think like that, the harder it is for anyone to stand on the NoHomo NoHetero land in-between. Yeah, I judge too.

You might think that's where I stand, the way I dress, what I do; some parallel middle ground, some NoMan NoWoman's land. And I like women, I think they're beautiful, I like to work with them and everything, but I don't want to *be* one, I want to be able to have the glamour and sensuality that women are allowed to have in our culture. But on me, on a man. A gay man who wants other men. And they have got to understand that, any guys that fancy me. They have to have that *insight*. And that's the first thing me and Jazz fight over.

'You're a man,' he says. 'Why d'you want to be a woman?'

'I don't want to be a woman, I just like how a lot of them beauties look, that's all.'

'But don't you get worried that no-one'll fancy you, I mean, they'll think you're too freaky?'

This from the boy who stole a horse to impress me, to get into my panties.

'No. Lots of people have. And you did.'

'Yeah,' he says. He doesn't pick up on the 'did'.

'Look, Jazz,' I say, getting up off the couch and facing him. 'Last night it didn't bother you. Tell the truth, man – the way I looked turned you on. And this morning you haven't tried to pull the rags out of my hair, you haven't wiped the lipstick off your chest. So what's the problem now?'

I'm raising my voice by now, my stupid fucking lisp furring up the words, getting angry cos I'm sure that when I stop he'll start laughing at me, *at the poor pathetic little drag queen who finally got laid, even finally got laid by someone who's halfway good-looking, who's halfway to being a real man. Stupid lisping little one-night-stand faggot.* I shut up.

He's not laughing. He stands and catches my hands in his.

'I'm sorry, man,' he says. 'There's some things, I find them hard to express. There's so many things I've never said, not to anyone, so even *trying* to explain them, even to you, it's really hard, man. The words often just skid away and I'm suddenly saying the wrong thing. But I do want to explain, man.'

He's staring into my eyes.

'So try again,' I whisper.

'I just want you to know, all I mean is, I want you as a man, a man wanting another man. So unless that's how you see things, then I just have to go.'

'And if that's how I see things, then you like the way I look?' I ask.

'No, man. I like how you look anyway. But if you don't see it the way I said, then I wouldn't want to stay with you, you

know what I'm saying? I don't want someone who's confused.'
He smiles a little smile. 'I'm confused enough for the two of us.'

'It's not shame, then?' I ask.

'How d'you mean, man?'

'Like walking down the street with me, like being seen with me and what it'll make people think,' I say.

'Yeah, well, it'll be the truth, won't it?' he says too lightly.

'Yeah. But have you got the guts?' I ask.

JAZZ

It's funny: I've done jobs, I've been in fights with bottles and knives, I've thrown bricks at the pigs, I've even shot a geezer, but he's right: have I got the guts to walk down the street with a boy like him? A *man* like him? The people I know, they'd shit on us. But maybe not all of them, and the ones left over, they'd be my real stars. My true brothers. And if that's none of them, then I'm the richer for knowing that.

And my mind is opened to a sense of total revolution, not of fighting in the streets (yes that also but that's a thing that can never be won), but of a true revolutionary consciousness, which is a vision of freedom taken as far as it can go, which in our times is still further than the eye can see. And it can start with two brothers like us. Visions of Black Power rush through my mind and spiral out around my head, Malcolm, Eldridge, Stokely, Bobby, Louis, fabulous and gleaming and proud and visionary, but now seen with their limitations also.

Now I can find a way forward.

See, with the shooting a whole part of my life ended and my revolutionary consciousness was fragmented. Now I'm trying to pull it back together I find that it has grown, in the same way that lifting weights tears muscles, making them bigger and stronger. And painful or not, humiliating or not, courting accusations of letting down the stereotypical idea of the Black Man or not, I have to pursue the truth, By Any Means Necessary.

By capillary action, new visions of revolutionary change are drawn into my mind, more compelling and more prophetic, the last reactionary traces burnt out leaving everything gleaming like newly smelted steel, the machismo broadened into some transcendental sexuality, all the constraints purified into freedoms.

This is the impulse I've been waiting for, for maybe the whole of my life. And maybe I don't have the courage but it's what I have to do so I'll just have to do what I can and fake the rest.

But genuinely.

'I've got the guts,' I say.

JOHNNY

So me cruising past Jason's block in me Merc, man, checking out the legs of the ladies of the evening out in the afternoon, when me see the shit-weirdest ting Ah ever seen, man, and Ah seen *enough* shit go down, you know?

Is Jason stepping down the street and beside him that cissyboy from next door to where him live, and them walking along like them stars fi true, you know what I'm sayin'? Man, things sure different since last night, ennit? So me wind down the window as me glide by 'em. The fag have white rags in him hair. Him wear one big polka-dot white shirt wit cuffs over him hands, black DMs, white socks and baggy lime-green shorts that almost looks like a skirt. What a fucking fag, man! The shirt open and him wearing like this woman's lacey shit.

Jazz, man! me shout out the car window, What you doin' wit that? Him no answer. You pimping for the battyboy-them, man? You selling ya own arsehole? Him still don't answering. People in the street looking round but me no care. Got a new lady to suck ya dick? me shout. Fucking pussy! Fucking cocksucker!

Rage sweep over me when me tink me did spend two years doing what some battyboy say. Man, me feel like him did have *me* sucking on his dick, you know? Me and them other fools-them Errol and Floyd. Oh, yeah, we was sharp, man, sharp as fucking butter: like we did have this battyman down with us and we never even guess! And alla that Black Power bullshit was just wank to grease we arseholes with, man. Man, was we fucked! Black Power a fe getting rid of alla that shit, you know what I'm saying? For getting back to something *righteous*.

Me pull the motor over sharp before me go hit someting. Everyting him ever done that piss me off shrinking down into a tiny white dot hot sharp like a laser beam and it sitting in the middle of me forehead. Me hand shaking slightly as me slide the key out the ignition. *Fucking faggots.* Me bounce outta the car. The white light it spread out until all that left in me mind is rage. *Dirty fucking freaks.* Me want to me want to – me hands-them clench and unclench. The lines of the street pour away from me on either side and in the middle the faggots. The power it flow out me head, out through me disblinded eyes. Jazz ain't nothing but a freak. Me heart pull me up like a hook through me chest. Me block him path. The other fag look nervous, him look down, look away but him no look at me. People at a bus-stop watch, pretending not to.

Battyboy, me say. And me touch him face the way me woulda touch a woman, like the skin baby-soft. *Cunt,* me whisper. Jason staring in me face and me look at him pussy-eyes and realise me oughtta always have known. Man, what a *fool* !

Get out the way, man, him say. I don't want no trouble.

You gonna get some, bitch, me answer. Me grab him crotch. *Battyman.* Me squeeze the soft shit there.

But me forget him have hate too, and anger; him no a pussy like Floyd. Him fist-them hit me stomach hard and before me know what happen him knee me in the gut also.

The sun glittering, the sky blue.

Me stumble to me knee-them, coughing and sick but not out, expecting the follow-up. But him no wanna mash it up wit me, you know? Full a arrogance. Or faggishness. Him walk away from me, the little faggot wit him, like me did drop through a hole in the ground and disappear. Me hawk and spit and jump to me feet. This time me go for the little faggot. Me give him a kick in the small of him back and send him skidding along the pavement, face-down like them like it. Me laugh, seeing him dirtied up and writhing on the ground.

Jazz turn and smack me in the mout hard and me don't laughing cos me lip split and one a me teet bust-up and me stumble over backwards, and him on me chest pinning me arms wit him knee-them, one hand digging in me throat, the other pointing at me eyes. Me see me blood on the gold a him ring-them.

I could fix it so you never see nothin' ever again, man, him whisper. A tear burst outta one a his eye-them, but him eyes cold. Stone-cold kill crazy. And me know when a man can be a killer, you know? And him could do it. A long second pass. Then him pull himself up and turn and go fi help him friend. The bwoy's knees them bleeding, so's him nose. Alla sudden me feel mean, yunno, like me did break a butterfly wings, like, for no reason. Me mout start to throb.

We all on we feet by the time the pigs-them arrive, call by some snooping motherfucker can't leave shit alone, you know? We all just standing around so one of the pigs must arx what seem to be the trouble.

There ain't no trouble until you show up, me tell him.

You seem to be bleeding, sir, him say. *Sir* like in *nigger*, you understand me?

Me trip pon some garbage and knock over this geezer and we both fall on we face-them, me say. Just a accident. Me look over at the roving eyes at the bus-stop like to say *If you stick your oar in me a take a machete and go chop it off.* Suddenly them all arrived just in the last thirty seconds, you know?

The pigs look at the bwoy. Is that so?

Him nod, still no make four with no-one. Yeah, him say thickly.

Because we had a fight reported to us, the pig continue.

We no fight each other, man, me say. We only fight the shitstem.

The pigs getting bored now, it being only nigger-on-nigger voilence. There's nothing for you here, Jazz say. Why don't you go catch some rapists and child-molesters instead of being in people's business?

A report was made, sir. We were obliged to investigate it.

Yeah, well now you have investigated it, him say.

The pigs take we names, then get back in them car, look we over like them shrewd or shit, then drive off, doing a U-turn that hold up other people going about them law-abiding business so as to feel them dicks bigger. Me see Jazz turn to him friend. Him touching the other bwoy's face where it bruise, touching him tears, touching him arm all gentle-like, different from how me ever seen him. Is weird, but seeing it, it don't bother me, you know? Is like the idea make me mad, but seeing it them have a kind of innocence, man. And them ain't the pigs or the BNP, you know what I'm sayin'? They someting else, man. Very much someting else. Them turn away.

Ey, me call, stopping the blood from me lip with a bit of tissue paper. Them no turn back. Hey, me call again. Them keep on walking. Me go after them, touch Jazz shoulder. Him spin round, expecting a fight and shit, but me just smile at him with what's left a me teeth. Me hold out me hand.

Ey, man, me say. Look, brothers should stick together, right? Me look at him friend. Right? me say to him. First time me ever look at him. Just a lad, after all. And who give a shit what a man want to do, eh? You just gotta do it, is all.

Me bunch me fingers and touch fists wit Jason. Him looking at me strange. Me turn to him friend.

What's your handle, mate? me arx.

Carl, him say.

Ow ya doing, Carlton, man? me arx, giving him me hand. Him have a firm grip.

We labrish a couplea minutes till a traffic warden starts eyeing me motor. Me no discuss business. Then Ah must be on me way. Me offer 'em a lift but Carl need to go clean himself up.

Sorry bout that, man, me say as me get back in the Merc, meaning the blood on him shirt. As me close the door me press down the window and call, me get you another one, man, a finer one!

CARL

It's not the first time I've been kicked in on the street, and I haven't normally got someone to stick up for me, to draw the violence away from me, you know? But it still hurts: The pain in my knees focusses and sinks inside, making me a little colder, chilling my heart.

See, normally I can just hate those people, sink them into a hell of violation and humiliation. And I can burn with hate until in my mind they char and flake and crumble into ash.

My Darkest Vision:

Like in Diamond Dogs I'm walking through the ruins of the city and rats as big as cats are eating six million dying peoploids and I'm walking in white as fine as Aladdin Sane and as fierce as RuPaul like a prophet of glamour. And the dying peoploids turn their faces up to me and beg me to help, their bloated and scabrous living bodies putrefying. But they brought it on themselves and there's nothing I can do so I don't even have to try. I just walk and walk until I'm in the green.

But now I have to try.

Johnny tosses his dyed red-green-and-yellow dreads and laughs with the blood streaming down his face out of his mouth. The dreads dance. I never even spoke to someone like that before and now he's grabbing my shoulders like we're best buddies.

Anyone fuck wit you, man, them fucking with me, he says.

I feel a whole lot safer, I'm thinking. But something I thought was solid is wire bound into a tight coil, and the coil's loosening and as it loosens it's starting to lose its shape.

MOLLY

Carly's late.

Maybe he's shopping.

Maybe he's taking in the sales, window-shopping. Trying stuff on that's too expensive to buy, Gucci, Versace, Hermes, like you do, stuff like that, feeling like class even if you don't have a penny, and laughing when shop assistants are rude because you go on and you're penniless but you're free and they have to stay and stay and they can't afford the clothes either, even with a staff discount.

Maybe he's been stabbed in an alley.

Maybe his new boyfriend's tied him up and is mutilating him.

Take some drugs, girl. Mellow out.

I make a pot of herbal tea because he usually arrives just as I'm pouring the water over the fragrant leaves.

JAZZ

He lets me wash his knees and face. I put a spot of Dettol in warm water and wipe the blood away with balls of cotton wool. All this time he hasn't said a word. I slip off his shirt and leave it to soak in a tub in the bathroom. He's just standing there in the middle of the room, as if he's in shock.

I feel as if everything I've ever done is to blame for this moment. I touch his waist. The texture of the lace and the warmth of his body behind it thrills my fingers. A shudder runs up him.

'Sorry,' I say. Because in the end it is my fault: my star, my lies, my bringing into being a situation where violence had to happen. And in the end it was Johnny who said the right thing, *Brothers should stick together.* Things came together then between us in a way they never did before. And of all of them, he was the one I least expected to come around to the reality of my situation in any way whatsoever.

We always used to fight, me and Johnny. We thought we wanted the same things and maybe we did, but for different reasons, fulfilling different visions. And the battles we needed to fight were never quite the same battles, which made it harder because we both have a vision of the Black man's struggle. Mine is here and now, always staring into the terrifying moment, resisting the weight of the stone that drags you down and drowns you in the past; his is Jah's, and Haile Selassie's, and gold-robed dreams of ancient Zimbabwe, kings and queens and emperors of distant empires. But these are just the two sides of the coin that is Yellow For The Gold That They Stole. We are both smelted in the same forge and hammered by the same hammer and the impurities in our ore too have the same source. I have the words and he has the music and there is a sort of love in that.

Now we know each other, we are both set free. But still, that is my struggle. Which is why I must apologise, I must atone.

'Sorry, man,' I say again. 'He's okay, Johnny.' I stand and take Carly in my arms, hold him. He shudders again. 'Do you want me to go?' I ask, holding him tighter than ever. He shakes his head.

'No,' he whispers. 'I just want you to love me.'

I'm going down on him fast when the telephone starts to ring, taking his circumcised head to the back of my throat, my nose touching the oil-smooth skin around the base of his dick where his pubic hair used to be. He reaches over and answers it. I don't stop blowing him.

'Hello?' he answers hoarsely. 'Molly?' He pauses to stop himself gasping. 'Yeah, yeah, I'm – fine. Yeah – I'll come over in

– half a hour.' His voice wavers. 'Can – I – bring – a – friend?' His fingers push through my hair, trying to stop me. I let him slip out of my mouth. His hard-on slaps against his belly and he gasps. I look up at his face which is comically embarrassed. 'Right now, girl,' he says in answer to some question over the phone. He hangs up.

'Well?' he asks, pushing his hips up a little. 'What did you stop for?'

MOLLY

'He's good-looking, girl,' I say, handing Carly an iced tea in a tall glass. 'That much I have to admit. But that gold tooth!' I gesture mouthwards. 'Girl, that's too much, too macho-thug. Not my thing at all. But then I guess that's what makes me a fag-hag.' I sigh, refill my own glass.

'Girlfriend, *please*,' Carly replies. 'You know the fags are butcher'n the straights these days.'

'Your beau proving the point, Carly, darling,' I reply, hoping to get a reaction. He pulls a few leaves off my potted mint plant, stirs them into his drink. Jason's out of the room taking a piss so we're just having a few moments of intensive girl-talk.

'Yeah, I guess,' he says. Then quickly: 'Molly, I think he might be the one.'

Before I can think of a reply, Jazz comes back into the room. I watch him go over to Carl so's I can make my mind up. You can measure like how bi a guy is, or how hetero he's going to go, by the way he touches his boyfriend in front of a woman, even if he doesn't fancy her. The less he touches, the more hetero he is. In my experience, anyway.

Jazz swings himself down onto the floor easily and sits between Carl's legs, hanging his bare lanky arms over Carl's thighs. He looks up at Carl's face and Carl bends down and kisses him on the lips. Jazz looks kind of serious the whole time so I only give him 99 per cent.

But lawks-a-mighty, Missy Scarlett, it must be a botheration bein' able to pass for straight.

Then Carl goes off to go for a piss and to check his make-up. He's still got the rags in his hair, and he's as cute as Bambi in an enormous baggy green check jacket (a homage to John Lydon, who we both love, this is Carly's post-punk Pistolette revival look) and baggy green shorts. He's wearing the paste-pearl choker I gave him his last birthday.

'How long have you known him?' Jazz asks me the moment Carly's out of the room, all charming and probing.

'Oh gosh, about six years,' I reply lightly.

'What's he like?' he asks. 'I mean, what's he been like?' There's something he obviously wants to dig out of me. But what? He's intense enough about it.

'How do you mean?' I ask him.

'Like,' he looks around to see if Carl's on his way back out, 'what sort of guys has he been out with? I mean, guys like me?'

Am I just one of a line of ersatz jack-the-lads? I guess he's asking, *am I nothing special?*

'All sorts,' I say brightly. 'Skinny, fat, macho, artistic, tall, short. Not camp, mostly, or at least not very. He did go out with a drag queen once, though. Mostly white too, except the drag queen. He was Japanese.'

'A Japanese drag queen,' Jazz repeats, choosing the one he fancies is most different from himself, between you and me. He thinks for a while, then he asks:

'Has he ever gone out with a girl?'

'He sort of went out with me for a while,' I say, slightly impressed that Jazz should be hip enough to ask that about a *feminine* man. 'We shared a flat and everything for a year-and-a-half, when he was at beauty school. It was a one-bedroom flat and we shared the bed. We had a rule, that you couldn't bring anyone back.'

'You weren't lovers, though?'

'Would it matter if we had been?'

He looks away from me.

'No,' he lies.

(I could tell him No, we never were, we just held hands, did each other's make-up and clothes, cooked and cleaned for each other, but why should I? Call me a hippy, but I think love is in the heart. I mean, why should fucking be the most important thing? But then, men think with their dicks, I guess. Even Carly.)

'Well, that's okay, then, isn't it?' I say, unable to resist being unhelpful. He looks back at me with an edge to his face. But anyway, since when did I have the right to blab out an unedited version of Carl's life-story? We've all done things we'd rather forget, even if that's not one of them. We've all done things that misrepresent us so much that telling the truth about them would be a sort of lying.

'What sort of guys do you like?' I ask.

'I dunno,' he says, not looking back at me.

There's a long silence until Carly comes back into the room.

'I love your new mirror,' he says to me.

'I think it's Victorian,' I say. 'I got it cheap cos there's a split in the frame. I just loved the pattern, all the fruit and urns. It made me think of Shelley.'

But Carl isn't into Shelley and stuff like that, only Stevie Smith. He knows I think it's romantic, though. If we're looking at old things, he sometimes goes, 'It's like Shelley, right?' And I laugh. Sometimes he means it though. I think that's what you get when you're black and the past's white. I dunno.

CARL

Finally we're going out, me and Jazz and Molly, dolled up to the nines, all of us. Down the West End I'm just another clubland starlet, a bit brighter than some of them but not so bright as others. I feel at home here; it's my people out here on these streets. And with Jazz at my side I feel like royalty, like we're the King and Queen and Queen and King of the West End, you know? I feel like everyone else knows it too, cos we don't bump into people; they move aside like dancers, like the streets around us are a big film set we're crossing and everything's choreographed around us.

At the door of Kudos I turn and shoot a look at Jazz, afraid he'll be afraid or, like, what would be worse, disgusted; afraid he'll be a closet-case after all, or that the violence I know fills him in some way that I don't understand yet will come sliding out of its sheath. But he slips past me and leads us in and down the stairs without batting a eyelid.

I watch him going to get the drinks, a snowball for me,

sweet white wine for Molly, a whisky for himself, maybe with water, nothing softer. I still feel nervous, wondering 'Will he get into a fight?' But he doesn't. Some handlebar-moustachioed period-revival leatherman knocks into him. They both just smile, friendly-like. I start to relax and have a good time.

The weird thing happens afterwards, in the club: The Fruit Machine at Heaven, a good mixed night.

Me and Molly been dancing, Jazz was leaning on the bar, watching us, watching me. I go for the grind and get some sweat on me. I think he's enjoying it even though he won't dance. He just wants to watch.

'That's the story of your life,' I say to him.

'Not now,' he says. But he still won't dance.

'Put on a show, girl,' Molly says to me. And we do.

We're sitting down after, having a drink, and me and Molly're having a rest. Suddenly I notice Jazz is looking up and staring at someone. I look round to see who it can be, and it's hard to tell but I think it's some middle-aged fat (white) guy in slacks and Caramac-brown shoes and a maroon leather jacket who's like eyeing Jazz up. But that isn't it exactly. There's a look on this guy's face and there's a look on Jazz's face like there's something between them or something.

'You know that guy?' I ask him.

Jazz looks at me, kind of shocked. 'No,' he says, shaking his head. And, seeing Jazz is with us, the guy doesn't come over, he just kind of gives him a look and moves off. Jazz blanks the whole thing like it hasn't happened, but for the whole of the rest of the evening he's on edge and not enjoying it. Actually, we don't stay for much longer, partly cos of that, and partly cos Molly's got a shoot in the morning.

'Night, girl,' she says to me at the front door of her building, kissing me on the lips.

'Night, boy,' she says to Jazz, kisses him on the cheek. At least she doesn't hate him like I thought she might. Maybe it was because she saw that he could be afraid. See, Molly wears all her faults on the outside and she likes other people to do the same or she gets frightened and resentful. And he did so she didn't. It's like, all the guys she's ever gone out with, they all always cried easier than she did. I'm the exception: I don't never cry. Not for love.

Don't want to smudge the eyeliner.

Molly's flat's only fifteen minutes from my place, so me and Jazz walk it. I almost say *Let's get a cab* but I don't want Jazz to think I'm a total bimbo. Beyond the yellow light in the perfect black, stars shine white like diamonds, like the sky's pearls pushed through by its hidden mother-of-pearl shell.

'Beautiful,' Jazz says, looking up. He looks like he owns the stars and the whole sky. He takes my hand in the street, his fingertips cool against my palm, squeezes it. And it's like everything the world's worth is curled up there in that little spot of warmth like some tiny animal, sleeping. It makes me realise that I've never been in love before. I mean, with Andy I suppose I thought it was love. But really I always knew it was just two boys together clinging.

You're wondering how I can say love after just two days? Well listen, you don't need to be married for fifty years to feel love, okay? And if it dies the day it was born, it's still love.

And for the first time, I really believe that.

JAZZ

I wanted to tell him, I *want* to tell him but man, the words aren't there. I've touched and I've touched but I've never been touched even though I felt things, such things as I do not want to remember. And now he's touched me and I'm so afraid. I should tell him, but I don't want to do anything that could drive him away.

Except lie.

I sit on the sill and stare out of the window at the moon, letting the sweat dry on my chest and back. The air in the room is heavy with breath and sleep. My body still tingles from where it slid over Carl's smooth-shaved skin. I rub a silk scarf over my face and my crotch. From somewhere the scent of honeysuckle is floating. Across the street in a flat a floor down from ours a Black man and a white woman are making love with the lights on and the curtains open. After a while the man gets out of bed and closes the curtains, his dick at half-mast. She is lighting a cigarette behind him.

I never smoked. It's dirty.

For once the violence of the city feels dispersed, like when the air's clean after a heavy storm, as if the rainwater's extinguished the burning buildings and hearts and minds and left them cool. It makes me realise that anger will not be the Storm, that the Storm will be precipitated by something quite different: by Love. And that's not sentiment, that's history: no revolution based on hate ever replaced anything bad with anything better, and anger has no vision except the Apocalypse.

So there's things I've got to tell Carly.

I start when I feel a touch on my shoulder. I look round and up into his face. My eyes are full, my lips too. I twist myself round and hold him tight around the waist. He is very warm, hot almost. I kiss his chest and he sighs a little sigh, sensing there's something wrong in me.

'What is it, Jazz?' he asks. I like the way he says my name, soft like velvet.

'Nothing, man,' I say. 'I'm just watching the moon. Sometimes... sometimes I don't sleep too well. So I watch the moon.' I let my breath out, try to shrink and be small. 'Look, man, look,' I'm still holding onto him with one arm and pointing out of the window with the other. 'Look, sometimes there are so many clouds you can't see the silver of it.'

'Is it me that's the clouds, then?' he asks, his voice too gentle for what he means.

'You're the moon,' I say. 'And the clouds, they're all inside me, behind my eyes.'

'You're a poet,' he says. 'But you're afraid of your poetry.'

Which is true.

'I've got something I have to tell you,' I say. 'Some things.' I'm talking into his belly, my lips brushing his skin. He runs his fingers through my hair and I shudder.

'What's wrong, baby?' he whispers.

'That geezer in the bar,' I say. 'The one who made out like he knew me?'

'Was he your lover?'

'No, man. Nothing like that. I told you, I've never had a lover. And I couldn't ever have a white lover anyway. I don't believe that's possible. Not for love.'

I know he's had white lovers, but he lets what I've said go

as a personal thing, not a grand statement, doesn't rise to it.

'So how *did* you know him, Jazz?'

'For cash, man. For cold cash.'

'You rented?'

'No, man!' I say sharply, my breath starting to hollow. 'It wasn't like that!' I pull away from him so I can look up at him, and claw my rising voice back down. 'What I did was, I heard from being around the scene that being a masseur, an escort, that kind of shit, that that could be easy money. I knew enough geezers who'd done it off and on, and even made like up to twelve hundred quid a week, they said. Without tax. So I made up this ad, saying *Call XXX-XXXX for Jason, Black raggamuffin, rough, tough and lean, XVWE,* and put it in and waited. See, I thought if they came to me then I could walk away with it: Money and myself, like with the stripping. The trick is, to walk away with yourself.'

'So that old guy was a client?'

A rented room in King's Cross, spartan but clean, not much furniture, nothing personal, a gas fire always on to drive away the damp, to make clothes seem like an encumbrance, the fumes making the atmosphere dopey, hustling, always hustling, grabbing hold and pushing away at the same time. Everything's a hustle, man, politics religion business sex. I had to prove I could keep cold, if I was cold I wasn't touched, if I was cold it wasn't me, if I was cold I was elsewhere, not – Like them voices on the phone people nothing oh –

'Yeah,' I say, looking down. I shake my head slightly. 'A client. Things turned out a bit differently from what I expected, man: Blokes falling for you, being *romantic* for fuck's sake, like they weren't paying you for it. I never saw any of them more than a couple of times because of that kind of shit. It was too – they'd try to give me stuff, clothes, jewellery, but I only wanted cash. Like I said, cold untainted impersonal dirty cash. And the more they fell for me, the more I despised them, you know?'

'You must of hated yourself a lot,' Carl says. And maybe he's right. No, there's no maybe. I know it's true. But he doesn't let go of me, he doesn't turn away or vomit or curse me out. In fact he squeezes me a little closer.

'They'd ask me for other shit, and if they gave me enough money I'd let them do certain acts, like blow me or lick my arse. But they could never touch me. Not for any money. Some of them wanted me to hit them and shit. And I would do that, man.'

Carly twitches against me when I say that. 'You did that stuff?' His voice is husky, brittle.

'Yeah,' I say, closing my eyes for a moment, holding him a little tighter too. Then I let him go a little, hold him looser, look up at him. 'Yeah, I did it, man,' I say. 'But I had to stop.'

'Why?' His voice is a little more solid now, less dessicated now he knows I had to stop.

I sigh, drag in a deep breath, let it out.

'I was enjoying it too much, man,' I say flatly. 'But something happened too, an actual thing. See, I thought I understood it, all the shit they wanted to do, the S&M shit. It was like Catholicism, like they wanted to atone for their whiteness, for the crimes that had been committed in the name of that. And I would hit them because that completed it, you know? Sick justice, but still...'

My voice trails off. *The studs the leather the clamps the belts the chains the straps often ill-fitting but they wouldn't care if it really fitted right hung right because it was the symbolism that mattered the symbol existing before the material and I knew it was crazy and I knew it was sick, it was making me sick but I felt I was like Eldridge, I thought it could be sanity out of madness. But if they* wanted *me to hit them, the ones who wanted that, where was justice or revenge then? And my dick got hard and I felt like it wasn't part of me but I knew, I knew it was and look at Eldridge practising on the sisters in the ghetto, so much rage but still but still I didn't stop I let the rage run through me like the rush of sperm the length of my dick it was so easy. Hate is easy. Anger is easy. It was all easy but it was all at least a simulacrum of sense until. Until.* I clear my mind and my throat.

'But then, but then this guy comes in, this middle-aged Black guy, handsome, proud, ex-army geezer. And he wanted me to beat him until he screamed. That was it. Until he screamed. And it couldn't be a white hitting him, it had to be a Black, and it couldn't be a woman, it had to be a man. And I needed the money so I did it.' I clear my throat again. 'Yeah, I did it. But I could feel the top of my head screwing upwards and outwards, you know? And it was like my brain was being torn out by red-hot hooks. And when he came screaming, man, *screaming,* then something changed in me.' *Reeling vomiting chromatic with tears my throat burning from his screams his pain and I rested my cheek on his back and the salt of my tears toughened the marks of the whip.*

'Stop snivelling you fucking cissy,' he said, tied down there on the bed. 'Don't wipe your snotty nose on me. Don't fucking touch me, boy. I'm not paying you to touch me.'

I pulled my head away, got up, got dressed and got out of there, left him there for hours and when I came back he was turned on again but I wouldn't do any more except untie him and tell him to get out, beg him knowing the whining would turn him off. And after he left I said, It's the army, the Uncle Tomming army, but I looked in the mirror and couldn't see my face looking any different. 'So I stopped. That's what made me stop.'

Carl bends down and kisses my forehead.

'Do you hate me?' I ask him, my searching eyes on his secret ones.

'I love you,' he says.

I breathe out. Oxygen is released from the crystallised air and the bands of fear around my chest are loosened.

I only have one secret left to lose.

ERROL

Floyd losing it freaked me out, man. I mean, it set me thinking about what happened in the worst way, you know what I'm sayin'? I know it's just paranoid, man, but I pick up the phone and punch in Jazz's number again. There still ain't no reply, not even after I let it ring for like five minutes. So he's out. Gone out. That's all.

But I can't stop from wondering, have the pigs kicked in the door? He's down the nick, you know what I'm sayin'? Having the shit kicked out of him?

Might be he's at his old man's, but I don't know the number so I call Johnny up instead. If shit's going down, Johnny'll know about it. Plus, I better warn him about Floyd. Man, that brother is *seriously* fucked.

Johnny's out also.

Shit, shit. I ring Jazz again. Still no fucking answer.

You could get ten years, not even for offing the pig, just

for being there on the wrong side of the fence, just for that, man. Don't get me wrong, Jazz wouldn't squeal, right. But Floyd, we gotta make sure Floyd keeps it shut.

Man, it's a bitch when you can't trust no-one.

Jazz Jazz Jazz answer the fucking phone, man.

We had this thing and it's all fucking falling apart. The Panther Posse. Man, that was the bomb. We stopped just hanging out, got serious, got political: too many brothers and sisters brutalise by the pigs, too many brothers and sisters behind bars. Jazz opened my eyes to that. I mean not to that it happened, cos we all know what's going down, right? But to *why* it happened, to the way history is made by the powerful, *reality* is made by the powerful (who can control what can be said, and where, who can determine the meaning of the words themselves and so suppress what can be *thought*). So like you had Black people thinking of Africa as savages with bones through their noses. And that's power. And that power-attitude trickles down through the state, the schools. The law. But within its cogs and mechanisms are necessary spaces where you can think different thoughts and draw breath for the battle. And raising that money for the Neville Latournaux fund, the yout with the bust arm who was mash up by the pigs, was a way of fighting the power, challenging it, damming some of the capillaries of power, you know what I'm sayin'? We was doing the jobs to get the money to do that, and for the first time I was doing something that mattered, you know? Something important. And now it's almost gone: What matters is holding on by its fingernails, and only just.

So I gotta reach Jason. But he ain't answering.

CARL

He stretches out like a panther. A black panther. Soft and dangerous.

'Love me,' he whispers. His voice disturbs the air. *Love me.* It's not like I have a choice: he's like a child, and you can't not love a child, can you?

I touch his hard-on and his whole body tenses with violence. I see it spread up and out through him. He pulls me down on top of him. Our bodies fuse. His fingers dig into my back. His eyes are screwed closed.

I kiss his chest and trembling stomach, push his thighs apart until his knees touch the mattress on either side. I go down on his rigid erection, letting it fill my mouth, and girl, that feels good. And then his hand's on the back of my head, forcing me down so I almost choke. I struggle and he grabs my plaits and pulls me up sharply. He's looking at me crazy.

'Don't do that, man, just don't do it.'

'Why not, Jazz?' I ask. 'You like doing it, right? And you like having it done.'

'No-one I like ever blows me, man,' he says. 'No-one I ever respect, just that bitch Judy and the faggots. I mean, if you pay, like, that makes you a faggot. To me. And if you go down on me, that makes you a faggot too.'

'So I'm just a faggot?' I say in response to this raving. My hard-on droops.

'No, man.' He touches my face, the side of my lip. 'I just don't want you to do that.'

'You're frightened,' I say, cupping his face with one hand, straddling him. 'Frightened of losing control.'

His eyes glaze slightly. He looks away, runs a hand down between my buttocks to the back of my balls, squeezes them. 'How many white guys laid you?' he asks. 'How many white cocks have been up you?' moving his fingers between my buns again. 'A dozen? A hundred? More?'

'What's it to you?' I say, turned on by the movement of his hand, turned off by what he's saying.

'All that whiteness,' he whispers. 'I want to fuck it out of you, man. Leave you pure and black and shining so we'll be one, fuck you clean with my dick.'

I pull away from him, pull his hand off my balls and my now totally-limp dick, stand up.

'No, man,' I say, my voice hard, loud, clear. 'I don't want that. I don't want to be *fucked*, alright? If we making love and part of that is you going into my body, that's one thing, maybe. But being *fucked*, being rammed, whatever you want to fucking call it, that's something else, Jazz. And I don't want it. And all this fucking white this and white that shit, what's that all about?' I grab at his clothes where they're lying on the floor, throw them at him. 'A cock's a cock's a cock, a man's a man's a man, skin is skin is skin and love is love is love and I don't regret nothing or no-one. And if you think shoving your dick up my butt's gonna alter the fact that I've slept with white guys, then I pity you cos you got a dick for a brain!'

I'm literally trembling with rage. At Jazz. At myself for letting him do this to me. I'll be asking Buju Banton for a date next. My gorge rises, strangling my voice in my throat. Upside my head there's a piercing, glass-shattering tone that slides forward like a helmet of white noise.

He stares at me, looking kind of hurt or surprised or something. I defocuss on what he's feeling. 'I didn't mean it like that,' he says quietly, trying to bring the level down. But it's too late.

'You did, though.' My voice is still loud. 'You fucking meant it just like that. And if you want to make me clean, you must think I'm pretty fucking dirty.' Tears are starting to roll down my cheeks and I don't want him to see them. 'Get the fuck out, Jazz. Just get the *fuck* out.'

Slowly he dresses, deliberately sexy, maybe. I don't know. It's just abstract. When he's dressed he comes over, tries to kiss me. I flinch away.

'Just go,' I say.

When he's gone I go and look in the mirror.

My eyeliner's run.

JAZZ

Crazy crazy *crazy*. It's like all the madness in me rose up like ink up the stem of a cut flower and flushed out through the petals, all the violence too. Christ, I wanted to hit him, I wanted to force him, I wanted to crush his flower into pulp, bloody the petals. What's wrong with me? I fucking *love* him. Man to man.

Maybe I don't have the guts.

It was easy looking out of the corner of my eye at Johnny groping his crotch or watching Floyd's arse peripherally when he bent over. It was easy imagining Floyd's perfect Black cock between my perfect Black lips, my hands cupping his buttocks to an exact sphere. And that's what I thought about when the old men blew me or kissed my arse or I whipped them. I could rise above it on that vision of perfection. And if they angered me with their presence I would choke them on my dick, smother them with my arse, or keep hitting them when they wanted me to stop.

And I thought I was keeping pure.

But when Carl did what he did, the dirt that I'd kept hidden, buried, unseen, poured out of me all over him, and I was terrified that he wasn't going to be perfect and that I had become *his* dirty little piece of shit. He was right. I had to have control. So I said those things, forced them on him. Forced him to kick me out.

It's easier this way.

I look round my room, wishing Johnny hadn't lifted my stack. The room feels very empty now; bare and stupid. Stupid because a fool lives in it. I want to go back and knock on his door, but I don't. Instead I lie down on my bed fully-clothed, one hand shoved down the front of my jock, and try to sleep.

But it all rushes through my mind too fast for sleep, the old visions of the battle where the Black man is always getting fucked but he fights back by never accepting it, by always feeling the pain. We have been fucked by guns and by gold, and the white man's pleasure has been our pain. But now I think about Carly, his arsehole opened by many white dicks and it cuts into me that the battle lines have become lost again because he was never *fucked*, so he says.

Just loved.

My own ugliness appalls me just as Carl's beauty shocks me. I feel the vibrant terror of life, the violence of my desire for him, the terrible naturalness of it, *exotic polished viridian mantisses chew at each others' heads as they mate, nature in red on green penetration a battle but is that so? But Carly was never* fucked. *I wish –*

It was my father who made me see battles. He's always made me fight, for everything. Taken out the anger he felt with himself (for climbing the ladder so high and no higher, for being so intelligent and no more, so powerful and no more, for throwing Sly up in the air, for dropping him, for not being able to do up what he'd undone and for feeling that made him not a man) taken that anger out on me, punching and shoving (but never touching or hugging) me, demanding that I fight back, attacking me all the more viciously for feeling my mother's eyes upon him finding him wanting.

Battles.

Sometimes being here being Black you have to shut your eyes and your ears to the white faces and white noise around you, the polluting element invading your nose and throat and lungs, permeating into your blood and brains. Sometimes. Other times you have to open them wide and take it all in: muggers rapists musicians sportsmen boxers runners businessmen with portable phones drug-dealers baby-fathers unable to reach out with their broken English some mutating into white niggers some into Black, invisible men all of them separated by things seen and unseen struggling not to go out of their minds, struggling not to become the mirror of the white state's vision of horror.

I shoot out beyond it and float in the cool Blackness before Doctor Yakob concocted his master plan.

So I bought the gun because it's a war. And I used it because things have to change: the balance has to be disturbed.

Last night I slept with a male, and the night before. I wanted to do it and I did. And I realised that I have never desired women. My father's my mother's the state's expectations have all been denied. I feel on the brink of a new revelation. I feel powerful. I feel freed from how I see myself. On my head is the Crown of the Future. In my mind I draw up a new set of battle-lines: Black, white, man, woman, gay, straight don't matter. All that matters is, are you for me or against me? I call for a Total Revolution, where all certainties are called into doubt, where we all have a chance to snatch freedom.

I shall begin by being free to love whomsoever I choose.

A shadow leaves me. I am in a hall where all the saints glitter with a highly-worked obsidian purity. And for the first time I belong there, dancing among the statues.

In between waking and sleeping I have a dream: I'm walking through the park with Carly, our arms wrapped around each others' waists. Maybe we're naked, I don't know. It feels like we are but there's no self-consciousness. Other people, couples, are strolling around us but we take no notice. It's the night-time but everything stands out clearly in shades of purple and blue. We come to a pond with urns at each corner, their surfaces crumbly with lichen. The water of the pond is very clear, so clear it glitters, and it is almost solid with glittering, wriggling golden carp. We sit at the edge, dangling our feet in the water, the carp cool and sensual all around them. We are born up on a bed of undulating solid gold and in the reflected light we become golden too. Carl's hand touches my chest.

When I wake up, the sheets are stained.

MOLLY

'Girl, I *told* you so! I know, I know, I promised I wouldn't say it but it just slipped out.'

But I can tell he's been crying so I don't play the line for all it's worth.

'He was just a closet-case,' I say.

'Maybe – ' he says.

'Girl, don't even think about it,' I say. 'He's just another No Good Man.'

'Yeah,' he replies sourly, sounding tired.

'Come round for a Snowball and a cuddle?' I ask. There's a long pause at the other end of the line. 'Go on,' I add. 'You know you want to...'

'Thanks, Molly,' he says, finally buckling on a cheerful voice. 'I'd like that. I'll come over now.'

We hang up. I go over to the mirror to fix my hair. It doesn't look its best after being lain on for three hours and then dragged upright at three a.m. I primp it with an Afro-comb. Now my head looks the right shape. I go for the cosmetics next. This situation positively demanding full-face as it does.

It's funny, a lot of people think putting make-up on makes you dishonest because it conceals things, but for me and for Carly it's like how you reveal the real you. It's like the mirror you hold up to your inner self. Or something. So if I wasn't made-up when he came around, it'd be like I was holding something back from him.

I put on sombre, autumnal colours, but not cold ones: they're all warm and golden. A mirror to how I want to make him feel.

I pop out to the 7-11 for some lemonade for the Snowballs

92

then come back and wait. I have the Creatures playing softly in the background in a flamenco mood: *It's funny to see How pathetic some men can be – Hah!*

Carly arrives all dressed in black: black mesh vest, black shirt, baggy black shorts and Voodoo top hat. Black lace gloves on his fingers, steel bangles on his wrists, designer punk earrings. I hand him a Snowball. He sips it holding the glass with both hands, like a little kid holding a glass that's too big for him. Sometimes the world does that to you, makes you feel small. His make-up is immaculate and has the cold formality of a geisha's. It's all matte: nothing shines or glitters or reflects. It's all kept within, and keeps the outside out. His eyes stand out starkly against that flatness. He looks me in the eye, smiles a little, looks away and a sigh slips out.

'I really thought – ' His voice chokes off for a moment. 'Girl, I really thought this was the one, you know?' Tears are shining on his face. I've never seen Carly cry, you know. I mean, I've heard him on the phone, sure, but I've never actually seen him cry before.

'It was the real thing, huh, baby?' I say, wrapping my arms around him. He quivers against me like some small wild animal.

'Yeah,' he whispers.

'Well, he's gone now, baby' – I'm whispering too – 'He's gone and everything'll be alright.'

FLOYD

I'm under me motor, adjusting the bearings when I feel this foot nudging me thigh. I roll out on me board and I'm looking up at Jazz. He's standing over me, the sun behind his head like Christ with a halo of corn. I squint up at him, wipe the grease off me face.

I thought you was dead, man, I say.

So did I, man, he says. But I'm back now.

Man, I could kiss you, I say, getting up. He smiles, funny-like. Something about him's changed, I dunno what.

You seen Johnny? he asks.

No, I say. He smiles again.

He's alright, Johnny, Jazz says. I reckon we should, like,

stay off the streets, you know what I'm saying? We've had enough heat, man. We don't need no more.

I nod. We touch fists. See you around, man, I say.

Later, he says.

And it's like the gun never really happened, man. Like it was all just a nightmare. The pigs ain't down on Jazz, they ain't down on no-one: I looked in all the papers. It was a front-page thing for a couple of days, yeah. Then it just faded out. And it ended up just a thing in the papers about as real as Hitler's car on the moon. Just a story. Or a dream. And the photo they used of the pig didn't look like how he looked on the night, guy. In the night flare white through the wire. The way he looked then was how soldiers must see the enemy, right? Just a casualty of war. Jazz was right after all.

See, last night I took some pills, man, and I didn't dream at all. I just woke up and it was just another day, with everything in the hands of God like it always is, and I felt okay, you know? Back balancing on the beam.

I watch Jazz walk away free as the breeze, like Christ or some African prince untouched by chains save by chains of destiny. Still I want to follow him, but man, the path he's taking, I don't think I can. So I watch him to the corner, then lay back on me board and slide back under the car. For a moment me eyes is dazzled, and all I can see is black on yellow, floating upwards.

JUDY

I open the door and it's Jazz standing there.

'Is Errol here,' he asks.

'No, man,' I say, 'I don't know where he is.'

He turns to go.

'Stay, man,' I say. 'Maybe I do know.'

He stands there watching me, looking sexy and lean. I imagine him firing the gun into the pig's open mouth, blowing it away red.

'Maybe I know about you,' I say.

'What do you know about me,' he says, his voice on one dead level.

'What I heard,' I say.

'What you heard,' he says.

'What's it worth,' I ask.

'A busted face,' he says. And I remember, this the guy that offed a pig. So I stop fooling around.

'Errol told me,' I say. 'About you shooting the pig and shit.'

He breathes out now, relieved like – why? – and turns to go.

'Is that it, man,' I say.

'Yeah, that's it,' he says.

You bastard, I'm thinking, watching his arse and shoulders as he goes.

JAZZ

I'm in the streets again, and Afrika is lowering over me like a vast storm cloud hurtling overhead but so long it never passes, only spreads above me. I'm re-entering all the castles of the past, the civilisations of Zimbabwe and Egypt shining in the white sun. But there's a tightness in my chest: I never look at the past, not my own, not any past. You might say, but he looks at history and that's the past. But I only look at history for the present, for what it makes today, for what it makes tomorrow. See, the past is old and haunted mansions, crumbling plantation clapboard edifices haunted by whiteness and black blood.

But Afrika is vast and heavy like some great ship on which I am not passenger nor crewman. I touch the leather medallion round my neck. It feels heavy, like a chain or burden.

But I don't take it off.

JOHNNY

Whey me a live the trains-them always going past, and the rattle of the wheels on the joints in the tracks them get into me dreams. Me must be always on the move, man, from job to job, from woman to woman, rattle rattle the wheels moving me on inna 4/4 time. Is why me car so important, man, why it must run sweet, you know? Cos that movement what Ah is, is me mirror, mirror in the chrome.

Me pump up the stereo and swing out the window onto the fire escape, stretch out looking down across the tracks. On a streetcorner a black girl in a floating pink dress waiting like she going to a wedding or ting. She hold her hat on her head cos the corner windy. Up here there ain't no wind, though. I imagine the dress blowing up, revealing her, and feel meself getting hard.

Not Jazz, man. Him don't interest. Had two gyal at once and him don't interest, ennit? Me lie back, rest me head against the warm bricks. See, the sun go down pon this side a the building each evening. The one good ting 'bout living here. Two gyal and don't interest. Me draw pon me spliff, taking the good shit all the way down, lightening me heart and brain, flowing wit the riddims, bewitch by Scientist. *What Is The Secret Of The Master Tape?* Old sounds the best, yunno.

Down below me me see Jazz coming along the back alley, picking him way over the trash and dirt, trying a keep him Timberland-them clean. From up here them look spotless yellow. Him jump up and grab the bottom rung a the fire-ladder, start to climb. A minute later him swing over the railing.

Ow ya doin', bredren? me say, high-fiving wit' him.

Not so bad, man, him say.

And ya star? me arx.

Jazz look away, squint at the sun which is low over the buildings now. Him don't say nothing. His tracksuit open and me look at the gold on him smooth, hard chest. Me pass him the spliff. Him draw it down to the roach and a evening breeze pulls the sweet smoke out of him mouth and nostrils.

We sit there not talking for, like, fifteen minutes, just letting the sun drop down out of sight, leaving the skyline black on red and pink.

Let's go inside, him say.

Me shrug and we climb in through the window. Jazz stares at this poster of Afrika me have over me bed, *staring*, man, like him did never see it before.

Afrika, me say, drawing the word out. *Afffriiikaaaa.*

Yeah, him say, and me wonder what him thinking. Him reach out and touch the poster. I look at the profile of him face, proud and Afrikan, like a sculpture, everyting elegant, wired like we all wired, like every yout on every street corner, waiting for the next card to be turn. Him swallow, still staring at the map. Me light up another spliff.

Them did have 'em, me say. In Afrika, man, them had 'em.

Jazz turn and look at me, kind of blank, like.

Like you, man, me say. Faggots, right? In Afrika. Since long time.

Yeah? him say, looking away again.

Yeah, man, me say. Me read it in this book me have. Like, there's always been faggots there, man. And it's like, often them was accepted, right? Like it weren't no big deal or noting, you know what I'm sayin'? And then the Christians-them come, the missionaries and shit, said all Afrikan tings was sinful. And then them turn Afrikans into slaves, which to them was no sin. Them Afrikan faggots, they was part a that culture too, man, part a that history – me touch Jazz shoulder – so be proud, man, cos you a faggot wit Afrikan blood inna ya veins. Don't forget your history, man. Cos it yours like it mine.

Me squeeze him shoulder.

I finished with him, Jazz says. His gold tooth glint like a pharoah's tear.

Shit, man, me say. What we gonna do wit you?

I wanna laugh, cos Jazz always seem so cool, so *down*, you know what I'm sayin'? and here him is not knowing what to do about a lickle bwoy trouble, what had two gyal hot for him at the same time. Shit. Him always seem so false before, all defence, not giving nothing. Ah mean, clever, sure, but coming from the mind, not the heart.

Is like him know that too. Even now, full of dread and anxiety, him more alive than him ever was, more really alive, you know what I'm sayin'? Tougher and more gentle at the same time, man, something like that. And to me, man, that's Black Power. It's like by letting go him grab hold of it. Not the idea but the heart, you know what I'm sayin'? Not the lightbulb but the light, right?

Him me bredren, man. And me wanna help him.

There's nothing to do, man, him say, touching his gold rings-them wit him fingertips.

What happened, bredren? me arx. Me go over to the fridge, get out a couplea Red Stripes. We crack 'em. You battle him or he battle you? Him don't answer me for a bit, just sip him lager.

It weren't like that, him say quiet-like. I made a fool of myself, him say.

We all do that, man, me say. When we in love, yunno.

Him look at me again. Hey, man, me say, what me know 'bout it, eh? Do your own shit, man, ain't nothing to me. But do it, man. Cos regrets ain't worth nothing, you know. Me start rolling another spliff. This shit is gear, me say. *Sensi*, me say. *Sensimilia*. Me change the tape, Jazz light up, draw the smoke down deep.

It's cos I wanted him to be like a woman with me, him say.

Yeah? me say. And him don't wanting it that way, yeah?

He wants something else, man, Jazz say, I dunno what. Just, something else.

And you, man. Is what you want? me arx, which is in me mind as being the whole point, right? Him no say noting. Me tink him don't heard, then him go, Don't want a woman, man. Don't want nothing like that.

So tell him what you do want, man, me say. Sound to me like you both wantin' the same shit anyway.

It's too late, him say.

You ain't dead, me say.

No, him say.

Then it ain't too late, man, me say, shaking me head cos him so slow. Gimme that smoke and shoot, man. You got places to go and people to see, ennit.

JAZZ

I'm in a call-box, dialling his number, my hands shaking, the receiver warm with sweat, germs reactivating; ready to cut off the call the moment he answers because I don't have anything to say but I've got to know he's there. The tone repeats and repeats all the drunks have used this place for a toilet as if it is to be made fitting for my humiliation, and the passing trucks keep the glass rattling the tone so quiet I have to strain to hear it. But even so, there's no answer.

No-one home.

MOLLY

I make some pancakes and only burn the first couple. We eat them in bed with lemon juice and golden syrup. My fillings ache but I don't want to go to the dentist cos they're all rip-offs, and anyway, how often do I eat globs of melted sugar anyhow? Carly's teeth look white and perfect. In their own right, I mean, not just compared with his chocolate skin.

'Girl, I'm going to burst if I eat another mouthful,' he says, stretching out on the bed in my red silk kimono and patting his stretched stomach. It's almost like old times, popping another broken heart in the shoebox on top of the wardrobe, getting your soul reheeled where the world snapped it off. And just carrying on walking. Almost, but not quite.

We're getting older.

I don't know if I ever believed in The Real Thing, not really. I mean, in the dark all cats are grey, right? And in the morning you've got your own stuff to do. What you offer is what you're given. Only stuff leaks out around the edges that you didn't mean to offer and that's painful but I guess it's what makes it worth doing in the end, or you might as well just be using your fingers. And that leaking stuff, that's what love is made of. Only watch out, cos you've only got so much, and once it's gone it's gone, and you're left like a dried-out beetle. With a pin through you, maybe, holding you onto the cork. If you're lucky.

Carly's leaking like a sieve. Love in all sorts of colours is staining the sheets into iridescence until the whole room's like the inside of a shell: mother-of-pearl. Looking at him and the room, I can't not believe in the Real Thing. Only right now it's mostly Real Pain.

'What *are* we going to do with you, girl?'

He shrugs his shoulders, looks down at the red of the kimono.

'Girl, I dunno,' he says, his voice quiet and tired. 'Right now I just want to be a stone, watching but not feeling.'

'A precious stone?' I say, a little tweely.

'Just some old rock,' he says. 'So I could just watch 'em all going crazy and not give a shit.' He closes his eyes. 'Jazz,' he says softly, like sighing. He catches himself, open his eyes, rolls them. 'Oh fuck, girl, it just came out – ' He sits up, takes one of my hands in his. 'See, I think, I want to think, Maybe I've got somewhere to go with him. Like, the good can change the bad and get rid of it. Which it should have to, cos the bad is real shitty. But maybe I'm just fooling myself, like, you know, married men don't never leave their wives.'

'Unless they do,' I say.

'Yeah, but how you'd trust them after they done it? Cos you'd be the wife then,' he says.

'It's not like that anyway between you and him,' I say, losing my grip on where the conversation's going. 'It's different.'

'It's the same,' he says. 'All you've got to ask is, can the leopard change his spots?'

'Does he want to?' I ask.

'Say he does.'

'Yeah. Well, maybe. I don't know. Maybe not. Well – oh, I don't know,' I say articulately and concisely. 'Only if he's not really a leopard and he's just having a hard time getting that out, you know?' Carly is giving me a kind of watery *bullshit walks* eyeball. He looks down, sniffs.

'I think,' he says, pauses, clears his throat, rubs his nose, then forces a smile. 'I think – ' He slips off the bed, undoes the kimono, lets it fall to the floor like any movie-star would, stands there naked, the blues discarded with the silk. 'I think my wardrobe needs a facelift.'

'Mine needs liposuction,' I say, pulling on some panties. 'But I hear Hype calling.'

'What's she saying?' Carly asks. I think for a moment.

'"Shopping is a duty",' I say. 'In a post-industrial post-ideological post-everything consumer-capitalist society, anyway.'

'You're crazy, girl,' Carl says.

'Not me,' I say. 'It's only me that's sane. Me, and the fish under the carpet.'

So we dress and we go out and we laugh our way around town, pissing off the snotty shop-assistants in the not-quite boutiques, getting them to unchain the £1500 leather jackets that I don't reckon anyone ever buys, they're just there to make the rest of the stuff look like a bargain. You can tell they don't want you to even touch the jackets, and they wouldn't let you except they're on commission and they can never be quite sure you won't buy one, not 100 percent sure. Like everything in life, I guess. So they just watch us like cobras, to try and put us off, which just makes us ask for all different sizes as well. We end up slumming it in Boy, where Carly buys a cheap and cheerful gold vest made out of shivery viscose, while I treat myself to a long, fine wool cardigan, black and very elegant, very Louise Brooks. But that's it. I guess neither of us felt like putting our flexible friends into traction today. Truth to tell, of course, neither of our minds were wholly on our consumerist obligations. We were both thinking, *What about Jason?*

Carly decides he wants to go home, be on his own for a bit. I kiss him goodbye outside Leicester Square tube.

'Whatever you do,' I say, 'just make sure it's what you want to do.' I pause for a moment, thinking *Did that make sense?* But Carl isn't looking puzzled so it probably did. Enough sense, anyway. 'Love you,' I say.

'Love you too,' he says, ready to go.

One day I will love a man who desires me and I will desire him too. Somehow they all turn into friends or screws. But never quite lovers. I watch Carly going down into the Tube and say a little prayer.

See, if he can do it, then so can other people. So can I.

'Girl,' I call. He looks back. 'Good luck.'

And he's gone.

CARL

Two stops down the line some ruffnecks get on and I think, Christ, not today, I can't take any mindless fucking abuse to-day. Fortunately, just before they get round to me these two sisters get on, dressed to tease, and get the youts' attention. Only when I'm getting off, one of them shouts,

'Hey, battyboy!'

Then the doors close and a few seconds later they're all swept away like shit being sucked down the toilet. I don't even feel angry, just tired. Where I live's not far from the Tube but every step I take I'm expecting a bottle to get smashed over my head or thrown at me out of a car window. Nothing actually happens, but still when I lock the door behind me I start to shiver. In the warmth I'm shivering.

Jason's flowers have all wilted in their bowls. I should throw them out, I suppose. But I'm tired cos I can't ever sleep in Molly's bed cos she thrashes about all night. She must dream a lot but she says she never remembers them.

I'll throw the flowers away after sleeping for a bit.

JAZZ

So I ring Caroline. Should get the mobile fixed, don't know why I haven't. Perhaps I need to be beyond contact right now. After a dozen rings, she answers.

'It's me,' I say. Silence. 'Okay,' I say. 'Just listen, okay?' More silence. I'm wondering why I called her. I don't reckon she can help me at all. But I don't hang up. 'If you loved someone, right? And they loved you too, you thought, but they didn't trust you.' Still silence. 'Caroline?'

'Yes.' She's there, hiding on the other end of the phone, hiding within the flat tone of a word.

'How would you get them to trust you?' I ask, wondering why I think a woman, a *white* woman, why I think she'd know the answer. I suppose I thought that women're supposed to know these sorts of things. Or that's what I've heard. I don't know if I believe it, though.

'You can't *get* trust,' she says, as if she's been expecting the question and rehearsed an answer. 'It can only be given to you. All you can do is try – ' her voice falters for a second ' – try to understand the other person. Not sympathise with them, not like them, just see what makes them how they are. And then open yourself to them inside and outside. Maybe then, they'll see and open up to you too. Jason – ' her voice catches a little ' – is she Black?'

I hang up.

On the way back to my flat I go into a bookshop and buy a big book, about Africa it is, not Afrika, a coffee-table book you'd call it. But still what it's taken from is *Afrika*. And what I want from it is Afrika, not Africa. Besides, I don't have a coffee-table.

The magazines I buy are not of the sort you leave on a coffee-table, nor the books. Some are political. Some are other things. But none of them needs a coffee-table.

Is she Black?

I shouldn't have phoned Caroline. I pick up the book and flick through it, not reading the white words, trying to see beyond the glossy whiteness framing the pictures, to the reality of Afrika. Looking at the pictures I feel a resonance, maybe not of the actual, geographical Afrika but of the Afrika within my mind, the landscape of my Blackness with its deserts and oases, mountains, forests, villages and cities, which is maybe just as real, maybe more so: my homeland, my centre of being. And the young men from the villages wear beads and frame their dark, smooth skins with shivering white feathers and peacock feathers, making themselves handsome and beautiful. And their faces and bodies are enhanced with colour, with make-up, darkening their eyes and celebrating their Afrikan skins under the cobalt-blue skies and golden sun. In their faces I see Carly's face, the white rags in his hair like Zulu feathers, and it reminds me that he too is a warrior, and that however much we belong here, however much we are Black British, we are also and always warriors in exile, and we must wear our plumes with pride.

We must always be proud.

The phone starts to ring. I'm going to leave it, but then I think, *Maybe it's Carl* and I answer it. It's Caroline.

'Sorry,' she says. Then there's a pause. Then she hangs up. I put the receiver down. I'm sorry too. It's funny, funny-peculiar; I thought I could take her on a journey, but now I realise it's a journey that I haven't even begun myself. And not back but forward. Forward to Afrika.

CAROLINE

The bag. I split the turf with the spade and folded it over, cut out a block of black earth and scattered it in the ditch through the wire fence, leaving just enough to pack in around the bag and cover it over. Then I folded the turf back down, trod it into place and left it as if it had never been disturbed. My breath misted the air in the predawn light. I put the spade back in the stables. The digging left little callouses on my palms. At that time I didn't wonder what was in the bag but now I know: a murdered future. And I buried it.

It must have been Jazz who stole Desdemona: who else would have stolen her and then just left her grazing in Hyde Park? Cruel and kind, like everything he does. But I don't say any of this to the Colonel, of course. He's bad enough already. I can just imagine Jazz leading Desdemona into an old furniture van at the bottom of the drive and rattling off with her inside.

But why did he do it?

Maybe it was a lesson, something about freedom, about setting things free. Perhaps he meant to show me that I must set him free. Or – no – he was showing me that I do not have the power to set him free, nor do I have the right to make that choice: It is he who chooses when and how to set himself free. And the lesson is, I too must choose to set myself free.

The bag is heavy in my mind, like a splinter in my finger: Sometimes you can forget it's there, but then you brush against it, and the feeling is sharp and unhealthy.

Tonight I shall pull it. Tonight I shall dig up the bag and open it.

And then I shall know how to set myself free.

CARL

I wake up and it's still light outside. I'm huddled up under my jacket on the bed, like a stranger in my own flat. Which I suppose I am right now. I lie there looking up at the ceiling not thinking, just letting my thoughts float over like summer clouds, looking at them but not doing anything with them. Even if they're all the fears and horrors in the world, from where I'm lying they're just clouds cool and pale and drifting.

The clouds cross the room from by the window to Jason's wall and slide through where the wall meets the ceiling like they're my dreams going where I know they want to. Where I want them to go.

I hear someone walking down the corridor. I hold my breath and listen. Keys rattling, then Jazz's door opens, closes.

Straightaway I feel like the whole flat is charging up with static. The hair on the back of my neck prickles up. I close my eyes and there's blue sparks in the corners.

I'm not going to go knock on his door. I'll just lie here, not making a sound, silent as my thoughts are.

And listen.

JUDY

I been screwing up at work, today. Well, it so dull and me mind was wandering. So lunchtime I go for a walk, tell Suzie and Di I was coming down with a migraine, need some air. Which ain't no lie. Di sort it out with the super. She got a honey tongue, man: she could smother ants and wasps with her words. Or it's not the words even, just something about the way her face looks when she's talking, you know?

Me, I just get up his nose.

So I get some fags from the boozer and take a little stroll, look at the ducks in the park, the trees. Shit like this. Kids playing. I look at 'em and think, Yeah, I could do that, be a mother, play house, you know? And then I'm thinking about Jazz again. Wild and crazy. Crazy bastard.

The park blacks out and Jazz is standing there, his gun pointing up from his waist, up at some faceless pig eyes never there, just shadows. And the ground is shattered from much violence, torn up into sharp dark hills. And on top of one of them hills is Jazz, his face a flag furl out in the warm wind. All about is rumours of war, the wind like whispering them.

The gun goes off and the pig's face opens like a red flower only sudden like a touch you ain't expecting. The petals is like fleshy and pink and red and fresh-looking. And in the middle there's white, like bone I suppose, gleaming. The pig's gone and only the flower is left. The gun gone too and Jazz standing there his fists clench and veins standing out in his arms.

Shit, I think to myself, woman, you cracking.

But still, me heart racing.

Steam covers the large, liver-spotted mirror over the sink. I wipe it away with my towel. Water runs down over the glass in rivulets. My reflection there looks frightened, young: a boy not a man. But becoming a man. I put the scissors on the bathroom shelf and take a deep breath. Behind me the bathwater steams. I wipe the mirror again, hang my towel up on the back of the door, so I'm standing there naked. The mirror frames me from the top of my head to the middle of my thighs. I pick up the can of shaving foam, spray a fat twist of it into the palm of my hand. Then I press it under my arms. It feels cool there. I pick up the razor, dunk it in the water in the sink.

I have to feel clean.

I run a finger up my smooth shaved armpit, across my smooth chest and it feels strange. Then I run the fingers of one hand down my belly down to the smooth base of my dick, cup the other under my shaved balls. They're like warm glass, and that feels even stranger. I fold my arms behind my head and look at myself in the mirror. It's like the first time I've ever seen myself, all streamlines, clean lines, smelted and pure, like I'm cast out of African bronze. I shave the sides of my head too so they're shiny and grey-blue.

And then I'm ready, my past shaved away and washed down the sink, spiralled down the plughole, all my shame and stupidity and the burden of being judged and the fear of being judged floating like the blade over my skin on the foam, my dick at half-mast like it's been ever since I drew the razor down my armpit.

I pull on my tracksuit and the silky fabric makes me shiver. It feels new and strange against my new, strange skin. I pull my Adidas's onto my bare feet, put gold around my neck, The Gold That They Stole.

The gold chills my skin.

I pick up the tape I've got ready and go to the door. The air in the corridor is cool against my face.

CARL

I hear his door opening. It makes me sit up and pull my jacket on. I sit on the bed with my arms wrap around my knees, waiting, wondering: will he go past my door or knock or what? And part of me wants him to knock and part of me hopes he'll walk out and never come back. I press my top hat onto the back of my head.

There's a knock on the door. It's not locked.

But I don't say that, I just sit there silent, still waiting. Slowly the knob turns, the door opens, and Jazz is standing there, looking fine like always, looking shy.

'Can I come in?' he asks. I don't nod but I don't shake my head either. 'Good,' he says, closing the door behind him. I watch him, wondering what he's bothering for. Isn't it easier just to let the flowers die and dry out until they're just dried flowers, just colour, or ghost flowers, skeletons without feeling or pain? Something you could even find halfway beautiful when you get old? My eyes feel wet, his eyes are shining too. He goes on over to my stack, puts in a tape he's been fiddling with ever since he came in, rewinds it. The laces of his trainers is undone, they drag on the shiny black floor. The music is Billie Holiday, singing *I must have that man* like sweet and sad. And Jason mimes to it, dancing slow and sensual:

My heart is broke and it won't ever mend

I ain't much caring just where it will end

But I must have that man...

He's pointing at me then. *I must have that man.* He unzips his tracksuit top, slides it off.

He's hot as Hades

Lady's not safe in his arms when she's kissed

And I'm afraid when he's cooled off

Maybe I'm ruled off his list

I'll never be missed...

He kicks off his shoes, slides down his tracksuit pants, steps out of them. There's tears in his eyes now, and the tears are saying *Look at me*. He spreads out his arms like they're angel wings and I see his smooth armpits and look down at his smooth crotch and I get to my feet.

I need that person much worse'n just bad
I'm half-alive and it's driving me mad
He's only human, if he's to be had
I must have that man.

He's so beautiful and so vulnerable, like a wounded angel. The gold round his neck glints as he goes over to my dressing table. He picks up a orange lipstick, draws a neon line across his face under his eyes, and another down his stomach, then a line of white across his face and diagonal lines and he circles his nipples creating a freaky African effect. I push off my hat and jacket, touch the tears out of my eyes, go up to him so close I can feel the heat of him.

'I need you, man,' he says, his eyes staying on mine. I look down.

'Yeah,' I say. 'Maybe I need you too.'

'C'mere,' he says. And we hug and move slowly to the music with our arms around each other. And I burst into tears and think *Jesus, I must look like shit.* But when I look up at him he's smiling. Which doesn't stop me crying but it makes me smile too.

JAZZ

If he hadn't come to me then I would have died, shrivelled up and died. See it sounds corny shit but my heart's like a bird, caged by my ribs. And if he hadn't stood up I reckon it would've broken its wings beating against the bars, but when he did it started to sing and the ribs became only ribs again and the song was freedom.

I must have that man.

Slowly he undresses too until we are both naked together. And we paint each other's bodies with African designs, the ones Carly does I don't know where they come from, the ones I do remembered from the book I bought and from dreams maybe. And when our bodies and faces are covered in bright bands and lines and circles of colour we kiss each other, caress each other, blurring the colours and patterns as we blur too, not playing man and woman or even man and man, just playing ourselves.

The way we're making love now, it feels so different from

how it did before: the way we touch, the way he lets my hands, my fingers move over him, explore him, feels so different. As I kiss his eyelids I realise why.

He trusts me.

CARL

In the morning we have a bath together, slide the soap over each other's bodies. I'm not afraid of him anymore, cos he's come over onto my side. All I'm afraid of is what he'll ask from me to show that I'm coming over to his side too. But right now that doesn't matter, right now it's just me and him, facing each other, his face like the mirror of my heart, like my face too I reckon, our warm thighs wrapped around each other's waists. We start kissing again.

'You gone out with a lot of guys like me, man?' he asks me softly.

'There's no-one like you, Jazz,' I say, touching one of his nipples.

'You think I'm a freak, man?' he whispers.

'I think you're a angel. A beautiful angel.'

He looks down, embarrassed. 'No,' he says. 'You're the angel.' He looks into my eyes and gets my heart pounding again.

'I never thought I was lucky before,' he says, tilting his head back and staring up at the maps on the damp-marked ceiling. 'All the shit in my life, all the fighting I had to do, just over who I was and who I wanted, you know? And now – I mean, the battles, they'll be outside of me now, man. And I know I'll have to fight, but I won't be fighting myself.' He touches my waist. 'And I know who I'll be fighting for.'

'Will there always be battles?' I ask. He turns and stares into space, working the visionary thing.

'One day,' he says, 'there will be peace.'

And I'm thinking, *When, girl, when?* But there's a hardness to his face, so I don't say anything, just get some foam in the palm of my hand, blow it so it lands on his cheek. He looks round and smiles, gold on white on pink on brown.

I've never felt about anyone the way I feel about him. But still I'm wondering, *Can it work out?* And still I'm wondering what *I'll* have to do, to prove I'm going as far as he is.

MOLLY

I get up at twelve feeling fat and sugary so I do ten boring and therefore virtuous minutes with Cher before having a shower. Step step step. Step step lumber whoops. Step step lurch twist. After drying my hair I give Carly a call, this must be around one.

No reply.

I picture him full of pancakes falling through darkness into cold water. A dozen other trashy scenarios tumble quickly through my mind then tumble out of my eyes and vanish in the light.

He's probably gone for a browse round the market: it's sunny outside.

It's only being inside, in the shadows, that's making me feel chilly.

JOHNNY

Mid-day me go along a Floyd's yard to see how him holding up, come pon him fixing up some fancy old car wit chrome trim and walnut panelling, fiddling around under the bonnet and shit. Errol sitting in the front seat, cuban heels on the dash, sipping a beer, listening to a song on the radio, *Can't get no satisfaction.*

The song as old as the fucking motor, man. Maybe it have a special old radio channel or shit. But the lyrics them right for how me feel right now.

Errol check me then. Him face harden. Him get out the car.

Floyd, man, him say, Johnny's here.

The tree a we touch skin. Errol shifting from one foot to the other, awkward-like. Me know him tink say me go arx him bout why him don't got the dollars off of Jazz.

Nice boots, me say.

Yeah, him say.

So what's up, guy, Floyd arx, unzipping his boiler-suit and taking a beer from the front seat a the car. Him don't offer me one. Him kinda nervous too, yunno. Me cough rough-like.

You want a beer, man? Me nod. Him hand me a can. Me crack it, take a sip.

So what's going down, man, Errol arx.

Is Jazz, me say.

You seen him? Errol arx. When?

Last evening, man.

You get the money, him say, tinking himself shrewd, beating me to it. And is true, me no arx Jazz for the money. But truth worth more than money, and truth me did get.

Him get himself a new star, me say enigmatically.

What you on about, Johnny, man?

Him have a lover, Errol, man. A *bwoy* friend.

'E turn battyman? Floyd face fall like the stuffing drop out of it.

Him always was, man! me say, laughing. Them gyals was just turned on cos them could smell him have someting them could never get!

Shit, man! You arsehole! Floyd shouting now. You're always dissing him, man! Why you're making this shit up? Fuckin' cunt!

And him go for me! *Floyd*! Me give him some licks before Errol get in between the two a we. Him turn to me.

What is this shit, man?

No believe me then, me say, shrugging. Then:

Arx Jazz.

ERROL

I'm getting seriously worried about Floyd, man. And about Johnny, pulling that weird shit about Jazz.

Arx Jazz.

I want to arx Johnny some shit first, yeah. Like, what about the money, bredren? Cos I can see Johnny getting my share of the dollars and just forgetting to pass it on, you know?

Floyd sips on his beer, winces. His lip don't bled much, and the blood there was was only on account of Johnny's ring.

He don't make four with Johnny and I don't blame him cos Johnny can be one crazy motherfucker, you know what I'm sayin'?

You was lying, man, Floyd says under his breath. Johnny don't say nothing.

Lying.

For a moment I reckon Johnny's gonna smack him again, but he don't.

We're all just standing there, waiting.

Then Johnny says, Me have business need seeing to, crushes his beercan, drops it in the gutter, and turns to go.

Later, man, I say.

Floyd don't say nothing, just keeps on looking at the ground. When Johnny's gone, he looks up, wipes a hand across his mouth.

Raasclot, he says.

You reckon it's true? I ask.

Naa, he says, pulling it together now, loosening his shoulders. He sniffs. No way, man.

But I know he's lying, man. But I don't say nothing cos I don't know what I think myself, you know? I remember something Judy said about screwing with Jazz, that he don't do it like other guys.

Judy knows, it comes to me. Even if she don't know it, she knows.

One way or the other, *someone's* giving the rest of us *enough* bullshit, you know what I'm sayin'?

Jazz turn battyboy. Shit.

Shit.

I'll go see Judy tonight, I'll find out everything.

FLOYD

Suddenly it's like everything he ever said is tainted, man, and every movement, every gesture, is a dirty lie. He thought he was motherfucking Jesus Christ, but now he's just some sick motherfucker shot-up-a-pig faggot. Shit.

If it's true.

Signs and clues fill my mind, wrists too limp, knees too

close together, eyes wandering, shit, looking at dick, wanting to get down on his knees or shit fucking sell-out fucking shit all he ever said just fag words and that fucking dead body dragging death and sickness twined together like the honeysuckle the smell making me wanna heave. My hand tightens round the monkey-wrench and I'm beating up and down with it bone cracking blood blood everywhere Jazz screaming like a woman like a animal and the screaming's winding me up tighter and tighter making the blows easier and slicker more like a well-oiled machine, a fag-killing machine. I see hooks tearing into his flesh, shredding it, shredding the lies Jazz told us while shredding his flesh and I'm the one who's screaming now.

Malcolm Eldridge Bobby Jazz you motherfucker!

And I can't stop screaming even though my hands're bleeding and my eyes are bleeding too. *Fucking pussy whore sell-out motherfucker.* He's been near me kid, man, motherfucker's been near me kid buying him shit giving him shit touching him and feeling his mind and his body while I was watching the fag, smiling at the fag, proud to have him under me roof.

I scream louder and harder, and all the windows shatter.

Faggot faggot faggot FAGGOT FAGGOT!

ERROL

I must've been gone a half-hour getting us some Kentucky Fried, but obviously a war broke out while I was away, cos Floyd's car all mashed up. Like, every window and all the lights is smashed, the hood's all dented up, the wing-mirror's ripped off. There's blood on the left-over bits of the windscreen like someone put their hand through it and the monkey-wrench is lying on the ground slippery red. The wind moves a little tuft of torn-out Afro hair along the pavement towards me. Floyd ain't nowhere to be seen.

He's lost it, man. In the worst way.

His front door's been left open, so I go inside. I better phone Johnny and Jazz, if nothing else for Floyd's sake before he does something really stupid. Upstairs I hear a baby crying. Floyd's kid. I feel indecisive for a moment.

Make the fucking calls, man, I say to meself.

But ain't neither of 'em answering. The baby's still crying but so what, we all got to suffer, right? I push buttons again, but still no answer. I slam the phone down. The baby's crying's getting on me nerves. I go upstairs. Poor kid, lying there in his cot, bars keeping him in like prison bars. He's wearing a blue romper-suit, s'how I know it's a boy.

I pick him up and he stops crying. Magic touch, right? Or maybe cos I just ain't insane. Floyd, Johnny, Jazz, sometimes it seems like they've all lost it, playing some weird mind-fuck game I don't understand. I rock the boy in me arms and he closes his eyes. A bit later and it seems like he's asleep. Gently I put him back in the cot. He don't wake up, just stirs a bit, then lays still. I sneak off downstairs, one step at a time.

I'm about to go when I see Floyd's keys sitting on the shelf by the front door. So now what do I do? If I shut the door he can't get back in, and this ain't the kind of street where you go out leaving your door unlocked. Not if you like having possessions and keeping the graffiti on the outside walls, you know what I'm sayin'?

So I close the door and go and put the kettle on for a cup of tea. At least I can try phoning Jazz and Johnny again. I get a mug out the cupboard and open the fridge.

No fucking milk.

JUDY

The air heavy like a storm coming though the sky a clear blue. I feel heavy and sweaty and tense like I always do just before my time. I sit down on a park bench and fancy I can feel the wetness of the blood against the fabric of me panties, spreading. Something big about to happen, I reckon. Me chest tightens.

Something red.

CARL

We stroll round Portobello Market together, our hands bumping and catching, little fingers hooking and unhooking, Jazz looking fine in his black Adidas tracksuit, black Adidas hi-tops and gold. The sides of his head are razor-smooth where he let me shave him this morning. Today he looks like he doesn't have a care in the world, looks like a boy.

The hardness is out of his eyes.

JAZZ

I buy him a white chocolate Magnum and we go up the market until we've left all the stalls and real shops behind and it's just rich tourists and antique shit. Carly's wearing a black lycra bra-top, skimpy black silk shorts and bike-boots under a flimsy black parachute-silk trenchcoat, with fingerless gloves. Catching glimpses of his smooth brown thighs and taut stomach turns me on, makes my dick twitch. He's wearing just a little eyeliner and the rags in his hair are black. A gust of wind catches his coat, spreading it out behind him like my kind of Marilyn Monroe. He arches his back, folds his arms behind his head, displaying himself for me, just for me. Then he yawns and brings his arms down, looks at me innocently as if he wasn't doing anything, just stretching. I want to make love right there and then, man.

Animal love.

Later we go on up to Hyde Park and hire a boat and row out to the middle of the lake. I take off my tracksuit top so Carly can admire my arms and chest while I'm working the oars. He lies back in the prow, coat open, thighs apart, one hand trailing in the water. I bend forward to kiss him, making the tiny row-boat tremble in the water. I slide on top of him, and I can feel his hard-on pressing against me through the slippery fabric of my tracksuit pants. We kiss deeply, then reluctantly I sit back in my seat. The boat trembles again and my thighs tense. I look down softly on Carly, framed by the light blue wood and the white-and-green flickering of the water, then over to the shore, to where people are walking their dogs, jogging and carrying on with their little lives not even knowing we're out here, floating free. A police van passes like a cloud flashing past the sun.

'Have you ever really loved a white guy?' I ask, thinking, Why the fuck did I just come out with that, now? Carly's body tenses, but he tries to keep it relaxed.

'Yeah,' he says. 'Not with everything I've got, but – yeah. And that wasn't to do with him being white, you know? Just, not being right.'

'I don't know how you could love a white guy, Carly,' I say. Maybe it's because we're close right now I feel I can push it. But it's still dangerous. But maybe I have to know.

'Cos a white guy loved me,' he says, too simply.

'But – '

'Look, Jazz, what do you want me to say? I'll just say what you want cos that's all you want to hear.' Carly's eyes flash and he pulls himself up onto his elbows.

'Just tell me the truth, man,' I say. 'I'll listen. I promise.' I smile too cutely.

Carly kisses his teeth. I turn off the smile and bend over and play with one of his bootstraps.

'You waste a lot of time blaming people,' he says.

'You reckon?' I say, looking down at his boots. The leather is seamed and splitting over the toes.

'You blame me for fancying white boys, and you blame white boys for fancying Black boys. Don't you think that's like half the trouble of the world, people going No, I ain't interested in him cos his skin's the wrong colour? I like people crossing barriers. It's what they're there for.'

'You can't just blank out all the history since slavery, man,' I say, because I think Carly's so fucking naive in a lot of ways. 'Sex won't blank it out, you know?'

'Yeah, but hate won't blank it out either, Jazz. Look – ' I look into his eyes – 'I've *seen* hate. I've *felt* hate. I've been threatened with *knives* cos of who I am. By Black *and* white, but I'm telling you Jazz, more by Black. So what do you think, I'm gonna tell the white guy who buys me roses to fuck off so I can wait for the Black guy who calls me battyboy and spits in my face? Or some dream *because* he's Black? Skin is skin is skin, Jazz.'

Maybe it's me who's naive. Sometimes hate *is* too easy. It's love is hard. Maybe there is a courage in what he does, and I just won't allow it.

'Hate won't blank it out,' I agree. 'Just, *how* can you love someone white?'

'Because people are people, yeah? They're not just lumps

116

of black or white. They're not just stereotypes. I mean, a guy who fancies me's not looking for no Ice-T, are they? They're looking for *me.*'

'Yeah, but it's easier cos you're, like' – like an obvious fag so they know what world you're in.

'Was it easier for you?'

I can't answer him. I look away. It's strange having this argument where for once I'm not all out to win, where I have to avoid the cheap shots and allow what Carly's saying to penetrate me, or else it's all pointless.

'But some white guys, they go for you for your skin, right?'

Carly shrugs.

'Right?'

'Why you're so judgemental, man?' he snaps, pulling himself up into a sitting position. '*You* only wanna sleep with Black boys.'

'Yeah, but that's – '

'Go on, man, say it. *Natural.* If that's what you go by, then what the fuck are you doing here with *me?*' Carly's eyes are hard and glinting. His mouth is set. My throat catches.

'Because I love you, man,' I whisper. Carly grips my chin and kisses me hotly on the mouth.

It feels, yeah – natural.

CARL

Walking back through the park, feeling close, we hold hands tight, daring the world to throw shade. Our hearts are so big and our chests are so broad nobody dares.

On the way we have some more serious talk. Jazz doesn't think I'm so much of a bimbo as he did when we was talking earlier.

'It bothers me, you being a racist,' I say, squeezing his hand.

'I'm not a racist, man,' he says quickly. I shrug, don't say anything.

'Look.' He stops me, turns me to face him, his eyes tearing at mine like he wants us to be telepathic, dark, fanatical eyes. I can see why the others listened to him, believed in him. But he knows I'm not going to believe what he says just cos he believes it. He knows he can't wing it on charm.

'All my life I've looked at shit and wondered why?' he says. 'And the more I looked, the more I wondered. Shit like, proportionally, why are five times as many Black men and four times as many Black women diagnosed as schizophrenics as white people? Why are so many of our people poor and under-achievers? Why do four policemen get together to stamp on a Black man's head? Break his neck? And what do I do with all the anger this awareness brings that's corroding my heart and soul? You know?'

I nod, thinking of the times I could've seen the world charred white and felt nothing. But hate makes me feel, like, ashamed, so I look down at the ground.

'I wanted to know so I looked into history, from slavery to the present day, and the more I read, the more I understood. And it made me very very angry not just that there were these people doing these things, but that there were all these people who just didn't do anything. And because they let all those *obscenities* just happen, for me they stopped being human beings. Like the nazis.' Jazz draws a ragged breath. 'There isn't a conspiracy, the world isn't paranoid. But for me there *is* debt, and yeah, there is blame when the world carries on as if none of it even *happened*, man. And, you know, they all get sweaty when shit the nazis stole from the Jews turns up – and they should, man, they should. But why is reparations to Black people just a joke, reparations to Africa, and to Black people in the West? All that shit is what makes me put Black people first, and if that makes me a racist, then I am one.'

He's kind of daring me to say something now.

'Why can't it just be the *human* race?' I say. 'Cos I could hate straight people cos of what they've done to gay people, but it was Molly who first took me on a Gay Pride march and she's straight. And I could hate white people cos of racism but then when some white thug went for me with a broken glass it was a white boy, a white friend who got in his way, who's got the scars on his arm that would've been on my face.'

I'm angry now too. It makes me realise that I put my anger on one side but that isn't the same as getting rid of it: it's storing it up, like in a over-full cupboard. And then you finally open the door and it all comes tumbling out.

'You're like some monk, Jazz. Some monk hiding away from people and sex and love and *everything.* Everything *human.*' My lisp makes me stammer and lose track of what I'm saying. So I say,

'If you haven't got love, you haven't got nothing.'

JAZZ

It's been a long time since I've been out of my depth. Just a few days ago the world was, well, yeah, Black and white.

But now everything's changed. Even my anger feels in its form like yesterday's anger. I think of Johnny, Errol and Floyd, stars, friends, I don't know, now maybe enemies. I know I want to put Black people first, but I wasn't there to put my arm between the broken glass and Carly's face. You can't be everywhere. Maybe hate and anger is just a way of not looking inside. Maybe a strong world-view is a simplistic world-view is a shallow world-view. Is a falsehood. Maybe you have to look from the inside out.

A heavy weight falls from me and sinks into deep water. The sense of freedom I first felt in Carly's touch returns to me. And in the battle freedom is both the weapon and the prize. I see clouds rushing across the sky and the sun darkens for a moment. So much of my life I've been avoiding shit: the pain of feeling, you understand me?

'I've got love,' I say.

CARL

At the edge of the park we still want to wander so we get a bus up into town. We don't hardly say a word, just press close in the love-seat at the back of the top deck. Jazz drapes his arm around me, doesn't move it even when the conductor, a ragga-looking black guy, asks for our tickets and gives us a look. But Jazz looks hard, so the look is just like a glance, really. Once the conductor's gone, he turns his head to look at me.

'Until I met you, I never knew how lonely I was,' he says, a small smile on his face, looking shy, not meeting my eyes. It makes me feel embarrass so I look down too.

But he knows I'm smiling.

CAROLINE

The bag is just where I left it, and only slightly damp and stained from having been buried. It sits on the white kitchen work-surface like a body on an autopsy table waiting for the surgeon. The clinical light dazzles my night-adjusted eyes. I thought it was going to be easy to open the bag but it isn't. I reach for the clasps then hesitate, turn and fix myself a cup of cappucino. The machine hisses noisily. I look at my watch. Rupert'll be home soon.

I've become troubled by the vague feeling that Rupert might have overheard Jazz telling me to bury the bag that night. I don't want Rupert to know it's here now.

I have to open it.

Slowly I push the clasps back. I reach inside, grasp something cold and hard, and draw it out. A sawn-off shot-gun. I run my fingertips over the shiny surface where the barrels have been filed off. I open the breach and send two spent cartridges flying. They rattle noisily on the terracotta tiles of the kitchen floor. I rummage around in the bottom of the bag and find six more cartridges, unused.

I put the shot-gun back in the bag along with the unused cartridges. Then I pick up the two used ones and put them back in as well.

I need to think.

JOHNNY

Me pass by Judy's yard, but me no say noting about Jazz. A fi-him business, yunno? And him drive she a little crazy, me tink. She arx me if me have seen Errol and me tell she him say him drop round later inna the evening. Me almost say, *So smarten yourself up, gyal,* cos she no look so fresh, yunno.

She look like she fever.

120

ERROL

About nine-thirty I'm knocking on Judy's door. I'm feeling racked off with Floyd, man: motherfucker never came back for his keys, innit, so I had to wait for fucking Astrid to saunter in from wherever she's fucking been, which weren't till gone seven.

Bitch weren't even fucking grateful.

When Judy finally answers the fucking door I can tell by the way she's slopping around she's already drunk which pisses me off some more. I feel like slapping her around but I don't. There's enough violence in the world without that sort of cheap shit. I fix her some coffee.

You seen Jazz around? I ask her.

She gives me this sideways look, sips holding the cup in both hands, shakes her head a little.

You and me, we been good friends, yeah, I say.

We been fucks, she says.

You got that right, I'm thinking. *What a fucking mess.* But I sit down on the bed beside her and put me arm around her shoulders.

She don't stop me.

JUDY

After we done it, laying there, Errol asks me about Jazz. Like, is him as good as Jazz in bed.

'Yeah,' I say, wanting him to shut up. 'Better.' Which is kind of a lie but it's what they wanna hear, innit?

Only he don't let up. 'Does he like, do stuff I don't do,' he asks. 'Like, *stuff.*'

'What the fuck you on about, man?' I say, leaning over him to get a fag.

'Does he do any freak shit?,' Errol persist.

'Look, man,' I say, tired of Errol – and Jazz, for that fucking matter. 'He ain't nothing special, you know. I don't reckon he likes girls that much.' I take a drag, sniff.

He don't like me that much, anyway.

ERROL

While she's talking I feel a weird cold thrill run down me, man. Suddenly I can't breathe, the room's too small. I climb outta bed and start pulling me clothes on. Judy starts whining. I kiss me teeth and tell her I got business to sort. She starts cursing me out, which don't exactly incline me towards dropping in again in the short term.

And anyway, her train's already reached the end of the line, you know?

Walking the streets the night air strips me lungs and sets me mind soaring. I try to think about Jazz but I can't get my mind around him, not yet.

One side of me's thinking, So what, man, fish or fowl, it's all flesh, yeah.

The other side's freaking out.

I wanna see him though, man. Get the truth of it. See what's gonna happen next.

JUDY

I'd call the pigs but they ain't gonna show no interest in what some black office-girl has to say except it's about offing one of their own so they'd probably listen real good maybe I'd even get one a them community community shit money *money* Jazz Errol Johnny I wouldn't never have to see them again just push push push the buttons and I ain't gonna remember nothing in the morning no sin no Errol no Jazz no Johnny no Floyd neither.

JAZZ

We climb the stairs quietly. I stop outside Carly's door but he takes my hand and leads me past his flat and along the corridor to the far end. Hand-in-hand we make our way up a couple of flights of emergency stairs. Carly's carrying a little bag of skin cleansers and stuff he picked up at Boots on the way back here.

The stairs to the roof are padlocked but one of the grills in the wire-mesh doorway has rusted loose. Carly folds it back and we squeeze through like kids sneaking into their den. I catch my tracksuit on a wire but the fabric doesn't tear. Then we're pushing the firedoor onto the roof open. It shudders, then gives.

It's a warm night for September, and the sky is very dark and clear above us, above the dull neon of the city. The high moon is a silver sickle not floating but standing still as a statue, standing as still as time is standing as I gaze into Carly's eyes. Softly we kiss, our tongues tasting each other, as delicate as hummingbirds' tongues slipping into the mouthes of rain-forest orchids. Carly unzips my tracksuit top and pushes the fabric off my shoulders, leaving them bare. I feel like a flower opening. I push his coat back and he lets it drop to the ground. I cradle his buttocks and pull him to me, hard. He gasps.

The tar of the roof is warm against my skin as I lie back on it, the heat left over from the day's sun stored in it. I stretch my arms above my head as Carly kisses my chest, teases my nipples, kisses my bulging crotch. I let him slide down my pants and pull down my jock. Then he swings round and buries my face in the silky crotch of his shorts. I slide them down to his ankles.

It's as I'm working my mouth on his smooth, sweet hard-on, feeling it slide to the back of my throat, that I realise he's working his mouth on me. And it doesn't feel like it did with the others, it doesn't feel like abuse or whoring, it just feels warm and good and his body feels so hot and hard and soft and we fuse into a single sculpture as my hips thrust up and his thrust down and I dig my fingers into his arse.

CARL

The moon's gone down when Jazz wakes me by nibbling on my tits. I push him away but not too much cos my dick's got hard again. He pins me down, playful-like, grabbing my wrists, nibbling my ear, making me wrinkle my nose.

'What do you want to do now?' he asks.

I pause for a beat then say, 'Look in the bag.'

He reaches over and rummages, pulls out the rubbers and the KY, grins strangely.

'Don't you trust me, man?' he says.

'We've all been young and foolish,' I say. 'You know?'

He laughs softly and shakes his head, but he hasn't got an argument.

My arsehole opens like a rosebud as Jazz slips two cool fingers inside me, the skin inside as smooth as petals. I move my hips down towards his knuckles.

'Oh yeah,' I moan, opening my thighs, making myself more available. Jazz swings me round so I can suck his dick some more, straddling my chest. I kiss his smooth, shaved crotch, take his warm, glassy balls into my mouth, tug on them gently. I shiver as he tastes the tip of my dick while he's working my arse.

I reach for the KY too, turn my fingers silver by the stars. I run them down Jazz's big butt. He clenches his buttocks, trapping my fingers, then relaxes. I slide my forefinger up him. He gasps. His body feels burning hot inside. I gently work in a second finger. He tightens, then relaxes. I push both fingers in to the knuckle.

See, I don't go for guys who just want to fuck me, you know? I don't let it go that way. Cos if they don't give it up too, then they're playing too straight-and-narrow and it's not a turn-on. And like I said to Jazz, I don't get *fucked*.

It's all or nothing.

Both ends or none.

JAZZ

Very gently Carly starts to work the head of his latex-covered dick into my arsehole. I try to relax. It hurts. He stops. I miss it being there. He shifts his angle just a bit. It feels too much but the pain stretches, thins and goes. There's a pressure that goes too. He moans and I moan too because he's just slid the whole length of his dick up inside me. He moves it back and forth and I writhe because the feeling is so *extreme*, man, so fucking extreme. I wish he'd stop never stop I never thought it could feel so complete.

So *exciting.*

It's because he's like he is that I can do this, you know? Not a stud, not a rapist, not a macho shit-hole, not some master/slavemaster. He's just my lover, inside my body.

And that's cool, man. It doesn't make me less of a man or anything, it doesn't compare with a man and a woman doing it. Not to me, anyway. His dick slides out of me with a soft sucking sound. I feel hot and turned on and wet and juicy and open.

Now I'm going to make Carly feel that good.

CARL

Girl *friend*! Molly, girl, you'd have been green with envy if you could of seen the way we were making out up on that rooftop. We were like a pair of crazy teenage kids. They say men can't have multiple orgasms, but don't you believe it, girl! I have living proof to the contrary! We do every position known to man and then some that aren't. He sits me on a air-vent and gets me to wrap my legs round his shoulders and slides right in and right out of my butt until I'm begging for him to stop but desperate for him to carry on.

I turn my head and see that maybe people on the top floor in the block across the street can see us cos we're near the edge of the roof but I feel so good I want them to see us, to see Jazz sliding his shiny dick up inside my bucking body. I feel like we're the night, me and Jazz, and our sweat is the stars.

Afterwards he cradles me so gently in his arms that I feel like in him there's all the love I've ever missed out on.

We fall to sleep on the roof, wrapped in my trenchcoat.

JAZZ

I'm woken by the crying of seagulls, just before dawn. The sky's pale-blue with yellow coming up round the corners. I'm lying naked and alone under Carly's coat. Next to me a note flutters, pinned by a bottle of moisturiser. I squint at it.

'*Gone 2 gett us brekfast. B-back soon. X X,*' written in eyeliner pencil. The weird spelling makes me smile. I sit up slowly and wince because my whole body feels like one big bruise. But in a good way.

A draft gets inside the coat, making my skin goose-pimple.

I bundle my clothes under it and quickly pull my jock and track-suit on. And wait.

The sun rises so it's morning. Little thrills of anxiety start to run through my chest.

Where's Carly got to?

FLOYD

The blood squeezes through the bandages when I grip the knife so I keep it held loose inside my coat. There was one time I was in this fairground thing, this like cylinder and it spun but it didn't feel like it was moving and then the floor dropped down leaving me hanging, stuck up on the wall. Like I'm hanging now, man, with everything fallen away, you know?

See, right now I ain't got shit left. I been set up, man, and I ain't gonna take it, yeah. I coulda been proud of what we was doing. But not now. What was I doing, man? What was I follow-ing? And even my kid don't make no difference, cos I ain't never done nothing I want him to know about, yeah. *Shit*.

Me hand's throbbing now. I try and pull the bandage tight but that only loosens it some, makes it feel worse. Some pigs eye me as they kerb-crawl past but they don't bother doing nothing. Filled their quota of niggers for tonight already. And I ain't waving no shot-gun.

Just a blade. And I'm gonna carve Jazz up, man, tear his fucking skin off so the outside match the inside, Krugerise him. So I can tell Zarjazz I did *something* right, you know what I'm sayin'?

I reach his block, knock back the half-bottle of whisky I got in me pocket. For a moment the dead pig's face flashes in front of me through the wire, blank and surprised. I laugh to meself, only it comes out more like dry-heaving.

His corridor's empty.

I push his front door open without knocking, and nose around. No-one's there. But maybe that's good, yeah. Cos it mean I can wait and *plan*, yeah.

I leave the door open a crack, so'se I can look out on the corridor. A white light's pounding behind me eyes in time with the blood in me hand. I grip the knife tight. It feels like part of me hand.

Jazz. Or the other fag. To make shit like it was before, man. You know what I'm sayin'? Like when we was gonna be heroes. In living Black-and-White. *They* understand – Louis, Eldridge, Rap. Fags ain't shit. Like the nazis had the right idea about some shit, man.

Like Pride, yeah? Pride in your skin.

Dawn's coming, man. I can tell.

MOLLY

I ring every half-hour till four a.m. Each time I punch Carly's number my stomach knots. Ten rings, then I hang up because I don't want to advertise to every passing burglar that nobody's home, do I? And he doesn't answer. All the black coffee's keeping my insides churning too. Maybe I'm just being paranoid.

Maybe I'm just sick of losing what I've got.

I don't want to lose Carly.

4.15 I call a cab from this lesbian cab company, cos I reckon if I'm going to be raped by the driver then at least it'll be a right-on rape. I'm wearing minimal make-up and a black bob wig, plus an ankle-length black wool coat, patent DMs, not heels.

I want to be ready for action.

They tell me three-quarters of an hour.

The woman's face is scrubbed and glowing, immediately giving me the guilts, which reminds me why I don't call their company more often. I tell her the address. She has a kind of Little Richard pompadour, so I guess some artifice is okay at least.

There's the beginnings of a pre-dawn lightness to the sky as I drag myself out of the cab outside Carly's block. It's not cold, but I pull my coat close as I look up, trying to count the windows, see if a light's burning.

'You okay?' the driver asks. She's not too interested, but I nod anyway. She pulls the door closed behind me, and then she's gone.

I hurry into the building, imagining rapists round every corner. I know, mostly you get raped by someone you know, usually your boyfriend or your husband. It's just a mature way of being scared of the dark, okay?

I call the lift and hear the doors closing high above me.

I've got the keys to Carly's flat but I knock first. I'm just about to let myself in to leave a note when I think of trying Jazz's, next door. I raise my hand to knock but the door's ajar and it swings open. It's dark inside. I step into the hall. From out of the shadows I hear a black guy's voice: 'I've been waiting for you, man.'

Shit, I think, as my stomach lurches into the room next-door. I put out a hand to steady myself and touch a light-switch. In the darkness I can hear the guy moving. I put my other hand up in front of my eyes and snap on the light.

It works. He's surprised, dazzled, and when he squints at me, surprised again because we don't even recognise each other. He's maybe in his mid-twenties, a boyish black man in hi-tops and a long corduroy jacket, spirals shaved into his scalp all over, and he's trying to push a big kitchen knife into one pocket with a badly-bandaged hand. He has a gold stud in his left ear. What's going on behind his eyes is so tangled it makes me want to reach out and hold him. But I don't. I'm afraid.

He breaks eye contact and shoves past me out into the hall. For a second as he passes his hand bites into my arm, and then he's gone. The room smells of whisky-breath. Very carefully I exhale. My knees feel weak and my bladder feels full, so after a minute I go and sit on the loo. Nothing comes out, but the weakness starts to leave me.

The bang of a firedoor makes me catch my breath. I pull up my panties and tights, reach to flush reflexively but stop myself before actually doing it and giving myself away and drowning whatever's outside out, and sneak over to the door. I peep out through the spyhole. A cute black boy in a pair of black silk shorts and not much else is walking away from me with black lace rags in his hair. I tear at the door to get it open.

'Carly,' I croak. He turns and smiles, then he really looks at me and the smile falls.

'Girlfriend?' he says.

Then we're hugging and the tears come rolling down my face.

CARL

We go and buy cream-cheese bagels and chocolate croissants for breakfast in the all-night deli. Molly makes me sit there over a cup of coffee while she tells me what happened to her. It makes me start to worry about Jazz, like what if he comes in off the roof? Molly sees me twitching, knocks back what's probably the nine-millionth cup of coffee she's already had today, and we hurry back to the block. The sun's up over something, anyway, cos by now it's morning.

I feel weird: happy and wild and frightened and still, all at the same time, you know?

JAZZ

I'm just about to actually go and see what's going on when the firedoor bangs open and Carly comes out onto the roof with a carrier bag and his friend Molly, which I can't help feeling a bit pissed-off about, you know what I'm saying?

But then Carly kisses me on the mouth and I taste him, and he huddles inside my arms and legs, and I just can't stay pissed-off. He rips a chocolatine in half and gives one bit to me, pops the other bit into his mouth.

And Molly tells me about it and I know it was Floyd, and I realise I've got to face it all out, that I can't just let things drift and see what turns up any more. I mean, what if it'd been Carly? Or even me? And I know how to damage someone physically.

Floyd Errol Judy Caroline. Shit.

Carly passes me a bagel. I put the night's madness out of my mind for a moment and kiss his nappy head, nibble his ear.

But I know it's all got to be sorted: there'll be time enough for sunsets after it's sorted.

CAROLINE

There must be a message in the gun, but what can it be? Perhaps something to do with crime. The sawn-off barrels. Or murder. Or suicide. Oh, I don't know, maybe it doesn't mean anything. Maybe it's just got something to do with that other girl, whoever and whatever she is, the one he needs to love him.

I thought of calling the police, telling them I found it somewhere, down some dark alley or something, bringing things to a close that way. No gun, no bag, no Jazz. But no.

Rupert's asked me to marry him. I've told him I'll have to think it over. Somehow it doesn't really seem very important. I don't even know what's made him ask.

Reflex, probably.

JUDY

I wake up with a splitting headache, can't hardly open me eyes. Can't remember nothing 'bout last night neither, 'cept telling Errol fuck off. And phoning the pigs. 'Cept I didn't.

But the phone's off the hook, you know? The tone sounding.

FLOYD

Death in me heart, I'm a blackheart man today. This is how Eldridge woulda wanted it, Eldridge and Buju and Minister Farrakhan, stopping 'em spreading fucking Aids ain't supposed to be no fucking Black fags cos we're better'n that, yeah.

Fucking kill 'em.

I feel so fucking – *dirtied up*, man.

JAZZ

I have to do this on my own. The burden is on me.

Or is that just cowardice? Not having the guts another way?

Maybe I do feel shame. Or I'd want him there with me.

But why would he want to come anyway? After Johnny, I don't think Carly's too thrilled about meeting the rest of the Posse. Or Judy. Or Caroline.

Or is it me who doesn't want him to meet Judy and Caroline? As my lover?

Or the others: Floyd, Errol. As my lover. My male lover. My homosexual/gay/queer/faggot/battyman boyfriend, the one who stripped me and didn't let me walk away with it, who didn't let me walk away, and through whom I'm shown naked, in my skin, and as I truly am.

Trying to play God, trying to play Hero, all it does is make you hide what makes you human, what makes you one man, one free man, which should be the real inspiration. All it does is make people hate you when you fall.

It's why Floyd hates me: of them all he was the one who most needed me to be a hero. But if I'm having to lose the easy belief I've had in my heroes (Eldridge, Stokely, Malcolm, Louis) and having to go through the anger I feel at them and accept their failings (which is what makes them human, makes them not monsters) and forgive them and survive, then he can too.

See, you must find within yourself everything you lean on heroes for, and become an individual. Become a fully human being. And see that all the rest of us are individuals too. Are human beings. All the evil in the world comes from people not doing that, from people being able to refuse to acknowledge that: Auschwitz, slavery, rape, war, racism.

Queerbashing.

I realise I need Carly to be there with me because he's lived it so much more than I have. Not the Black thing: the gay thing. Being gay. Queer. On the streets.

He knows the arguments.

I know I can't afford to lose.

The sun's shining dazzling bright over the tops of the blocks of flats opposite now. I feel Carly's lips brush my cheek and I turn my head and look into his eyes. They look at me more gently, and with more love, than any eyes I've ever seen. He smiles a little smile, made momentarily unsure by the intentness of my gaze. I want to say, 'I love you,' but I feel choked.

Carly puts his arms around me and hugs me, his smooth brown embrace shielding me from the wildness of the world.

Right now, just for a moment, I feel safe, for probably the first time ever.

CARL

Back in my flat Jazz asks me to come with him on his big Coming Out tour, which is kind of flattering. But gruelling: his friends being not the most caring-sitcom crowd you're ever going to meet, you know?

I say yes anyway.

But what should I wear? Something that isn't no Sell-Out but not anything Too Much?

Girl I'm not out of the shower and I'm stinking of compromise. I'll take the advice Molly'd give me if she was here:

Dress To Kill, girlfriend. Power-Dress.

But under the circumstances, wear flats...

MOLLY

It's strange the way Jason's influencing Carly; there's something serious about him in a way there didn't used to be. And there's a kind of directness he's getting too, which is weird because Jazz can't actually *be* direct about a lot of things.

But he wants to be, and I guess that draws it out of Carly. It's almost like a male-female thing, but then I hate myself for thinking that; that men are all up-front but emotionally deep-frozen, and women are all sensitive and blah but can't make the tough decisions when trouble hits.

Makes us all sound like we ought to be in analysis.

Analysis never did anything for me.

It's too weird, though. I mean, *Carly* going off to war, and *me* left waving a hanky as the train pulls out. Surprisingly Mills & Boon, or as near as I'm going to get to it, anyway.

'Luck, girl.'

'Love you.'

JAZZ

'Who're we going to visit first?' Carly asks me. He's wearing a black lycra minidress, black-and-steel bike-boots. His make-up is light, but stylised war-paint fashion around the eyes, making him look kind of like a Grace Jones doll. Steel flashes in his ears and I realise that this could be one of the worst days of my life.

Or one of the best. When I can stop sweating and stop my guts turning over in 4/4 time.

'Johnny,' I say. Carly looks round at me, surprised.

'I thought we'd done him,' he says, an edge to his voice.

'Don't worry, man,' I say. 'Once Johnny's made up his mind about someone he's solid. It's the truth,' I add, seeing Carly pull a face. 'Trust me.'

CAROLINE

A cold thrill of anger runs through me. Was love – brotherly love, sister-brother love – was even that really so much to ask for? I think about the gun, semi-safely put away in the utility cupboard, the two spent cartridges. I think of ghetto girls as seen on TV, covering for their men, whoring for them.

Have I been no more than an intellectual whore? Well, moderately intellectual? Selling myself for ideas, and to someone else's destiny?

For a moment I picture myself loading the shot-gun, snapping it shut and going to find Jazz. To end it. To end everything. And it would be a cheap and foolish thing to do, but right now I feel rather cheap and very foolish. My mind plunges into a chaos and darkness that is far from liberating, since it threatens to liberate me only from the things I most need to cling on to. Rupert touches my arm gently.

'Well?' he asks softly, his voice, his face, his touch a seductive mirror reflecting the possibility of an easy, conflict-free life. And yet one as hollow and brittle as a Christmas bauble. I look up at him. In his Harrow-then-Polytechnic way he's so simple, a child who knows nothing except the world of his own wants. He sees a full glass, I see an empty one.

'I still need time to think,' I say quietly, as his eyes meet mine.

JOHNNY

Me just get back a yard from fixing a little business needed sorting when me see Jazz and Carlton down at the bottom a me fire escape.

Come up nuh, me call, and them start to climb.

Looking pretty, Carlton, me say, rolling a spliff. Him look ill-at-ease. Sit down nuh, man, me tell him. Look what me did get you. And me reach over for disya carrier bag, trow it to him. Him catch it up and look inside like him looking in a shark mout, frighten him a get bit up. Him pull out the shirt me did get. Is flame red wit black polka-dot on it, and silk.

Him like it, me tink.

Is cos a the other day, me say. Try it on, man.

Him look sweet in it. Me smile at Jazz. Him *embarrass*, man! But him enjoying seeing him star look so fine. Him keep on making four wit me then look away.

Thanks, Carlton say, still a little awkward. Relax, man, chill, me tell him. Me pass him the spliff. Him toke, pass it on. You come fi hear labrish, innit? me say, already knowing the answer. Jazz nods. Round him neck him wearing a black-edge pink triangle me reckon Carlton give him, along wit him Afrika disc.

You seen Floyd, him arx. Me shake me head.

Me did speak wit Errol, me say. Him bell me last night, full a grief and tribulation bout Floyd. Him say him mind snap. That him dangerous, you know? *Bad.*

He's psychotic, Jazz say. Me shrug. Me no psychiatrist, you know? And no man should be a judge on this earth. *Psychotic*, Jazz repeat, passing the spliff. Me inhale deeply, put on a tape. The boss rhythms fill me head and chest, fill me heart.

Maybe him wit him gyal and pickney, me say after a pause, shrugging.

Yeah, Jazz say. Then: How about Errol, man.

Me laugh. Him more worry bout Floyd than bout you turn battyman, me say, laughing still.

Yeah, but –

Speak to him, man. Is what you must do. Then you will know.

134

Johnny, man.

Yes, star.

Why did you tell them, man? About me.

Cos me believe in truthfulness, man, me say. Like you, innit. We both searchers for the truth.

We touch fists, smiling, him smile a little – force.

CARL

Jazz is gagging that Johnny gave me that shirt even more than I am, I can tell, even though he doesn't mention it.

'Where to next?' I ask, trying to sound light.

Jazz wavers.

'Pick a easy one,' I say. He shoots me a nasty look. 'Try one of the girls. They're usually less hysterical about gay things.'

'Even when the source of the hysteria's been fucking 'em, man?' he says, unpleasant-like.

I shrug, look away.

'Sorry, man,' Jazz says, touching my arm. 'I just – ' And then we're hugging in Tottenham Court Road, blanking the tourists and the office boys and girls on their lunch-breaks, the shoppers, the suits, the shopworkers and the street-hawkers. Even through his jacket I can feel the knots in Jazz's back. He's holding me so tight I can hardly breathe.

Sometimes he really is as innocent as a child.

'So who're we going to see next?' I ask softly as his arms relax around me, my lips brushing against his hot, sculpted ear.

'Errol,' he says.

JAZZ

I'm going at this all wrong: I'm ready to fight, ready to argue, at least my heart is ready. But I don't know the words, I don't know if the words will come.

They always came before.

But I knew the arguments before, had rehearsed them in my mind ten thousand times, and practised them before sympathetic minds willing me to show them wisdom. Not this time.

My mind spins, my thoughts prismatic, dazzling, disorientating, my confidence crumbling like a sandcastle lapped by a rising tide. What I believed – what I *believe* – is seething in my mind like boiling oil, the contradictions acting like sodium in water. But somehow I'm just about keeping them all in tension, in one unified field.

One mind, maybe.

One heart, fi true.

CARL

Jazz is holding up pretty well, considering. I guess he has got guts, girl. I mean, when my problems got too much I just ran away to the big city, you know? I didn't face them out or nothing. But then I was just a kid then, Jazz is a grown man. And I face stuff out now. Every day, you know? Specially, girl-friend, especially today.

Guess I've got guts too.

I'm expecting fists to go flying the second Errol opens the door, particularly seeing as how he's the one who slammed me up against the wall that time and it was Jazz stopped him roughing me up. He does look kind of weird, but not totally gone.

'Errol,' Jazz says.

'Jazz, man.' They touch skin, but just barely, kind of a ragga version of a Hollywood kiss, then Errol lets us go in the house. I can't help shrinking away from him as I pass by, but he doesn't seem to notice.

It's a good-sized council flat in a brick block. The decor's all that one-step-up-from-MFI black-and-chrome minimalism. Ikea-stylee. A portable phone sits on a smoked-glass coffee-table. Toni Braxton is playing on the stack. Errol picks up a remote, turns it down, stands there looking kind of lost.

'I'm Carl,' I say, holding out a hand. On reflex he grips it in his. I do my firm-and-manly handshake so as not to set a stereotypical tone to the proceedings. Well.

He doesn't wipe it on his trousers after.

This could be interesting.

ERROL

They sit there side-by-side on the sofa while I fix some coffee. Shit, man, right now I feel weirder'n I did the time I saw my old lady doing it with some geezer who weren't me dad after church. Doggy-style. But this guy looked real like him, you know? It made me think, Why's she bothering for the exact same shit, you know?

Right now I feel kind of like I did then. Like, it's Jazz, but then it ain't, you know what I'm sayin'? Jazz doggy-style. But then, who gives a shit?

Me. Maybe. I dunno, man. It's on him, you know what I'm sayin'? He's gotta prove what he is. What he ain't.

I don't want to talk or nothing like *Do you take sugar etcetera* so I stick the mugs on a tray with the milk and sugar and spoons and shit and just bring it through. The other thing I'm feeling like is from when I used to went to church, you know? And after, when you couldn't just say what was on your mind, you had to be all picky-picky.

Like now.

We all sip we coffee.

JAZZ

Well, it isn't getting any easier, so I put down my mug and say, 'There's things we need to talk about, man. Serious things. Deep things.'

'Yeah,' he says.

He's looking out through the open window over an overgrown garden. Honeysuckle is dragging a disintegrating trellis off a far wall of grey breezeblocks. For a moment the ghost of the scent of it fills my nostrils. *One more thing*, I remember, and it seems like today will never be over because there's always going to be one more thing.

Errol's waiting for me to say something, but I don't know how to begin.

'You want me to go?' Carly asks softly, maybe giving me the choice to be ashamed without him having to know about it, without a witness.

'No,' I say, gripping his hand. It's sweaty. I squeeze it for a moment, then let go.

CARL

So finally Jazz is actually going to say something, just before I wet myself from tension-clenching.

'I know you're feeling pissed-off and let down, guy,' he says, speaking low like he's reciting a speech. 'And you're thinking, he's dissed me man, he's a liar, to us and to himself. Yeah? Tell me I ain't right, man?'

Errol nods, almost just a twitch really, doesn't say anything.

'All I can say is, I couldn't tell you. Because I didn't know myself. I mean, I knew some bits. Like I know the Black bits of me real well. But the other bits, what could I say, guy? I'm going with these two girls but really I'd rather be going with another brother? *I* didn't understand it. How could I have expected you to?'

Errol's looking down, looking like he's gonna burst.

'Say something, man.'

Errol looks up, straight into Jazz's eyes. 'Didn't it ever bother you, man, being such a fucking hypocrite?' he asks.

I feel like I'm in a boxing match, wanting my bloke to get a good one in, wanting to jump in the ring with him, even if I ain't no fighter.

'I never said a word I didn't believe in, Errol, man.'

'Yeah, but it ain't the words is the problem, guy.' Errol's got a pile of stuff to say after all that sitting around in silence. 'It's like the whole thing, yeah. The big picture. Like' – for a moment he's tongue-tied, maybe like when you meet someone who used to teach you at school in a night-club – 'like all those ideas, man, Black Power, the whole thing, yeah? Uplift the Race, yeah? Ain't that about getting something good and pure? Getting drugs outta the community, getting business in? Getting rid of all the pimping and selling and white decadent shit, building something that ain't been degraded?'

'So?'

That's all Jazz says. *So.* It's not good enough, and if he doesn't realise it, we're both in shit.

'So where you fit in, man? You turn battyman, white man's disease, his style, your needs before the Black community's. It don't fit, man. Like, is you one a them, or one of us?'

'Both, man,' Jazz says. 'I got the same commitments I had two weeks ago. Nothing's changed.'

'You still a proud Black man?'

'Course I am, man. I ain't ashamed.'

JAZZ

Shit shit *shit.* Excess affirmation reveals a fundamental lack of conviction but what else could I have said? We've hit a stalemate if it isn't just a brick wall, me and Errol. Maybe it's too high to climb and too long to get round. All of a sudden I realise I could just jump up and run out of the room. Never see Errol again. Grab Carly's arm and run. I can't catch my breath I need to get some air to stand on top of some mountain –

And then Carly speaks. I don't know, I suppose I thought he'd be too shy to say anything. And I suppose I thought I could handle it all myself. Carl looks Errol dead in the eye.

'Why've you got a problem with gay people?' he asks.

'I ain't got no problem, man. You got the fuckin' problem,' Errol snaps.

'My problem is people like you.' Carly talks real quiet, pulls Errol's shouting down to just talking. 'Bigots.'

'I ain't no bigot, man.'

'You once grabbed hold of me outside my flat and banged me up against a wall. I think what you said was, *You fucking faggot.* Isn't that being a bigot? Doing that just cos I was gay?'

'I didn't mean shit by it, man.'

'Why'd you do it, then? You can't control yourself?'

Errol looks away. 'We was talking bout Jazz, yeah,' he says.

'When we're talking about people who can't be true about who they are, we're talking about the people who keep them shut up in lies. People like you.'

'Stop saying that, man.' Errol's angry now. My legs and

arms are aching from being tensed to jump up and get in-between them if Errol loses it.

'Why? It isn't true, then?'

'Just stop saying it, man!'

'If I was knifed cos of my skin colour, you'd be out there shouting about it,' Carly says, and I realise as he speaks that he's also exorcising anger with me too. 'But if I was knifed cos of my sexuality, you'd just go, *One less battyboy soiling God's or Allah's or whoever's Christian or whatever creation.* ' He pauses. Then: 'It would still be me.'

There is a silence. Errol squirms irritably. 'So which are you, man? Black or gay?'

'Both. Always. Which are you, Black or straight?'

'That don't mean shit, man.'

'Yeah, it *don't* mean shit. But it's supposed to for me and all the other hundred of thousands of Black gay men?'

'Cos it ain't natural, man.'

'It's natural for me, yeah. I never wanted to sleep with a woman, not really. It's natural for Jazz. It's what he wanted to do. It's natural that some people are always gonna turn out gay. Just cos you're straight don't make it natural for me, but we're both natural, man. You mean normal, and that's a So What.'

'Yeah? You reckon?'

'Yeah. Cos what does normal mean?'

There's a silence because Errol's expecting Carly to rattle right on instead of waiting for an answer. It's strange to hear him throwing down this way; I guess there's always been a side of me that thinks he's a bubble-head. He's still waiting for Errol's answer.

'Well, what people are, innit,' Errol grumbles. 'What most people do is what's normal, yeah?'

'And that's why it's not normal to be gay?'

'Yeah.'

'Most people in this country are white, aren't they?' Carly says quietly. 'Does that mean it isn't normal to be Black?'

'That don't mean shit, man. That's bullshit.'

'Why're you so full of anger about racism, but then you think it's nothing and it's a laugh to spit on me? To hurt me? To fucking *murder* me?'

Carly's eyes are glittering wet but hard as diamonds. This

is his moment of revenge and also of revelation – that he too is a visionary. And the anger he keeps always so nicely chilled, so immaculately made-over, is hot and writhing now.

'My people – gay people – were cut up alive and put in the gas ovens, yeah. And my people – Black people – were branded, mutilated and seven million of us died on the Middle Passage. Don't ever give me no shit about fucking *choosing*, yeah! Don't tell me about making no fucking *choice*!'

Carly's eyes are fixed on Errol's, gentle eyes but at this exact moment eyes totally devoid of pity.

'I'm proud of who I am,' Carly says. *And you better believe it, man.*

There's a pause that's long enough for stars to be born, go nova and cave into black holes and die in. 'That go for you too, man?' Errol says finally, looking over at me, his eyes opaque. I nod impassively, feeling tense and shrivelled up inside. More silence. All the words of the last few minutes buzz around the room like bluebottles, sometimes hitting each other and falling stunned to the carpet.

'We better be going, man,' I say finally, my voice dense, compressed.

'No, man,' Errol says as I get to my feet. 'Wait.'

I keep my eyes on his, shrug, keep my arms loose, hanging tough. We're exactly the same height, me and Errol. An even match. If it comes to it.

I'm not afraid anymore.

He asked us to wait.

Errol looks away from me, away from Carly, shakes his head. 'Shit, man,' he says with a dead half-laugh. 'I need a drink.'

ERROL

Oh, man, this is freaky shit and I feel so fucking weird I can't hardly express it, you know what I'm sayin'? I mean what they do and shit, you know? Shit I can't even *comprehend*, man. And everything's changed, man, and I can't comprehend that either, you know what I'm sayin'? Not yet.

Fuck it, man. Okay, I'm curious. Yeah, I admit it, okay? I'm really fucking curious. You gonna tell me you wouldn't be?

Guess I must be a pervert too.

CARL

We sit in Errol's house talking and talking and even laughing in a hysterical sort of way, and drinking Cockspur, which loosens us all up and for the first time ever I'm having a good time with a straight black guy who knows I'm gay. I try to teach Errol how to Snap and he does it better than Jazz which sparks off a bit of a nature-nurture debate.

Errol's chat makes me realise he's one of those people who wants to see and feel and understand everything in the world but he's only ever had what's pitched up on his doorstep. Jazz of course. And now, strange as it may seem, girl, me.

Some people do want a bigger, wider world after all.

Later, mid-afternoon, Jazz says we'd better be moving on. Lots of drunkenly sentimental embraces later, the two of us stagger out the door. Jazz and Errol smile at each other awkwardly.

'You're a dark horse, man,' Errol says. 'A real fuckin' dark horse.'

He grips my hand. 'Luck,' he says, then hugs me drunkenly. I know we'll probably never be this close again, but it doesn't matter. We turn at the gate and wave, drunk under the glittering afternoon sun.

JOHNNY

Must be 'bout one when Floyd come sniffing round me yard. Him clothes them dutty and him eyes them sticking out like chameleon eyes. Me 'spect one a start moving different direction from the other.

You miss him by tree hours, man, me say. Him give me a look, then go skulk off somewhere else. It make me skin crawl. What make some men so weak that them must break under the slightest lickle ting?

JAZZ

We stop at a McDonalds to get some food and coffee. I didn't mean to get so drunk, none of us did I reckon, but then we were all so relieved that we had somewhere to go, that it wasn't just a dead end.

I feel strengthened. Bovine steroids and caffeine flush through my system.

'You up to another one?' I ask.

'Another McMadburger?'

I kiss my teeth and shake my head. Carly nods, his expression serious. 'Who's it gonna be?'

I sigh. 'Caroline,' I say. Again perhaps, no, no perhaps about it, *because* she's a woman I feel ashamed in front of Carly. But then that's my penance for abusing her, and proof to Carly that I'm totally his.

As if he didn't know by now.

ERROL

After they've gone I have a bit of a doze. I get woke up around five by the tone on me mobile. It's Johnny.

Ow you doing, man, I ask.

Ting sweet yunno, he says. Jazz and him star them did come by you?

Yeah, I say.

Well? he says, teasing me.

It was okay, I say. Yeah. It was okay.

Seen, he says. Later, me bredren.

And hangs up.

A minute later and it's Astrid on the line, hassling me with *Do I know where Floyd is.* Being Astrid, she don't sound worried, just pissed-off.

It's just I'm going to a blues down Brixton and I need someone to mind the kid, she says. Maybe she's fishing for me to do it, I dunno, but I just say I ain't seen Floyd since yesterday. Then I hang up.

That bwoy, that Carly really made me think, man. Use

me brain. Exercise me mind. It makes him someone good to know, you know? Cos your mind's a muscle like the rest. You gotta work it to keep it firm and make it grow. There's enough fatheads around already, man. Look at the world and let's face it:

More people need to be thinking, innit.

CARL

On the way Jazz tells me the story of how he met Lady Caroline, dishes the whole lot right down to the not-sex sex, and right down to how he got off on feeling that he was her salvation from a meaningless life of pampered indolence.

I guess Jazz'll never lose that puritan streak. But that's alright.

We walk quietly and hand-in-hand down the sort of leafy and secluded roads black people don't normally get to go down unless they're burglarising the houses or maybe they're African diplomats or Iman or stuff.

But I could live here, you know? I could deal with it. All I'd need is a chauffeur-driven limo to take me door-to-door so I wouldn't never have to step out onto the neighbourhood-vigilante tarmac.

We get to the front door without being ambushed, Sussed or peppered with buckshot. Lady Caroline lives in a – not a flat – a *apartment* – in, of course, a exclusive apartment-block. Jazz presses the intercom by the wrought-iron-and-brass entry-door. Truth to tell, girl, I've never been nowhere this posh. Molly'd like it. It's like Shelley. Kind of.

A man's voice answers, gagging on a plum. 'Hello?'

Jazz punches the wall softly, making the ivy-leaves rustle. 'Who is this?'

'Is Caroline there, man?' Jazz asks aggressive-like. There's a pause. Jazz's about to add on something else when a woman's voice comes on, well-spoken, but not gagging on a plum.

'Jason?' she says, maybe the only person who ever calls him that. A little quiver of – not jealousy exactly but it's nearer to that than anything else, maybe just being excluded cos I'm not a woman or something – anyway, it runs through me and I wasn't expecting it.

'Yeah. It's me,' he says.

'You want to come in?' she asks. Girl, this conversation is *flagging.*

'It's important,' Jazz says.

'Yes,' Caroline's voice says. There's a buzz and a sharp click, and Jazz pushes the curly brass gate open. We steal into the stone-flagged courtyard like cats or cat-burglars. Jazz glances up at a bow-window yellow in the blue dusk high up above us and I look up there too, into the faraway face of a young man with a flick of straw hair and kind of GQ-modelly chiselled features, looking down on us.

'The fiancé,' Jazz grunts.

Oh, better and better, I think. But I say nothing.

RUPERT

I have a feeling it will all be over tonight. Yes, one way or another, it will all be over. I knock back an indifferent malt and listen to Caroline rummaging in a cupboard in the kitchen. I assume she's trying to avoid having to talk to me, I suppose because she knows I'll have to ask her about, you know, my proposal again.

Tonight wasn't going to be anything special, but then the intercom went, and the moment I heard the silence, I *knew.* And then, looking out of the window and seeing *him* and I suppose his girlfriend – she looks good enough for more than a one-nighter, a fit little piece – I knew. Time for Caroline to stop playing Jane with the jungle bunnies and stop wanting to get speared on the Big Black Dick.

People should stick with their own. I mean, Christ, what if she'd got pregnant, for God's sake? I don't think I could marry a girl who'd had an abortion.

Perhaps I should have sorted it out myself, sent him running back to whatever sleazy night-spot he emerged from. But then, he might have had a knife. He's the sort that would. Pimps, crack-dealers, immigration racketeers, you know.

I have a strong feeling Caroline wants to be on her own when he gets here, that she'd rather I left. But actually it's become quite important to me to see her drop him, to hear the exact words she uses to say, This Is The End.

It's quiet in the kitchen.

CAROLINE

I get the bag down from behind some old hi-fi boxes and put it on a shelf where it'll be easy to reach, then close the cupboard doors on it.

Then I go and stare out of the black kitchen window. I find myself looking into a flat in the block across from ours, Rose Court Mansions, but a floor lower. Only the kitchen light is on. A girl who looks like me only younger is sitting at a pristine breakfast bar, dressed in a white satin night-dress. She's taking pills, interspersed with sips of water from a cut-crystal whisky tumbler.

One... two... three...

I have a feeling she's been doing this for some time, that she's taking an overdose. Turning away from the window, I feel strangely reassured.

CARL

We climb the stairs, the carpet so thick and soft, like a fat cat, that our feet don't make a sound. The only sound is like the swish of the parachute-silk of Jazz's tracksuit. We don't meet anyone coming up or down.

It's so quiet here it's creepy.

Then we're at Caroline's door. I dunno, maybe there's static build-up or something in the air cos by the time we get there the air is crackling with tension.

At least with Errol I knew the kind of shit to expect.

JAZZ

Caroline opens the door to us without a word. She looks at Carly a moment, takes it all in, susses the whole situation, then steps back to let us in. It makes me feel like turning round and leaving directly because once you've said it all, you know? But that would be just too weird, too rude.

Standing there in the best dull tailoring money can be thrown away on, Rupert's just about clocking that Carly's a man. I watch peripherally with a kind of detached curiosity as the cogs turn over while I wait for Caroline to say something. Always gracious, she extends a hand to Carly.

'I'm Caroline,' she says.

'Carl,' he says, shaking it.

There's no malice seeping out into her voice, she really is always gracious. But there's blood behind the alabaster. Anger. And she's right to feel it.

'Something to drink?' she asks.

CARL

She's classy, girl. Classy. She isn't a beauty, not really, but how she is makes her beautiful. And, unlike most people, she got manners, you know?

Plus, she's one of these white people who *likes* black people. She's not afraid like some people who think you're always just about to bottle 'em so they're all nicey-nicey. Just, like, our being black is a plus cos we're in touch with the outside, we're part of the tribe of warriors and outlaws. Which is looking-glass-land status, but status just the same.

The fiancé's creepy though, girlfriend. Up close everything's just that bit too out of place to hit the GQ thing, so so much for that Brideshead moment. Slimy eyes. Or maybe it's just the way they're sliming over my body that's making me think that way.

He's the sort of guy who'd suggest a foursome or shit.

I sip my Evian and blank him, look round the room. Lots of cool grey and white, then gold. Like, gold brocade curtains,a gold-filigreed green marble fireplace.

You can tell I read *House & Garden*, innit?

If someone don't say something, I'm going to *scream*.

'I love your ear-rings,' I say to Caroline in desparation – though actually, I do. She smiles softly.

'They're my grandmother's,' she says. 'I never used to wear them, I was so afraid of losing them, but now I just think – ' She shrugs, looks quickly at Jazz, then looks away. 'Well, it doesn't matter that much. In the end.'

Silence.

Oh well, I tried.

JAZZ

Okay, so I don't want Rupie here, but I'm just going to have to do this shit anyway. I take a deep breath.

'Caroline – '

But she touches a finger to my lips. Her mouth is smiling a little, her eyes are a little sad, but although her expressions are small, there is a radiance of grief about her.

'You never had a place for me,' she says softly.

'No,' I say.

'Do you think I'm a fool?' she asks, her voice without guile.

'I only just learnt it myself,' I answer.

'What did you learn?'

'That I don't have a place for any woman. Not that way. Maybe – '

'Yes?'

'Maybe we could be friends.'

'Not yet,' she says. 'I'm still too angry.'

'With me?'

'No.' She looks up at me, stares deep into my eyes, her eyes so blue, all depth and all surface, that blueness. 'Yes.' We hold each other close, almost like I imagine a brother and sister would.

'Who are you?' she says, as she lets go of me.

'Just myself,' I say. 'Jazz.'

She smiles. 'Perhaps – ' she says, then goes out to the kitchen. She comes back carrying the carpet-bag with the sawn-off, holds it out. 'You left this here one time.'

And she hands it to me.

148

CARL

Deep shit is happening here, girlfriend! Jazz takes the bag, knocks back his whisky.

'C'mon, man. Time we were going, yeah.'

Caroline opens the door for us. I tell her goodbye and she smiles. Jazz hurries down the stairs ahead of me. Just as I'm about to follow him, Caroline touches my arm. When I look at her I see her face is flushed in the low light.

'What's it like,' she whispers, 'to really know him?'

'The best,' I say softly.

The best.

JAZZ

One a.m. and we're crossing the Thames, Hungerford Bridge. There are no trains going by, and there's no-one but us the entire length of the walkway. I calmly reach out towards the iron mesh and gridding between the railway bridge and the pedestrian one with the bag, and drop it into the black void between. It makes no sound, and the wind swallows its impact on the water. There are no boats on the river.

'What was in there?' Carly asks.

'Bad memories,' I say.

He lets this pretentious answer pass, and we walk on in silence.

'What're we going to do tonight?' Carly asks me as we near the Embankment side.

'How d'you mean?' I say.

'That geezer with the knife or whatever was in your flat, Jazz. And if he's not in yours then he's probably in mine waiting to jump us if we go back to yours, yeah?'

Indecision floods through me. I shrug, suddenly weary, feeling the mark of Cain upon my forehead, livid and weeping and highly visible, ineradicable.

'I don't know,' I say.

I hug him tight. It feels so good to hold him, to smell the scent in his hair, the cocoa butter on his skin. I kiss his soft lips firmly, and my hard-on presses painfully against the waist of my jock.

All above the river, on Hungerford Bridge.

MOLLY

So guess who pitches up on my doorstep at two a.m.? Right, and right again. They look beat but not beaten up, so I guess today didn't go too badly for Jazz. I kiss Carly on the lips, Jazz on the cheek.

'Well?' I ask, over a cup of steaming grapefruit tea.

'Errol's solid,' Jazz says. 'I didn't think he was going to be, but he was.'

'The crazy guy, you mean?' I ask, arching a sceptical eyebrow. Jazz shakes his head. 'Oh,' I say to myself, sipping my tea. I hate forgetting people's names. It's like you're forgetting the person.

'We need a place to crash, girlfriend,' Carly says. 'Is it okay if we use your sofa?'

I dig out some sheets, an eiderdown from the seventies covered in purple-and-white paisley hexagons that even now doesn't cut the mustard as retro-chic, and some rugs and pillows, and spread them out on the slightly too-short sofa, which is conveniently missing an arm at one end. It looks cosy though, specially when I turn out the main light and plug in an old lamp with a pink shade that casts a rosy glow. But it still makes me wonder how I can put up with having so much junk around the whole time. I mean, especially now I'm finally making a bit of money.

I guess I must have a tatty nature.

CARL

Molly grabs the bathroom first, then disappears through the bead curtain into her bedroom. I'm so tired I drop the toothbrush in the sink. Jazz embraces me from behind.

'Hey, baby,' he says. Then he literally sweeps me off my feet and carries me through to the sofa. I hold him round the neck. He grunts as he kneels to put me down.

'You putting on weight, man?' he asks.

I kiss my teeth, pretending to be annoyed. 'Get your sweet arse stripped and under these covers, man,' he orders. We wriggle out of our clothes fast, then slide under the sheets together. Jazz pulls me to him, his hot skin electric against mine. I shudder.

'You okay, man?'

'Yeah,' I whisper, holding him tight. 'Yeah, I'm – fine.'

He rocks me slowly in his arms, humming a tune. After a bit he looks in my eyes and starts to sing a little, very softly, not very in tune, but still sweetly.

I ain't much caring just where it will end
But I must have that man...

MOLLY

Okay, so tea at two is probably a mistake, no *definitely* a mistake if you've got a bladder the size of a brontosaurus brain. There's no point in me trying to sleep on it, so I swing out of bed to go to the bathroom. I don't need to put my light on because the lamp in the front room's still on. I think, oh fine, I'll just tiptoe past the sleeping babes, but then I see they're not sleeping.

They're making out. Making love. Whatever.

Okay, so I know I shouldn't watch but, well, I'm not going to be able to sleep anyway, and there's no point in me going back to bed just so I can lie there staring at the ceiling till dawn, is there? Anyway don't *you* ever wonder how your friends make love?

Well, *I* do.

They're sixty-nining on the sofa, Jazz mostly on top of Carly, twining sinuous and naked and smooth and lean, beautiful like men ought to be. In the soft light they look so perfect I wonder how any sculptor could have ever had the nerve to even try to catch it. Carly slides round and straddles Jazz's chest. I look at his shaved crotch while he pumps his hard-on into Jazz's eager mouth. Jazz moves his head forward, taking as much of Carly as he can. Seeing the rapture on Carly's face, the ecstasy in every tensing muscle I ought to feel jealous, but I don't because I'm watching, which is a kind of sharing in its way. And because Jazz is so beautiful too. And because he loves Carly so much.

I don't feel jealous, I just get very turned on. I slip a hand inside my panties. Jazz's crotch is shaved too, making them look like Masai warriors, if Masai warriors make out with each other, which I daresay they do sometimes, maybe often for all I know, though probably not usually on sofas.

Carly's fingers glisten with lubricant as he slides them in and out of Jazz's body. Jazz is on all fours. Carly is moving his other hand in a fist slowly up and down on Jazz's dick, in time with the back-and-forth of his fingers. Jazz moves his hips backwards, sitting down on Carly's fingers and fiddles with a small foil packet, rips it open.

'C'mere, man,' he whispers throatily. Carly goes and stands in front of him and lets Jazz roll the condom down the length of his rigid erection. Then Jazz puts his head between his hands as Carly climbs up behind him.

'*Yeah*,' he moans as Carly's well-lubricated dick slides into his body. Carly starts to move his hips against Jazz's big butt, Jazz gasping with each thrust. I suppose I thought it would be the other way round, but then I guess it's so often the straight ones, the tight ones, that most need to lose control, to trust someone else. And you hardly need eyes to see that Carly's loving letting Jazz lose control, loving that he trusts him enough to lose control.

Loving that feeling of being up Jazz's beautiful big muscular butt too, of course, loving Jazz's moans of pleasure.

Suddenly Jazz looks up, eyes glazed, mouth open, gold tooth flaring, his face so strange and so radiant and so handsome, glittering with dreams. Maybe every guy looks best being fucked up the arse.

No. Being made love to.

And then I realise he can see me standing there, a hand down my pants, gawping and hot. I catch my breath, ready to burn down to the stump with embarrassment, but somehow it just doesn't happen. Because *he* isn't ashamed.

He isn't ashamed.

When he puts his head down on his arms again, I slip away and go and lie on my bed.

I'm sweating.

JAZZ

The next morning I feel full of energy, get up early. I'm eating cornflakes when Molly slops into the kitchen bundled up in a big old dressing-gown, a green silk thing with embroidery on it. Carly's still asleep. Molly looks awkward.

'Cup of tea?' she offers.

I nod. She potters around filling the kettle, putting it on the stove, still awkward. The cornflakes crunch noisily in my mouth. Outside I can hear gulls crying.

'Um, about last night – ' she begins apologetically.

'You don't have to say anything,' I say quickly, and she stops. So I don't have to say the rest, which is, *Maybe I wanted you to see Carly fucking me, or at least me getting fucked, so you'd understand, so you'd know me on my own terms, without lies, half-truths or evasions.* Maybe.

Or maybe I'm just an exhibitionist.

But even if I am, that was just the way of showing her the truth that turned me on the most. And, one way or the other, we all do that. Molly doesn't push the point, she just pours the tea.

'You were very beautiful together,' she says. I look down at my cereal and shake my head, my face flushing.

Now I *am* embarrassed.

CARL

Molly and Jazz are already up and got breakfast on the table before I'm out of the bathroom, so now they're doing the crossword. They're just about done by the time I finally sit down. We chat for a bit, then Molly has to get off to get some stuff for a shoot, leaving us to clear out in our own time.

'So who we gonna do today?' I ask, once we've said good-bye to Molly. Jazz's brow clouds over.

'Judy, I suppose,' he says, avoiding my eyes. 'And then there's Floyd.' He rubs his face, suddenly weary. 'I don't know.'

'What about your folks?'

Jazz raises a eyebrow, looks round the room. The idea obviously didn't occur to him until it tumbled out of my mouth. He presses his palms together and stares into space, blows out his cheeks. I go over and stand behind him, push the tracksuit top off his shoulders, and start to knead them. They're tense, but not as bad as they were yesterday.

'Maybe later,' he says quietly. I keep on kneading.

JAZZ

Maybe your folks.

Yeah, I can see it now: my old man clapping me on the shoulder, *So you're a battyboy, man? You're a queer and your brother's a fucking mental retard, eh?* and we crack a couple of beers and laugh about the way things turn out.

I see him throw Sly up in the air, laughing, stoned, maybe drunk, maybe just happy for once, too happy. And the bulb shatters and Sly hits the bare boards and lies there silent as a stone and my old man's skin turns grey. It seems like my mother's been screaming a long time, like she's screaming at him now however silent she is.

She never let him touch me after that. I was six.

Carly kneads my shoulders and just to feel his hands on me gives me inexpressible relief: Sometimes I feel so scarred I'm surprised people don't turn away from me in the streets.

You bitch, you made this happen, he'd be shouting by now, *you stopped me making a man out of him*, always afraid she'll say, *Like you did the other one? Me a change the nappies on that man three times a day*, but knowing she never will say that because she's lost the gift of being direct.

I think maybe once my father kissed me. But maybe it was a dream.

And then there'd be my old lady's hurt eyes as she says, *Jason, son, what did we do wrong?* And I'd say, *Nothing, ma, at least not the way you mean*, and we'd sit there not looking at each other properly. Then she'd say something like, *At least you're not in prison*, and I'd want to say, *So why do you make me feel like I am, then?* but I couldn't because. Well, just because.

'Maybe later,' I say to Carly. He lets it pass.

Carly's old man broke his arm when he found out. Just like mine would do, if I wasn't too strong and too hard. He thinks he's strong, my old man, but if he tried it I'd break *his* fucking arm.

One for all the gay kids whose parents beat on them.

Rage surges through me. Why the fuck *should* I tell them? Telling because you think you should is like confessing is like admitting there's a sin to be confessed, and there isn't.

I think of the way Judy's looked at me sometimes and feel my gut turn over.

CAROLINE

I woke up with the strangest feeling this morning; that I'm pregnant. I don't know how I know this. I don't even know *if* I know it, but I feel very certain.

Rupert's. It has to be.

If only –

I potter round the kitchen, fix myself an espresso. Across the way the blinds are down in the flat I was watching the girl in last night. I wonder what she did? Somehow it seems to be an event immeasurably distant in time.

Pregnant.

The espresso seems stronger and more bitter than usual.

Pregnant.

Rupert's. It must be.

Pregnant.

From this morning? Surely not. Surely I couldn't feel anything this soon, couldn't *know* anything. *If only* yes, say it, *if only it were Jason's*. That would be something another man couldn't give him, that *I* could give him. But it has to be Rupert's.

Except.

Except for that time. That evening a month ago. When Jazz seemed colder – I now see lonelier – than he ever had before. We talked about power, the power of power, for a long time.

Prejudice will never die, bigotry will never die , he said, *not only because it is endorsed by the institutions that control this coun-*

try but because it's part of the structure of the system. It's inside the terms. Like, you can't think about just thought in the abstract. Like, you can't step back from time and watch it pass and stay where you are because where you are is a place in time. That's why the efforts of people of goodwill within the system can never end prejudice.

It's not a matter of rooting out rotten apples. It's a matter of junking the barrel.

In the small hours, as he stood to go, I stood with him and let my hand brush his crotch. I could feel his stiffness through the soft, rough denim. He inhaled sharply but didn't move away. I ran my hand over his bulge again. He looked away, but didn't stop me. Finally I unzipped his fly and reached inside, slid my hand inside his briefs. It was burning hot in there. I wrapped my fingers around him and he felt large and heavy, though feeling makes things seem bigger than they really are. As I moved my hand on him, I slipped my other hand between my legs. It was the closest we ever came physically.

But thinking, just now, I remember that afterwards I took the fingers that were sticky with him and slid them inside my wetness, just momentarily.

Just to seal the connection.

So maybe –

But I'm probably not even pregnant. It's probably just a kind of perverse wishful thinking. And even if I am, it's almost guaranteed to be Rupert's.

I'll get a tester kit from the chemist's. It's probably just nothing. It wouldn't be the first time, after all, that something's turned out to be nothing really.

CARL

We take the tube up to the West End and go into one of the big bookshops down Charing Cross Road. I drag Jazz over to the **GAY** section and he's like too embarassed or too holy to look.

'What're we doing in here, man?' he asks me, sounding tense.

'You like to understand stuff from books,' I say. 'You like all that learning arguments stuff, don't you?' And I buy him

156

two books, *In The Life* and *Brother to Brother*, and give them to him, still in the bag. And wait to see if he bites.

It takes until we're on the bus to some print-shop in Aldgate Jazz knows to get some leaflets printed up. He starts on *Brother to Brother*, it being the more macho-sounding title, and blanks me out so totally I wish I'd bought the new *Uomo Vogue*. Instead I just stare out the window and watch the city going by. It's grey, but the greyness is bright and full of hidden colour, like mother-of-pearl as you turn it in the light. Jazz's thigh is pressed against mine, and just realising that gives me a hard-on. The usually nauseating vibration of the bus's engine seems like a turn-on too. As we pass by a park the sun breaks through the clouds and dazzles me with gold on ochre, scarlet, green and russet.

It's not the usual London Transport Experience.

Jazz writes notes in the margins of the book! Shit, I mean like a real scholar! Girl *friend*!

I don't know where we're going and Jazz is so glued into his book that we miss our stop and the conductor starts giving us a hard time, doing this *Just cos we're all black don't mean I'm doing you no favours, man* performance art-piece, all over twenty pence, you know?

'You got shares in the company, man?' Jazz says. 'You on a percentage?'

'You gone too far on your ticket, you must pay the extra. And don't *man* me, bwoy. Just pay the fare.'

The bus is stuck at the traffic lights. Jazz grabs my arm and drags me off with him.

'Ey – ' the conductor goes as the lights change. 'Don't walk away from me, man!'

'You've walked away from yourself, man!' Jazz shouts back, a bit too upmarket for the situation, I'm thinking, and for the company, considering I didn't get it either.

'S'good,' Jazz says, waving the book around. 'It makes – connections, you know? Like, sometimes things that look like they're coming head-on, when you look at them from another angle, really they're following parallel lines. Things that look incompatible can create harmonies. There doesn't have to be a conflict.'

Which Jazz, being a heavily-conflicted man, needs to hear,

you know?

'Like you can be a revolutionary, you can take all that with you, and still love who you like, it doesn't matter who they are. Just it has to be strong. It has to be – ' he starts flicking through the book.

'Fierce,' I say.

'Yeah, man,' he says. '*Fierce.*'

Hearing Jazz practising these arguments, where bits of them make sense and bits don't, or they only make sense to him, it's like watching a actor or, I don't know, maybe like watching a poet, which is what Jazz really is. A revolutionary poet.

'Yeah, our nature being that of desiring another person of the same sex' – he practises some more – 'it isn't a moral state. It's a psychological state or a state of the soul, yeah? It's not moral and it's not an indulgence, therefore it's not decadent. All revolutionaries tend to oppose homosexuality because it's made out to be a decadent ruling-class vice. But that's just dishonest shit. Reactionary shit, looking back to old, chained times. A revolution's meant to set people free, right? We need a revolution of the mind. I remember – '

He stops for a moment, like there's something personal he doesn't quite want to reveal.

'I remember Eldridge Cleaver saying some shit about James Baldwin wanting to have the white man's baby. Well, I'm a man who loves other men,' Jazz says assertively. (There's no-one on the upper deck at this point, I should say.) 'And what is that shit all about?'

Not having read the book in question, I can only shrug. He takes a breath, lets it out. It's weird to watch someone learn. Under the anger I can feel his frightening innocence. I mean, he's older than me, a little, but he's younger in my world, you know? Just like I'm younger in his.

'So what're these leaflets about?' I ask him.

ERROL

It's just gone eleven when the phone wakes me up. It's Jazz, calling from a call-box. Wanting me to meet him down Portobello and do some leafletting. Panther Posse stuff.

What about Floyd, man? I ask.

He needs time to chill, Jazz says, which is one way of saying *I don't know what to do there, man.*

Johnny a be there?

I can't reach him, Jazz says. I'll try his gaff later.

One side of me don't give a shit if he reaches Johnny or not, but Johnny's also a total motherfucker and he could sort Floyd, it don't matter how crazy Floyd stand. I know Jazz thinks he can sort Floyd too, but Jazz ain't insane. He's tough, guy, but he ain't insane.

I saw the blood on the windscreen. And the floating hair.

I'll hook with you later, yeah, I say.

Later, man, he says. One, yeah?

Sweet.

I hang up, put on some sweet Soul. Boyz II Men. In the shower I think about Judy. Man, I don't know why I keep seeing her. I mean, I don't even *like* the bitch, you know? She's crazy. Like all the rest of 'em.

The weird shit is, I start envying Jazz. I mean, not in detail, you know, cos I don't swing that way, but just having someone who gives a shit about you, the real you. And then I think, well what if that person was a geezer? What I'd do?

I guess the answer is I'd probably do what Jazz did with Judy and Princess C: try to take a bit and not give none yourself and end up screwing 'em over along with yourself at the same time.

But face it, guy. A geezer just ain't that likely.

The phone goes again just as I'm slapping on the cocoa butter. It's Astrid. She don't waste time on hellos or shit.

Is that prick round there? she screeches. I want to say, You want to get some manners, man, but she'd only go curse me out too.

No, he ain't, I say, and start to hang up.

Errol – she says quickly and quietly, like it's a different person. *Errol.*

What? I say. Suddenly I think, *She's about to cry, man.*

Zarjazz, she whispers, her voice dry like polystyrene. He's taken him.

CARL

The leaflet reads:

Neville Latournaux is being charged with assaulting a police officer during one of the illegal stop-and-searches still routinely used by the police to repress and oppress and harass Black peoples and other minorities. The officer supposedly assaulted suffered no apparent injuries. Neville Latournaux has a broken arm, a fractured skull and a broken cheekbone. His sight in one eye may be permanently damaged.

Then there's this photo of the boy looking wistful, quite nice-looking in a homely kind of way, and under that:

FIGHT RACISM

FIGHT INJUSTICE

JAIL CORRUPT POLICE NOT INNOCENT YOUTH

and then some stuff about a meeting Jazz is planning to get money to get a lawyer for the guy to sue the police with and support the family.

I got Jazz to put in the 'and other minorities' line just as like a reminder that the police shit on all kinds of people in all kinds of ways, even if this time it's a skin-colour thing, you know? And I say that, but we don't know what actually went down between this guy and the police. I mean, maybe *he's* gay and it turns out it was a gay thing, you know? A gay thing with a black man who still ought to get the money to sue the police with.

Jazz gets the point, anyway.

JAZZ

We pass by Carly's gaff quickly, expecting Floyd to come springing out of the woodwork at any moment, like the last sequel before the cycle dries up, but somehow knowing he isn't there at all. I force myself to be careful, despite this feeling: intuition can be treacherous. Or, more truly, hope, despair and delusion have straight enough hair to pass for intuition. While Carly changes I read more of the book.

He comes out in kind of revolutionary drag, camouflage

trousers hugging his butt, DM boots, and a figure-hugging camouflage vest. A candy-pink beret sits on the back of his head. The effect is alternately masculinising and feminising. He wears a hint of lip-gloss and a little eyeliner round his Kohl-black eyes, a diamond stud in one ear. He leans against the door-frame, hips aslant.

'What d'you reckon?' he says.

I look up at him and smile, excited and a little frightened.

CARL

I float down to Portobello on an uneasy high. I was going to wear my Raybans for the total Revolutionary look but Jazz said no, people won't connect with you if they can't see your eyes. Which I couldn't argue with.

I notice that Jazz is only handing out leaflets to other black people. I'm handing them out to all sorts of people, which I know is pissing him off cos he thinks they won't turn up to the meeting or give any money. I know he's mostly right but that's my stand on my principles, you know? I mean, if I've got to be black to think racism matters, and gay to think homophobia matters, or a woman to think sexism matters, then why should anyone else give a shit? Because all I'm displaying is self-interest. Not principles, just looking out for number one. Which is, let's face it girl, something the people at the top of the pile are pretty good at. Which is why the world is the way it is.

Jazz'll make me a deep thinker yet.

I can tell people're wondering if I'm a boy or a girl but it's hip and trendy Portobello on a Saturday so they don't lose it like they would down Westbourne Park way. A couple of raggas check me, but when they check the leaflet they give me the benefit of the doubt. I look through them as I hold out the fan of paper, defocuss so I won't have to say anything.

The one with the black leather X-cap perching on top of a Japanese-flag headscarf points towards the last line.

'Ah be there, guy,' he says.

'Great,' I say. We touch fists. 'Later,' I say.

'You got a lisp like Chris Eubank,' he says.

I don't say anything. He laughs. 'Later, man,' he says, flashing a golden smile like Jazz's, and turns and ambles off.

Memo, girlfriend: Macho Drag Has Its Uses.

Jazz touches my arm, flashing his gold cap. 'You okay, man?' he asks. I nod. He looks down, then looks straight into my eyes. 'Thanks for being here with me, man,' he says. 'I know you won't believe it, but you belong here.'

I'm trying to think of a reply to this bullshit/deeply disturbing and possibly insightful remark when Jazz calls, 'Yo, Errol, man!'

JAZZ

Straightaway I see Errol's got business. We've barely touched skin before he's telling us about Floyd taking Zarjazz. Again I feel everything slithering away from me. I feel hungry and sick at the same time. It's the only moment I've ever thought, *What if I'd never seen Carly, what if I'd just gone on juggling the people I know with the pieces of my personality* . But I know that eventually you fumble something and the whole lot goes down. It's just a matter of sooner or later. And anyway, life's too short for regrets, let alone regretting the good things, you know?

Two pigs are watching us, watching the way we're talking so intensely, three Black men on a street corner. One of them starts to speak into his walkie-talkie, maybe about us, maybe not.

'C'mon,' I say, shooting the pig a look to say Just Try Us, Motherfuckers.

We stroll up under the canopy, start down to Ladbroke Grove. The pigs haven't followed. Errol catches my eye and I look away sharply *red flower the shot shatters the night life bone I –*

'He won't hurt the kid, man,' I say.

'Motherfucker's crazy,' Errol replies.

ERROL

So okay, I'm mostly angry with myself, yeah. Cos I knew Floyd was not like just pissed off with Jazz for like dissing him, you know? I saw the blood and the hair and shit, the spare wrench was missing, my fucking wrench and you don't take a wrench less you got a use for it, a plan for it.

A place for it.

And Astrid, she didn't know that shit, she just thought he was jerking around with his homiez or playing the field instead of playing family man, and I didn't tell her no different and now shit, the kid's missing. If I'd have told her she would've maybe stayed home, yeah, would've been there and then he couldn't have taken the kid. Like, this innocent kid getting caught in this screw-up. In the crossfire. I didn't tell Astrid and I didn't do nothing myself, man. Shit.

I owe her foul mouth a apology, innit.

Well, almost, yeah.

JAZZ

Motherfucker's crazy, man, but even if he wasn't, it makes me realise I've never known him, not in himself, just in relation to me, and I've changed so much I don't know him in relation to myself anymore. Or, I've changed the angle of my self to reveal a different diffraction of the crystal, but either way he doesn't know what he sees, and seen from a new angle he shows me new and unrecognisable facets too.

He won't hurt the kid, man but that's just wishful thinking even if it turns out to be true. I never thought about him having that kid, being a father, what it might mean. What kind of man that made him. And it makes me think that I would like to have a child too, to undo what my father did to me.

No, a son.

Not very likely now.

Carly's hand finds mine, and as our fingers lock together I realise that I could never have been a father anyway, not before, just like my old man never was, because you've got to know love to love another, and you've got to love yourself to let another love you.

I feel cold air drifting in my chest, and grip Carly's hand tighter. In the bustle of the market no-one notices, or if they do, they don't care enough to say anything.

Floyd loved me.

FLOYD

Me hand's throbbing man, numb and painful at the same time. Like the hand of an avenger ought to feel. I feel so fucking – there's a pain sawing through me head, a cry Zarjazz his pain my pain you know? Shit, I'm so dirty – seeing his old man so dirty – shame shit I –

Son, son, I whisper. He looks up at me afraid, so afraid, like no Black Man ought to have to be. *There ain't nothing to be scared of.* But he is even though my hand I'm reaching out with ain't me death hand, ain't holding no sword of fire. He starts shrieking louder than ever. But there ain't no-one to hear. Not down here. Used to be a club called shit, Shaol's? *Shaol.* Some geezer's name or shit. Just a burnt-out blackened shell now, insurance shit or shit, dirty money shit, *Don't cry, man.* I can't take no tears. *Be a man. Shit.*

I could start laughing right now, but I don't. I swallow it and it's bitter, man, so fucking bitter. But I'm a man, I'm this kid's old man, so I take it, yeah.

Buju was right I say, educating for once, yeah. *Off the motherfucking queers, motherfucking* don't *motherfucking* swear in front of the kid, Astrid, *Astrid* it ain't easy being a man. Shit, what the fuck you'd know about being a man? she said. You're just a child. Don't swear in front of the kid, I said.

Shoot the queers but I ain't got a gun but I got a knife, fucking butcher's knife. Any murders we'll know who to look for the girl in the shop said, and I got the wrench too, but.

But Jazz got a gun.

But there's other weapons also.

I'm cold and cramped, man. Time to move. Sun's still high but it's getting dark.

CARL

There's something between Jazz and Errol Jazz hasn't told me about. I don't mean a sex thing or anything like that, but *something.*

I don't reckon I've ever even seen Floyd, so I don't offer a profile on how many cups short of a cupboard he is, I just hold Jazz's hand tight and dare the world. Maybe it's *my* bone-china's cracked, you know?

We hand out the last few leaflets as we stroll down to Ladbroke Grove.

'We need flyposters too,' Jazz says.

Me and Errol nod, but right now our minds are not entirely on it.

'You think he could kill someone?' I ask.

'What do you mean, could *I* kill someone?' Jazz says unexpectedly, looking paranoid.

'Not *you,*' I say. 'You're not a killer. *Floyd.*'

'Yeah,' he says, but not in answer to my question. Then, 'I don't know, man.' His voice is tight. He shoots Errol another look. Again something passes between them, but this time it strikes my flint, you know?

'Look, don't Mina Harker me, Jazz,' I say sharply. He looks at me with a puzzled expression. *Snap snap snap* I go in front of his face. 'Don't not tell me what's going on because you think I'm too fragile to take it, okay? It killed Mina,' I add, just in case my sparkling literary-filmic analogy still eludes him, you know? 'The vampire got her.'

Jazz looking aggressively puzzled now. 'What you talking about, Carl, man?' he says, nervy and irritable. He tries to wrestle his hand free from mine but I don't let it go.

'I don't know,' I say.

JAZZ

One more secret left to lose. But not now, not today. Not with everything that might happen, that might make the rest *even that* not matter any more.

'Later,' I say quietly. 'Just – later, okay, star?' I force the wild hunt out of my blood, the dervish dance out of my mind, and catch Carly's eye. He looks me straight back. His eyes are dark and clear and open and I feel a little ashamed as I try to match their honesty.

'You said we got to sort the hall for the meeting,' he says, changing the subject. I feel like a kite, grateful he's chosen not to wind me in out of the high winds.

I feel strange.

There's a tension in the atmosphere, a smell of static, rubber. A storm coming.

I say that I'll go and sort the hall out, and I'll phone Errol later and see Carly round at Molly's when I'm through.

'Be careful, man,' Errol says, gripping my shoulder. Carly doesn't say anything. I kiss him lightly on the lips, trying not to wonder what other people are thinking. because it's what I want to do.

It's so difficult, so surprisingly difficult to do what you want. Except man is a social animal, he wants pack approval more than anything, so perhaps it's not surprising at all. Like the reserve troops who were called out to round up and shoot the Jews in Jazefou in Poland, send tens of thousands to the gas ovens of Treblinka. Only ten percent of those ordinary German men refused to do these things. And why? Because it was easier for them to murder unarmed and defenceless people than to go against pack approval.

I go and sort out the hall. It's in a large old brick church called Our Lady of Lourdes down the Uxbridge Road. The room we're getting is big, probably too big because it could seat over a hundred and if we get more than twelve we've done well, but the smaller room I wanted is full of old pews rescued from some other church that was being demolished.

'A result of the – now upturning – spiritual recession,' the Father says in that smarmy churchy way.

I think of the new hordes of scared, ignorant fools rushing to kiss the Virgin Mary's flat arse, but since the Father's not charging anything for the hall, I push out a low-voltage smile.

'Just leave it as you found it,' he says magnanimously.

The stubble on my arse is starting to itch.

CARL

I window-shop on my way back to Molly's, knowing she won't be back until at least six. I pick up this month's *Interview*

166

and go and sit with all the other queens in the Compton Street Cafe over a Raspberry Canadian Springwater. Because I'm seeing someone, guys come on to me like hummingbirds round a orchid, some even very good-looking. Honey, ain't life a bitch? I smile blandly and let conversations flag.

But somehow it all seems a bit – so what, you know? I mean, right now *All About Barbra* is just not going to give my life that extra essential missing ingredient. Not when my crazy and beautiful lover, and my crazy and beautiful self while we're at it, are being menaced by a kid-kidnapping psycho homophobe.

That is a drama, girl-friend. You know what I'm saying?

Still wishing to immerse my troubled soul in a 100-percent queer ambience, I go down to Harvey Nicks in Knightsbridge and browse some Hermes scarves. I could mop one, but I just feel too conspicuous today.

Anyway, I already have five.

After once-overing the designer womenswear, I head back to Molly's. She's just got back from a shoot ('C&A,' she says. 'Never mind,' I reply) when I arrive, and is unwinding over a cup of grapefruit tea.

'Can me and Jazz stay another night?' I ask her.

'Is Mr Crazy still out there?'

I nod. She gestures towards the couch. 'Thanks,' I say.

'And what have you been up to today?' she asks.

I tell her about Floyd and the kid. 'Shouldn't you call the police?' she says. I shrug. I also tell her about the meeting.

'Can you come, girl?' I ask.

She looks away. 'Raoul's invited me to dinner tomorrow night,' she says. I feel like going 1, Cancel. And 2, What, you mean the one who beat you up on slammers when you told him his stuff was derivative of Baselitz or whoever rip-off painter it was, but probably that one, I can't think of any others who get off sticking broken plates on blue velvet, which I don't say and 3, Tell him you'll be late. But I don't say that either. I just say, 'No problem, girl.'

She smiles. But it is a problem.

CAROLINE

The paddle turns pink.

I feel water trickling down inside me. My breathing is a little shallow. *I love Jazz. Still.* I say that but it's different, you know? He's given me something, finally. *If it's his*, but I'm not thinking that, it's not even a thought.

A baby born of black and white, man and woman, gay and straight, elite and proletariat, all those things in their commonplace way rare metals and precious stones, or if not, if common in themselves, rare in their alloys; a hope of synthesis above dilution or compromise. A baby, a child. A person.

I said I'd marry Rupert.

An outrageous sequence of thoughts flashes through my mind: if I'm having Jazz's – a black man's – baby, I can't marry Rupert. Not because he wouldn't have me, and perhaps he wouldn't, but because it would turn me into one of those well-off white women who enjoy black men for a little down-and-dirty fun and then marry a nice white peer to ensure that they haven't really been dragged down into the dirt.

But Jazz has crossed over to the other side of the court, and the outrageous part is that I start to think, *Well, Errol always had a glint in his eye for me.* Because that would be like a form of integrity, on one level, at least. But on a more immediate level it's so crass that I blush at having thought it.

Then I really think, *What if it's Rupert's baby?*

I mean Rupert's and mine, of course.

ERROL

Some brother cruises by in a white XR3i, 'Boom By By' blasting out the motor system, telling us kill battyboy, shoot 'em up and shit.

I feel angry and ashamed, like everyone on the street's looking at me.

Shit, man. Easy targets, you know? Why ain't he did a rap about killing the Klan or shit? Shit.

We gotta break open these circles of violence, man. Fuck's

sake, this shit is so – unavoidable – you know what I'm saying?

JAZZ

On the bus back from the print-shop I start in on the second book Carly gave me, really the first one, *In The Life*, but I can't concentrate. I've got a show set up tonight, in a new West End gay bar. I feel strange about it, mainly because of my shaved arse and crotch and armpits, which will make me give more of myself away than before. Which I ordinarily wouldn't like. But then I like myself more than I did, so I think that's why it just feels strange. I get a hard-on on the bus thinking of Carly shaving me, thinking of being up on stage, everyone looking at what they can't have.

But for a new reason now.

And maybe there is an incongruity in paying for political posters by grinding your arse in some club, in the decadent yielding the radical. But if you step back, if you look at it from a different angle, you'll see that parallel lines do cross. Because to me the only decadence is cruelty, and the radical who tries to impose a harsh, judgemental value-system on a people powerless to choose not to accept it, is reactionary, is just a mirror-land tyrant. White God to Black Allah. Checkmate.

Plus, name me a job that isn't the top job that isn't a polished form of slavery, you follow me? A glossy version of prostitution.

(The seduction of being a drug-dealer, a pimp; transcending the most obvious of the chains. The same for an artist or a poet. And ultimately, a revolutionary.)

CARL

Molly's prattling on about her day and I'm not listening, I'm thinking about Jazz fucking me. My dick gets embarrassingly stiff and my arsehole feels warm and relaxed. I feel like a battery sitting on a charger, you know?

'How awful!' I say quickly, cos Molly's stopped talking, and the tone of her voice was mid-volume moan.

Molly nods, which means I fooled her. Or at least enough for her to carry on without inhibition. 'I mean, without make-up, most of those girls are just *nothing*,' she says. 'Or they're even actually ugly.'

I nod, imagining pumping my arse on Jazz's cock. Some straight boy I knew, or closet or liar, once asked me did I get fucked that way? When I said 'Yeah,' he said, 'Man, I don't know how you could let 'em do it to you.' Which was, like, the man's point of view on it, you know? To the extreme. I just shrugged, didn't say anything. But later on (of course) I thought of what I ought to have said: 'Because it feels so *good*, girlfriend.'

Which Jazz gets, despite his more macho aspects.

I guess I used to fantasise about the totally manly man, you know? The totally obvious verging-on-showing-myself-up-as-a-self-hating-fag 101-percent male manly man. With me Geisha-girling it and doing all that girlier-'n-the-girls routine. Jazz a manly-man type, but there're a lot of currents drifting, there's a lot of undertow, you know? And that means there's understanding there, not just use. A *sophisticated* turn-on, you know?

I suppose when I was a kid I wanted a man who'd take me away from all the shit, in his UFO or on his Harley or just in his Capri, and just completely look after me like my old man wouldn't.

But now I'm a man too. A man who goes with his feminine aspect, but a hundred percent a man. A adult. And that means controlling my situation, and I couldn't give up that control, you know? Not in that total way I fantasised as a kid. It'd be like wanting to be a happy slave.

If love isn't setting you free, it isn't love. To me.

When's Jazz getting back?

'*Dishwater* blonde,' Molly's saying. 'I told her that's her natural colour. Not honey blonde at all.'

Women're lucky. They can take dick and not get read on it. I mean, a lot of even *gay* men think you're letting the side down if you like to take it too much, you know?

Jazz is right, girlfriend: Change is *sorely* needed.

There's a knock on the door. I know it's Jazz before Molly's even dragged herself up to get it.

My battery is now fully charged.

JAZZ

I kiss Carly and realise that both our dicks are already rock-hard. I know it's Molly's flat, but I want to shove her out of the door. I feel breathless and out of control.

'Come to the bathroom,' Carly says. 'I'll show you the new skin-care stuff I picked up today.'

'Yeah,' I say, letting him lead me out of the living-room.

I close the bathroom door and ram the lock into place. Then I fall on my knees, cradling Carly's arse in my hands and burying my face in his crotch. He gasps sharply.

CARL

We make fierce love, wild and hot and noisy, Jazz taking me so deeply at one point I'm crying out with each thrust, his dick all the way in me, then all the way out, then up to its base again.

When we finally emerge literally a hour and a half later my arse and dick so warm I feel like I'm melting, a good well-used soreness there. My thighs and arms and every muscle ache so much I can hardly walk.

I stumble out in just a pair of Calvins to apologise to Molly for keeping her off the can, but she's gone out. She's left a note which says, *Felt I ought to leave in case my presence was inhibiting you.* I don't know if it's a joke or if she's heavily pissed-off at me.

Actually, I feel too well-fucked to care.

Jazz comes up behind me and takes me in his arms, nuzzles my ear. His embrace is hot and soft and tender, his dick incredibly soft between my buns. I wriggle round to face him, planning to say, 'I love you.'

But right then I love him so much I can't say anything.

We kiss so softly it's like melting and flowing into each other. For a moment we really are one. But *really*. It's the most amazing feeling I've ever –

It's just the most amazing feeling.

ERROL

Jazz calls me, tells me everything's set up for Thursday night. He's like the Black monolith in *2001*, you know what I'm saying? He makes shit happen. He makes *change* happen.

You hear anything from Astrid, he asks.

No, I shake me head even though he can't see me.

Change for better *or* worse, you know what I'm saying?

JAZZ

The sky is heavy and bruised but no rain comes. Staring out over the thrusting towers of the city I feel apocalyptic.

'Our people built the pyramids, man,' I say to Carly, watching his reflection yellow against the deepening blue of the glass. A rising wind rattles the dry-rotted frame.

'Slaves built the pyramids,' he answers.

Somewhere a car alarm starts to scream. The apocalypse is just man's vanity after all; nothing is ever really resolved.

'Yeah,' I say with a shrug, curl a dumbell I found by Molly's sofa up to my chest, looking down at the smooth bulge of my bicep.

About seven we go round to speak to Mrs Honor Ann Churchill, Neville Latournaux's grandmother. His mother's dead, his father's inside for glassing someone. Neville was supporting his grandmother. She's a fragile, bird-like woman, elegant except for hands warped by rheumatism. One of the points of the Panther Posse is to make sure she's okay while Neville's awaiting trial, and to fix things up for her if he goes down.

CARL

Mrs Honor Ann Churchill opens the door to us on the chain, sees it's Jazz, lets us in. Jazz is wearing all black – black Nation of Islam suit but with a yellow tie, conservative black shoes and he's carrying a briefcase. There's a gold X in one of his ears, a tiny pink triangle with a gold border in the other. I'm in black too, a lycra cyclist's one-piece with fluorescent green up the sides, black leather bum-bag, black lo-tops, kind of high-tech nudism with no VPL thanks to a Calvin Klein jock. Jazz corn-rowed my hair earlier, and I'm wearing minimal make-up – gloss on the eyelids, eye-liner, a blush of foundation, the tints a hint metallic, a touch transhuman. In my bum-bag are a pair of wraparound shades, but I'm not wearing them now. Lycra covering me from wrist to ankle, I'm in kind of Marvel comic-book drag, you know?

So as to set the world to rights.

On my back a small Cross-Colours back-pack, containing other essentials.

Jazz introduces me as 'Carlton'. He asks her if everything's okay, tells her about the meeting and says the posse can do her a loan for anything, asks will she need a cab to get there. She tells him no, but he puts a fiver on the mantlepiece anyway.

'Give it me back at the meeting if you don't have a use for it,' he says.

'It's good to know there are some good Christians out there,' she says.

Jazz looks down. 'Just good people,' he says, then kind of goes back on it – 'Just people.' He shrugs a little shrug.

'Thank you anyway,' she says. 'For Neville.' There is a shine to her eyes that looks like hope and tears, a little smile on her lips like she thinks we're young and naive and godless, but we're also all she's got.

The best she's got.

MOLLY

When I get back they've gone out. On the back of my note Carly's written 'Gone to seee a show – have spear key Love C.'

So long as it's only the spear *key,* I think to myself as I flop down on the couch. The couch makes me think of sex, not surprisingly. But when I think about Jazz and Carly I don't feel turned on anymore, I feel – motherly, damn it.

I'll be waiting up for them next.

CARL

Jazz gets me into the club for free, as his personal stylist. He could've just said Guest, you know? But it does mean I get to go and mingle with the 'stars' in the compact confines of the dressing-room/broom-cupboard. Actually I say mingling, but we were mingling very much lat-to-pec if you know what I mean, posing-pouch-to-bubble-butt, so I slip out (literally, on baby oil) and go to the bar, get a rum & Diet Coke to sip.

Some of the guys were real dogs, you know? I guess they probably put on the best shows cos they know they've got to *work*. The cute ones know they're cute so they think they can just strut about. Like guys with great big cocks who think you'll be just so excited they won't have to do anything to get your juices going, you know? Except say something like *I'm gonna shove this big M-F up your arse* etcetera.

Which could be sexy, but is kind of presuming, you know?

It goes without saying, of course, that Jazz is good-looking, well-built *and* puts on a good show.

Actually, it's very professional and slick and it gives me a hard-on, but it's not crazy like Molly said he was before. I guess he still likes doing it, you know? But he's not so repressed, so it's not his only let-out anymore.

I mean, why fuck with a bunch of pissed suburban queens when you could fuck with *me*?

JAZZ

I'm in a house where I used to live as a kid. It looks like the house where I met Caroline for the first time, but it's my childhood home, and my old man's sent me to find the jewels under the floorboards. I'm prising the dirty rotten boards up with a crowbar. The sharp metal edges of the crowbar are cutting my hands but I carry on because I don't want my father to – I don't want him to – I find the gun which is what it turns out I'm looking for and I'm in a church but it's like a bad film-set church. Then I shoot someone and it's just like it was and it's a street and it's Carly and he's dead but when I go up closer I see it isn't him it's my father and I feel so relieved.

I wake up and Carly's nuzzling against my chest, smooth and warm and trusting. A drop of sweat runs down my smooth arm-pit. He mumbles something, snuggles closer. I hold him a little tighter, rest my nose on a clean cane-row, its soft scent disguised by a skein of smoke from the club. For no reason, for every reason, a tear slides out of the corner of my eye and down my cheek.

It's four a.m. and I don't want to sleep.

CARL

We drag out of bed at seven to go flyposting. I'm wearing navy-blue overalls that are tight over the butt, and Raybans to shield my sensitive eyes from the precommuting glare. Jazz has a dark blue Adidas tracksuit. We don't talk much. He has us jumping on and off buses so we can't get caught up with by the pigs.

We finish about nine and this girl's arms are well and truly worn out! No weight-lifting happening today, girlfriend! Them dumbells staying dumb and down on the ground! The only workout considerable is a strictly intimate one. I look at the bulge in Jazz's pants as he stands up to get out change for the teas we been drinking.

Eyes on the prize, girl, I think, dragging my tired arse up off the moulded plastic.

As we stroll along, hand-in-hand in the yellow morning light, I ask Jazz what the meeting tonight is actually going to be about.

'Telling people what happened, what's going to happen, what we're going to do about it, and how they can help if they *can* help. Giving their time, money, writing letters and what have you.'

Which brings that conversation to a close. Jazz is tense, I can feel it in his fingers.

'What's wrong?' I ask.

'Nothing,' he says.

Except tonight's the night it all converges: the Panther Posse, Neville Latournaux, the point of it all, what I've been trying to make happen.

And I've got to stand up there. As a Black Man. As an Afrikan male. But also and more problematically as a Homosexual Afrikan-Black Man. And if someone calls me on that, I've got to stand up for it. Stand by it and hold everything else together, all those threads which in my hand may become the tangled strands that hang down below a Portuguese man-o-war, paralysing and possibly deadly.

I want to be like Malcolm (charismatic, handsome, original, and a truth-teller, a struggler against the beast, who wouldn't want to be like that?), I want to be like Malcolm except some voice can shout out 'faggot', 'queer', 'battyboy' and there's no way out, there's no way forward except right through them. And I can't say '*Malcolm* had sex with men, because even though that is, I read somewhere, an open African-American secret, even if it were admitted to, all that would be said is, 'Sure, when he was a pimp, dealt drugs, pulled burglaries, slept with white women, before he purified himself and became a Moslem.' To which I could not say, 'pimped out then by Elijah Mohammed,' any more than I could point out that his early life is implicate in the broader vision he was creating at the end, because I would just be one more person trying to make Malcolm mine.

The answer is obvious in words, if not in meaning: *Don't try to be Malcolm, then.*

Suddenly I have this flash of – fantasy – precognition? I see myself being shot at the meeting, just like Malcolm except exactly like real life, exactly how it happened when I pulled the trigger.

The bag drops noiselessly into the darkness.

Has Floyd got a gun? Were the flyposters destiny's calling card? I'm ashamed of my sense of self-importance: the gap between striving to make a better world and thinking your striving's what's keeping the world turning is so narrow there is no gap. Maybe there's even an overlap. I clear my throat.

'Really, man. Nothing's wrong. Just, I hope somebody

shows up apart from us, you know?'

Carly nods. 'What're you going to wear?' he asks.

CARL

Jazz laughs, flashing gold and white, then shakes his head.

'I hadn't thought about it,' he says, still smiling because he knows I know he's lying.

'What could be more African than adornment?' I say, which is probably the title of a *Vogue* spread, but it sounds more meaningful in the context of two Gay African male warrior urban children like ourselves.

'A little of the Gold That They Stole,' Jazz says quietly.

JOHNNY

Two p.m. Jazz reach me on the phone, tell bout the meeting fix up, see if me a be there.

Seen, me say. Him arx me go collect the grandmother in me BMW, say she frighten to go out on she own.

Tell she me come round seven, me say.

Okay, him say.

Him about to hang up. Jazz, me say.

Yeah, him say.

Peace and love to Carlton, man. Tell him me get him a gift, yeah.

There a pause.

See you later, Johnny, man.

Him hang up.

ERROL

About six the rain starts coming down, like just when I'm setting off, no fucking surprise there, guy. Sheets of the fucking stuff, blinding you in the wind. It's been getting up to come down for days. Even if there was like sunshine this morning, the air's been waiting for days.

The rain's so heavy you can't use a umbrella, it just gets ripped right inside-out. I pull the hood on me leather parka down tight, push me hands down deep into me pockets and lean into the wind. A busted pop-up umbrella rolls by like a fucking tumbleweed and the thunder's rumbling like God got diarrhea. Me Timberlands go from yellow to black. The rain's still getting blown up in me face, making me feel like I'm drowning.

I pass by a kid in a sleeping-bag in a shop doorway, chalk-white face and hands, everything else soaked black, but I don't got no change. And I got me own to take care of, you know what I'm sayin'?

The leather smells strong under the hood, and no rain ain't soaked through to me scalp so far.

JAZZ

We run for it from the Tube. I catch hold of Carly's hand and drag him across the busy road. Everything's glittering and hallucinatory, car headlights making the rain explode from battering blackness into a spray of diamonds, soaking you as quickly as jumping into the sea.

I feel wild and crazy and elated even though I realise this probably means no-one'll show up at all.

CARL

The hall is warm and dust-dry and silent. I take off my Jones hooded raincoat and hold it, thinking where can I put it where it won't get ripped off.

Jazz gets busy pulling chairs around, pulling tables together and shit. He looks over at me.

'Leave it up there with my stuff,' he says. 'No-one'll nick it from there.'

I shrug and climb up onto the stage and look out over a hundred empty seats, a kid's inflatable, empty Coke cans and crisp packets. Jazz's dragged six chairs onto the stage.

'Who're they for?' I ask.

'You, me, Mrs Churchill, Errol, Johnny,' he says.

'There's six,' I say.

He shrugs and looks at me weird. 'A spare, okay?'

I let him play drama queen. I mean, he's got to perform tonight, and if you don't have drama, you don't have a show, right? And you need a show cos there's no such thing as natural beauty when it comes to parading the truth.

Varnish that truth, girlfriend.

Jazz has gone for unpretentious drag – yellow Timberlands, black leather trousers, black tee-shirt with a red-gold-&-green map of Africa on it. There is gold on his fingers and wrists, the pink triangle I give him in one earlobe.

My man looks *fierce*.

No more Malcolm X wannabeing.

His black leather parka is hung over a chair, same as mine. I'm in the cycle-lycra one-piece, hi-tops, black leather fingerless gloves. There's a diamond stud in my right ear and I'm wearing Carl Lewis make-up – like, you know, subdued but obvious. Plus I got on clear plastic wraparounds, I suppose to put a barrier between me and the world, you know?

JAZZ

Half-past seven Johnny arrives with Mrs Churchill, acting the charming gentleman in a white tracksuit and fun-fur white gangsta bowler, escorting her from his car with a rasta-colour golf umbrella. Her face is fixed in an unfocussed benign expression, a look to deal with surprising success or flat-on-its-face failure, and she's dressed Sunday-smartly in navy-blue and white. She seems a strong and brave person, and I feel sick when I imagine her consigning me and Carly to the gas ovens as the next best thing to hellfire. I draw a deep breath, clarify my mind: if you seek after justice, you do not do it to be liked; you do not do it to earn justice in return.

CARL

The kettle's boiled but there's no coffee. Well, there probably is, but it's padlocked in a little dresser the mugs and things are sitting on.

'You fixing we some coffee, man?'

It's Johnny. I try not to look startled. He smiles warmly, well it's meant to be warm. He claps me on the shoulder. I tense.

'Relax, man,' he says, squeezing me, then letting go. 'You me star, nuh? Me a protect you, man.'

I wonder *Is he coming on to me?* but I don't think he is, it's just his way of being friendly.

'It's the cupboard. It's locked.'

'You have a hairpin pon you?'

I rummage in my bum-bag and find one and hand it to him. It's like watching a pantomime or a magic show or something because he bends one arm of the pin halfway down, gets down on one knee and starts to fiddle in the lock.

'Time me, nuh,' he says.

Before I've pulled the lycra back off my Bart Simpson watch, the lock's sprung. 'That's got to be a record,' I say. He smiles, puts the jar of instant by the kettle, and stands up. 'How do you like it?'

'Strong and black and sweet,' he says, handing me back my bent pin. 'The way you like your men-them.'

Just as he's about to go back into the main bit of the hall, he turns and catches my eye. He brings a small crepe-paper packet out of his tracksuit pocket, holds it out to me. 'Ah did bring this for you, yeah,' he says softly. I open it tentatively. It's a gold earring in the shape of a revolver.

'Cos you a warrior, guy.'

And before I know what's happening he's unscrewing the butterfly and slipping it into my ear. He leans back. 'Is pretty, yunno. You like it?'

'Yeah, sure, ah – very much,' I blab. He smiles, then turns and goes. I switch the kettle back on. My heart's still racing. Chemically more than romantically. I mean, I always expect to be murdered by someone like that, not rained on with gold and silk, you know what I'm sayin'?

My hand's trembling so much I spill the sugar.

JAZZ

At eight-twenty I decide that's it, there aren't going to be late-comers. Fourteen people have come, which is good considering the weather. Twelve Black, two white: four solid fly-girls, three ragga boys, two churchy couples, a tall, sexy, shaven-headed brother with a white girlfriend, a slightly punky white boy with a nose-stud.

A smaller room would've been better, more intimate.

No Floyd. Yet.

As I stand to speak another premonition/neurosis/movie-memory flicks through my mind – the baby wailing in his arms as Floyd drags up the aisle, rain dripping from his soaking body. He pulls the gun up in one easy movement and my chest explodes. Black.

'Thank you all for coming,' I begin.

JOHNNY

Jazz start working him charm. Me did forget the skill him have, you know? The voice. Him tell 'em fi no forget this injustice just cos is so commonplace inna thisya Babylon. Him introduce the Churchill lady and shi tell all a them Neville a good boy. Jazz know just the time to stop she before we tinking a saint like that belong with the angels-them, you know?

Floyd no appear. So far.

JAZZ

'All we're asking you tonight is, if you can give money that's good and that's important, but if you can write letters, and get friends to write letters to your local MPs, that's even more important. And if you want to write to Neville, to let him know that people out there *do* care that an injustice has happened, and that we do care and are doing something about it, I have addresses and sample letters you can take away with you. I know he would appreciate that.

'Thanks for coming out in the storm. Peace and justice.'

The churchy people go and chat with Mrs Churchill. The ragga boys and the fly-girls take some letters and forms and slop out without talking or interacting with anyone, except for a pretty girl with gold-dusted braids chewing gum who turns at the door and flashes a smile at us.

'Later, yeah,' she says.

I smile back.

CARL

Well, I thought there was quite a lot of people turned up. Jazz was like very simple and straightforward, kept it moving along, like a good director. People give forty pounds and Errol, all professional, writes them out receipts for contributing to (rubber stamp) The Panther Posse Fighting Fund.

It doesn't seem much, you know? I guess I was expecting kind of a Blonde Ambition tour show-stopper kind of thing. Or like banners waving the air hot with rocket-fuel smells anticipating some revolution.

I guess this is the real Real. Or part of it, anyhow.

I guess it feels good.

Johnny's just helping Mrs Churchill on with her coat (she hasn't invited us onto more familiar terms), when she turns to Jazz and asks what it means, the pink triangle in his ear.

'It means I'm gay,' he says blandly, bravely.

'Ah,' she nods. There's an awkward pause. 'Yes.' Then, 'My brother is – too.' She feels too awkward to wrestle the word out. 'He's a good man,' she adds quickly. 'He helped me raise my son. He made a fine man of him. It was only when he came here – my son – Well.' She smiles a smile sweet for her brother, bitter for the times, I guess. 'Are you all – ?' she says suddenly, looking round at the rest of us. Johnny laughs, Jazz shakes his head.

'We are – ' he indicates himself and me. 'They're not – ' Johnny and Errol. Errol looks embarrassed, but funny-embarrassed, not insane-with-humiliation embarrassed. You know?

Mrs Churchill smiles and we all laugh a little. I guess she

thinks even more we're strange lost children in a upside-down world. But it was Jazz read the story about her grandson and got her number and everything, so what can you say, you know?

How can you judge?

Floyd steps out from behind the curtain hanging just behind us.

His parka's dry and dusty which means he must've been hiding there for hours and hours. He's holding a fucking butcher's knife a foot along and his eyes are scary and dead. He's moving like a cripple, jerky, unpredictable. His eyes roll over me and Jazz. Everyone's paralysed. Then Jazz speaks. His voice is warmed-up, clear.

'Where's the kid, Floyd, man?'

'Wanna interfere with him do ya, battyboy?' Floyd spits, baring his teeth, his face distorting with uncontrollable emotions.

'Where's Zarjazz? Is he okay?' Jazz edges a bit closer. *Don't,* I'm thinking. The knife is sharp and wicked. Floyd smells bad.

'Fuck you, battyboy. Faggot.'

Jazz's voice gets more powerful, more direct. 'Where's the kid, man?' A drop of sweat runs down the side of his shaved scalp. Off to stage left Johnny's making sure Mrs Churchill is behind him, Errol is standing frozen stage right. Jazz takes another step towards where Floyd's standing.

'The kid's at home, alright with you, mister battyboy?' Floyd sneers. 'Mister fuckin' – ' he slashes threateningly at Jazz face, Jazz steps back quickly ' – battyboy!' I can smell the whisky he's been drinking.

JAZZ

Floyd's madness clouds the air. His eyeballs are moving in rapid little movements. I have to control this.

'What do you want, Floyd, man?' I open my hands, extend my arms in kind of the echo of an embrace.

Floyd doesn't answer. I force my breathing to be regular.

'Do you want to hurt someone?' I harden my voice. 'Do you want to hurt me?' Floyd shifts slightly. I force my eyes onto his, lock them there. His eyes are blank as wood, and as

183

hard. He's waiting for a trigger. A movement. A word. Maybe just another word from me. But:

'Do you hate me?' I say. And before he can answer, before the feeling can become an action I continue: 'You might hate me but you've got to be a *man* now,' I tell him, threaten him. His pupils contract to pinpricks. Still waiting. 'You've got a woman. You've got a child. Don't fuck it up, man. Just don't fuck it up. You hear what I'm saying? You haven't done nothing yet, man. Nothing we can't sort out. Between us, man. Between *us*.'

I gesture the space between him and me. And maybe silence is the trigger, but I have nothing else to say. I keep my eyes on his and I keep my arms open. His wooden eyes start to move rapidly again. He ducks his head, can't meet my gaze, looks down at the knife in his hand. 'Me, Johnny, Errol,' he mumbles. 'You had us all sucking on your dick, man. You was... you was – '

The gold flashes on Johnny's rings as he tightens his grip on the back of one of the stacking chairs we've been sitting on. I see the movement almost peripherally, but Floyd catches the tiny flicker of my eyeballs and inhales sharply, gripping the knife tightly again.

Johnny pulls the chair up and jabs it viciously at Floyd, legs-first. One leg catches him on the cheek-bone, one in the crotch. He cries out in a high voice and the knife goes skittering off over the edge of the stage. His pain tears at me, his fear thrills through me.

Love and darkness they can both tear your world apart turn it inside out and the fear the fear is terrible – love for me darkness for Floyd God plays with dice crooked dice chaos the meaning we chisel through will alone the meaning we must carve chisel construct.

I shoulder into him. He stumbles back, half-turns, trips over another chair and falls. I can smell his bad breath and stale, damp clothes as I straddle him with my knees on the points of his armpits. His eyes are the eyes of a stranger.

Perhaps for always.

I touch the side of his face. It's already livid. He struggles for a moment, then goes limp. Tears slide out of the sides of his stranger's eyes and I don't know what or who they're for.

His chest rises and falls under my spread thighs and crotch.

Neither of us could have won.

His eyes meet mine again, and I think I see a recognition there. But maybe it's only a reflection. Maybe I'm only seeing myself.

JOHNNY

After Jazz let him up, Errol take Floyd go sit him down. Carlton embrace him star, them squeeze each other tight. Me put me arm round Mrs Churchill, guide she toward the door. Me hope she no have no weak heart or noting cos she skin the colour a ash.

Johnny! Is Carlton call me name. Me turn to face him. Him only come and plant a lickle kiss pon me fucking cheek, man!

Thanks, him say. Me slap him neck, give it a squeeze. Skin soft, smooth. Then me go leave wit the old lady.

In the car me laugh, yunno. Cos the bwoy finally trust me.

JAZZ

Carly's tremblings gradually melt into my body. We slowly let each other go. I'm suddenly bursting for a piss but I can't just slope off to use the toilet. Then I look round and see I can because Johnny's dealing with Mrs Churchill, Errol's dealing with Floyd.

My brothers.

FLOYD

Errol's face is like in a dream.

Whassup, man? he's saying.

I didn't have the bottle, man, I say.

Didn't want to have the bottle.

You better talk with Jazz, yeah.

I can't, man.

Sure you can, guy. He ain't mad at you, yeah, except over

Zarjazz, right. And I'm mad at you over that too, yeah. He *understands*. He ain't no fool. Carlton ain't no fool neither.

You tight with 'em, star?

Yeah, I'm tight with 'em. They're tight with me. Like with Johnny.

Shit, man...

What they do in bed ain't our business, guy, so long as they're up there for Black people.

Shit, man. You're just turned on by that freak shit.

You're talking shit, star. Talk sense or keep your mouth shut, yeah. Don't go dissing people who give a shit, you know what I'm sayin'?

It ain't natural, man.

What, like kissing?

What you on about, man? Like man and woman, yeah?

Yeah.

Course it's natural.

There's tribes in Africa where they don't kiss, man. They think it's gross. Dirty.

Who gives a fuck, man?

You saying they ain't natural?

Bullshit, man.

They're natural or not, man?

Yeah, yeah, what you on about?

Just, it looks to me like natural don't mean nothing except what we want it to mean, star.

Who cares, man? Ain't nothing but words, yeah.

Like nigger'n faggot are just words, man?

Shut up, man.

I try and get up but me legs are so fucking tired and I just want to sleep or fucking die or whatever. I feel so cold I start shivering.

I'll get you some tea, man.

Thanks.

The high-five so weak it's a fucking low-five, man. I feel a hundred years old, and I ain't slept for seventy-eight of 'em, you know what I'm sayin'?

I can't look in Errol's eyes, man. Cos if I look I'll see it ain't nothing to him. Shitting on the Bible. Not that I believe in that shit or nothing, you know? So I look at Jazz out the sides of me eyes instead. Man, that's a *dirty* way to be, man. When he was on me I felt sick, you know what I'm sayin'? Like I was going to puke. Like I was a bitch too.

Shit, man. Why don't it bother them none? They're all battyboy too? Nah, Johnny ain't no – Errol ain't one neither.

He was on top of me, man. *On top of me.*

Shit.

I'm so fucking tired, man. *Astrid Zarjazz Jazz* no.

Cut him I'd've got fucking Aids, man.

On top of me. Moving about like he could do anything, man. I can't accept that, man. Whatever the fuck the others wanna do I ain't gonna accept that. *I* ain't gonna – it makes me sick, man. *On top of me.* Makes me *sick.*

Shit.

On top of me –

ERROL

Floyd puts one hand up, covers his eyes, hunches over. On the top of his head, off on one side, there's a bald patch and a scab. Shit –

Cousin of mine, he was a schizo. He used to turn up looking like Floyd looks outside me auntie's yard. Scream stuff. They'd lock him up, let him out, lock him up, let him out, you know? In the end he done himself in.

Man, the first official action of the Panther Posse been *one* event, you know what I'm saying?

I look over at Jazz. He's wired, man. Nervous like a racehorse. Carly too. Me? I just feel whacked, guy. I just want to get home to me bed, get under the covers, smoke some smoke.

And for once I'm thanking God I ain't got no-one to share it with.

CARL

Jazz disappears off to find the toilet, so I go and sit by Errol, on the other side of him to Floyd.

'You okay, man?' Errol asks me.

I nod slightly, look round him at Floyd. He's got quite a sweet face in a homely kind of way, Floyd, big slanty eyes, dimples, but beat-up looking at present. Like some kid sent off to war come back again.

But all the same there's a hardness in my heart against him, you know? All the others, Jazz included, want to just let him off the hook. But I can't just forget, you know? Not the knife. Or the words. Cos that stands for something, for all the shit I've ever faced in my life. Or ever run away from.

It's like what it must be like when you're a Jew and you meet some old guy from the SS and they're just this old guy but they've also done these things and gone along with these things. So, like, one way they're just this person you can maybe even feel sorry for, but another way you can't ever forgive them. Or, to be more gruelling, they're someone you maybe could fancy and then they've done these things.

But I'm no Christian, girlfriend, for better or worse. I don't read no Leviticus, and I don't turn no other cheek.

If there's one thing this world's got to spare, it's bigots, you know?

JAZZ

Outside the rain's stopped and the stars are out. The air's still heavy with water vapour but the storm's passed. Water fills puddles like glass, slides down drains. I breathe in the ozone, stretch my tight chest.

After I lock up the hall and drop off the key we walk to the tube station, four beautiful Black men, side by side.

Errol catches Floyd's shoulder. 'Need somewhere to crash, guy?' Floyd nods. Then he touches skin with me. 'I'll bell you, man.'

'Later,' I say.

Errol puts up his palm. Carly meets it. 'Later, man.'

They pass by the empty ticket-booth on up the stairs to the platform. Just as they disappear from sight a train rumbles in overhead.

I feel like I should just go home and be quiet but the star-light's filling my heart and I want to run wild. I can tell Carly needs a bit of wildness too. It feels as if nights have rolled by, but it's only ten o'clock.

A stone's been lifted from my back: not just the weight of Floyd's threat of violence but the fear that the others wouldn't stand by me, by me and Carly, in the face of that violence, that straight man's terror and rage.

Things will never be the same again. But then, I don't want them to be.

I feel *fierce.*

CARL

Jazz grabs my hand and we're running through the night-time streets, our sneakers scattering chandeliers, our breath ragging in the cold air. There are no shadows, there's only the velvet drapes of night like the city's a fashion show and we're the Future Supermodels.

Jazz hails a cab and it actually stops for two niggers. We go over to Molly's, pick up our stuff. Then finally we're going back to our block. Since my flat has a lock on it, we go in there. I still feel, like, a atmosphere of danger. *But it was Johnny who kicked in Jazz's door,* that's why that. *And the crazy after us was Floyd who's presumably at least no longer hiding behind curtains with kitchen knives to carve up homos.* So what's left to be frightened of?

The ten thousand other Floyds in this city, girlfriend, that's what. Black, white, young, old, whatever class or sex or even fucked-up sexuality. Breaking 'em down one at a time just isn't fast enough, you know?

Jazz, he's a optimist. Maybe I'm just not one, you know?

JAZZ

I'm still feeling elated as I stretch out on Carly's bed but he's come down fast. I get up and slide round behind him, grab him round the waist and nibble his ear.

'What's the matter, man?'

He doesn't answer for a moment. 'The way you just let

him off, Jazz. You know?' His voice is harsh. 'I don't know how you could do it, that's all.'

'Because he loved me,' I answer him. I feel his body tense against mine. I don't really want to explain it, but I know I'll have to try. I sigh softly. 'Floyd loved me, man, that's all. He admired me. I was like a teacher to him. We were friends, but I was also this educator. As well as that I had these two women dangling – ' My voice catches. 'Anyway, anyway he looked up to me and was always loyal to me. Like a brother. There was that brotherly love.' Or what I imagine brotherly love must be like. 'A hero.' I shrug. 'I guess maybe there was some subconscious sex thing going on too. So when he found out about me, it blew a fuse. But the madness happened because he loved me. Which is why I forgave him.'

'But he might've killed you, or slashed you. Or me, you know?'

And all I can say is, 'But he didn't, Carly.'

It's his turn to sigh. 'Does he still love you, then?' he asks, an edge to his voice. I shrug again.

'It's something me and him will have to work out between us. If we can. If he wants to. But I can't just – shut him out, that's all. Not if he really needs me – '

'Jazz – '

'I know, I know, man.' I hug Carly tighter, close my eyes. 'But I *need* him to need me, you know? Me as I really am. D'you – ?'

But I know Carly does.

CARL

The club is hot and heaving. Sweat runs down the walls. Girl, the children are fierce tonight! Even the dancefloor packed crotch to ass. And Jazz is ripping it up, I'm telling you, in just black leather shorts, long and Black-Panther-comic-book-lean and gliding oil and sweat, working it, girl. There's gold on his fingers, his eyelids, crimson and gold on his lips, my twin brother-sister-lover-friend. He tosses his head, his mouth white and pink and gold, and works his butt, his dark eyes on mine, shining and wild and free and not afraid of anything.

Work it, girl. On the runway –

And I forget he's been a stripper, like there's that trashy side to him. And it isn't just throwaway, just body, just surface, it comes from all the way down, you know? From the place which you can never run away from cos it's what you really are. What Jazz is. Like not in Black Revolutionary Drag, yeah? But really A Black Revolutionary in Drag.

Or – yeah – A Black Drag Revolutionary.

If you need a box to put him in.

Jazz grinds his crotch against mine and we melt into each other. Bits of us melt into the other people on the dancefloor. Shit, girlfriend, *this* is the *real* Real.

JAZZ

It's all so – for once it all makes sense; the stripper, the performer, the speaker, the activist, are simply stretched along a continuum. There doesn't have to be an inherent contradiction, not to me, even if there will always seem to be one to others.

But then freedom isn't easy. It isn't safe. It isn't always even sane.

If Floyd could see me now. I realise I wish he could see me this way, wreathed in freedom, crossing barriers to find myself, playing with this drag and glamour unafraid because I am a man. And since my masculinity does not reside in these things they cannot rob me of it, any more than Carly inside my body firm against my prostate turns my open arsehole into a vagina.

What does rob you of it, then? Floyd asks, his voice edged in my imagination.

Thinking other people's thoughts, man, I say. *Living other people's lives. Shit like that that keeps you as a child.*

You got a weird idea of what makes you a man, he says, shaking his head.

Yeah? I say. But he's grinning. Unsure, but grinning.

When Carly made me up it seemed to pull out something from inside me. Each time I flicked a glance in the side mirror on his dressing-table my face would be altered and telling a slightly different tale. Showing a different facet.

You can't always reach for truth directly, you see: sometimes you have to catch it out of the corner of your eye.

It's strange as well that something someone else paints onto your skin can open up something inside you: I had a sense of revealed unity. Not of plastering over cracks but of seeing that from the right angle, and in the right light, everything was in harmony. Is in harmony.

I think of Sly, damaged Sly, and for the first time in my life I acknowledge that we are twins.

And also for the first time, I pity him.

Shame is a terrible thing.

CARL

We taxi home at four a.m. The geezer's black with a attitude and at first I think he's got a problem, you know? But then from the way he catches my eye in the rear-view mirror I decide it's more like a interest.

One of the many who fancy a dip but don't want to get wet. Or they would if they'd brought a towel etcetera.

Jazz doesn't notice. Or maybe as a ex-closet-case he doesn't want to be reminded of how other brothers are not so sorted out as he reckons he is.

Paying for the ride, I smile at the guy and he smiles back. There's a diamond in the smile. He touches a finger to his white funfur flat cap and pulls out.

Yardie drag.

'He was into it,' Jazz says with a quiet chuckle as we wait for the lift. He catches my eye shyly, then looks down. Scrub my earlier asssessment. But there's something else.

'What's up, man?' I ask him as the lift doors open.

'You don't – ' He looks away for a second. 'Just because I tried this – ' he gestures at his made-up face, then abruptly: 'You wouldn't've rather gone with him?'

Jazz looks so worried I can't resist reading him a bit: 'I thought that doesn't make you less of a man or anything.'

'It doesn't,' he says quickly. 'But it might. To you.'

I take his hand. A tremor runs through his hooked fingers. I earth it. 'I love you,' I say. 'and it doesn't make a difference. Like the sister says, *We come into the world naked. All the rest is drag.'*

I consider chucking in a snappy line of the *Anyway I bet he doesn't shave it and I don't fancy getting pubic hairs stuck between my teeth* variety, but I don't.

I just kiss Jazz hard and wrap my arms around his broad, well-muscled back as the lift starts to rise.

'Make love to me, Jazz,' I whisper hoarsely, going for a Technicolor moment.

JAZZ

It's six when the sirens wake me. I snap upright in bed with a sharp suck of breath. Carly's nappy head slips from my belly to my crotch. He murmurs something but doesn't wake up. Sweat trickles down my shaven armpits as I hear car doors slam outside, the sound carries to my ears with preternatural sharpness, so clear it's heightened, like a dream I once had where a bunch of my teeth broke and snapped and fell out and I held one in the palm of my hand wishing it could be what it was, a dream. But knowing it wasn't one because the tooth felt too real, realer than real.

But this is no dream.

Fire-doors bang.

The lift whirs and moves.

I blink and exhale, not moving.

And the door bursts open and they twist my arms up behind my back and they see my shaved body and they go he's a pervert he's got drugs up there and they stick a truncheon up me until something bursts inside and they go he's loving it the other one'll love it too and I try to stop them but they go pervert cop-killer and I don't feel like no Ice-T as they smash Carly's face on the corner of a table destroying an eye –

My heart cramps and my tongue welds to the roof of my mouth. I slip out from under Carly, cradling his head in one hand. *Do that much right, man.* He mumbles some more but he's not awake. I try to say something about a glass of water but my mouth is too dry.

No-one's going to touch my baby, my man , I think as I pull on black sweat-pants, jam my feet into a pair of Timberlands *hard shoes.* I slip out into the corridor, pulling the flat's front door closed behind me.

I can hear the pigs on the stairs; words I can't understand, radios farting static. I can't breath and I'm bursting for a shit from all our fucking. I ought to run but I don't, I just stand there, letting fate fuck me over, abdicating free will. *But they won't touch Carly. At least that.*

A door bangs below me. There's shouting, scuffling, feet clattering up concrete steps. They're getting to this floor. Other doors slam. Somewhere a woman is screaming, a white woman, and the feet in the stairwell are Uzis firing in South Central. The firedoor at the end of the passage judders violently open and a white geezer drunk and big and crazy with fucked-up tattoos on his face and blood all down the front of his grubby white vest explodes out of it, behind him pigs in dark blue and black.

I'm so tense I let out a yell and spring back into the doorway. A burly pig brings the white guy down like a rugby pro just five feet from where I'm standing. Then the other pigs are all over him. The drunk's snarling like a wild animal and they're none too gentle. But it wasn't *his* blood, you know what I'm saying?

And for once I'm invisible to them, watching it all like Ra, affecting cool, my heart pounding *not me not me not me they didn't want me*, a whisper of a smile on my papery lips as the pigs wrestle clumsily with the drunk, rolling around in a lame manner that looks almost funny.

Not how they'd do it for TV.

Suddenly Carly steps out into the corridor, wild-eyed and beautiful, smooth brown satin in white Calvin Kleins, vulnerable as a startled deer. I put a bare arm around his bare shoulders to pull him to me, and we're both invisible now.

We watch the gradually slowing scrum for a moment. Then I realise that any second now the pigs are going to get interested in the two of us standing there so I say 'C'mon' to Carly and we slip back into the flat. I lock the door behind us.

CARL

Jazz so tough, but when the door closed he starts to like

shudder. Not even just tremble, you know? And I was scared but I'm not scared now so I hold him tight.

'It's alright, bwoy,' I whisper.

'I'm just tired,' he says, his voice catching. But he doesn't let go of me, just holds me tighter. We stand that way until the sounds of footsteps and police cars and radios all fade away, skins chilling in the five a.m. air.

'I'm getting cold, baby,' I say softly. 'Let's go back to bed.'

Jazz slowly releases me, lets me lead him to the bedroom, his fingers a butterfly's tongue in the petals of my hand. The light from the bedside lamp catches smudges of silver on his cheeks. I reach up to smear them away with the heel of my hand, thinking they're make-up. But they aren't.

They're tears.

JAZZ

Fear of failure. Like my father.

A vivid snapshot of my childhood: *My old man holding me under the arms, around my chest, I feel so warm and safe as he whirls me around in the park among the scarlet, amber and rust of the autumn leaves. A vortex – no – no memory, a fantasy, not even that, just TV ad images retinted. Reality: Carly holding me under the arms, pulling my shoulders back, I feel so warm and safe as he slides inside me, in and out of me, I feel so loved.*

Sly on the kitchen lino. A little glass from the shattered light-bulb, but no blood. Just his eyes funny and dead. Shuttered from inside. A mirror broken.

The man, the Black man who wanted me to beat him till he screamed, it was so easy, too easy, he was so like my old man. In that room where he's tied to the bed with stuff he bought and I'm using the belt he gave me on him and wearing shit I'm embarrassed to be wearing because the pain and the humiliation and self-laceration are my father's gifts and I'm paying them back. One for Sly one for my mother her personality erased too One for me, oh yeah. And he screamed but I didn't stop until I was finished. And then I was finished.

And Carly is a way off that narrow path of masculinity that seemed like the whole world when I was walking it, a way

195

out. The moment I kissed him I didn't need my old man any more.

To love or hate.

I drift off to sleep in Carly's arms.

CARL

By ten I just can't sleep any more. The sun's glittering like diamante through a crack in the curtains, like the world's a diamond, waiting to be worn. I leave Jazz snoring, have a bath, shave my butt, crotch, armpits, legs, everything. Perfect like a piece of Lalique glass and *twice* as smooth, girl. Sat in front of my dressing-table I get a androgynous intuition there's going to be battles today, so I go for fashion heavy metals; silver on me eyelids and lips, outline in charcoal. Stainless steel slot-eyed disco wraparounds, plate-metal junk-jewellery. Cane-rows still tight against my scalp, silver on my fingernails.

I wriggle into a silver lycra mini-dress, pull on steel-plate-fronted bike-boots, check myself in the mirror. *Snap snap snap* ain't no-one gonna mess with me, girlfriend! I accessorise with a matte silver clutch-bag before sashaying out to pick up a classy and expensive romantic breakfast for two from M&S. I'm thinking Naomi as the lift doors open but as this girl hits the courtyard it's pure Grace.

Slave to the rhythm of 'My Jamaican Guy', even if I don't have no bulletproof heart, you know?

It's a beautiful warm autumn day and I feel high and floaty and I guess I'm also getting off on kind of a reaction against the more macho drags of the previous few days also.

On a street corner two fly sisters are shaking it down to the ground to a Walkman with two pairs of headphones. They giggle as I pass.

'Sashay, Shante,' they call, working their booties to the beat. Girls got back, you know? I throw my shoulders back cos the streets are *my* runway, you know?

It's one of those days people seem to leave the homophobia at home for once, you know? Probably plugged in to recharge but I can deal with that.

Just not *every* second of *every* day, you know?

JAZZ

When I finally jump out of bed I find a note from Carly written in soft silver pencil saying he's gone to get us some food. I feel *awake*; everything seems crystalline. I feel like I've had the best sleep I've had for years as well. But still there's a tension in the atmosphere, like a dangerous resonance in the crystal, a kind of low-energy hum that could make something fracture.

I put on a CD to drown it out, one from Carly's almost non-existent rap collection, the truly phat Disposable Heroes of Hiphoprisy, and groove around the flat while my bath runs.

'Dehumanising the victim makes things easier/ It's like breathing with a respirator' I shout, getting down to the only rap outfit who've ever challenged homophobia and hit because they throw down the truth like a gauntlet, guy!

'Eases the conscience of even the most conscious/ And calculating violator/ But death is the silence/ In this cycle of violence.'

'Tell it like it is, man!' I respond, cranking up the volume. Then I remember my bath, and sprint through to turn it off just before it causes an un-neighbourly disputation by overflowing and pouring through to the floor below.

I'm just shaving my balls when I realise someone's thumping on the front door. Of course I immediately feel embarrassed that someone's there while this is what I'm doing. And then I think it's probably the music except the only people in this block who are old enough to complain are usually too drunk to notice.

The thumping carries on. With a sigh and a grunt I pull myself out of the bath.

'Who is it?' I shout, thinking maybe Carly forgot his keys. There's no reply but the thumping stops. So of course that makes me curious. Before opening the door I knot a large black-and-white towel round my waist. In a flashback to the last few days I also slide open a Stanley knife and place it on a shelf behind the door where I can grab it up easily.

I open the door.

It's Judy.

I'm in Carly's flat.

The flat, the towel, the stubble under my balls, she's got three edges and she's not even in the room. She doesn't move or speak, she just looks me up and down, then kisses her teeth. But her eyes aren't filled with contempt, there's something else there, something cold and lambent. She's dressed smartly, for an office job, for whatever job she's got now.

'I was on me way to work,' she says tonelessly, stops. Then, 'I just come to see if it was true.'

'What?'

'What Errol said.'

'What did Errol say?'

She spits in my face but there's not much there. It lands on one side of my nose. I blink. I don't punch her out. I expect her to turn and go but she doesn't. She just keeps standing there. My shaved legs and arse goosebump.

'Ain't you gonna arx me in?' she says.

I shrug, let her pass inside. I owe her this. Unless she tries to hurt Carly in any way.

I expected anger but she's not giving me anger. Anger's easy for me to deal with. It's like a bright jacket, it's like a mirror. I look into her eyes again. There's no reflection; they're matte-black flat, or pits. *The bathwater's getting cold*, I'm thinking.

Judy looks round Carly's flat disinterestedly.

JUDY

He's still so beautiful it makes me hate meself. Makes me remember stories of women who did think them did know angels, but it turn out they was demons, just silvery and deceiving of the eye. I'm turned on I'm white with rage I'm dead.

Why why why any of it, man? *Why?*

It was so hard to come here. So fucking hard.

I don't know what I'm going to do or say. What I want. Nothing. Because I'm nothing. So I just watch. And listen.

And suddenly it's easy.

JAZZ

I close the door behind her.

'I've got to go finish in the bathroom,' I say. She probably nods, but it's just a shiver of flesh. I lock the bathroom door, dunk my arse in the tub and rapidly finish off.

I quickly rub cocoa butter into my smooth skin as the bathwater sucks away, then pull on my Nike tracksuit pants and a pair of black Fila hi-tops. I can move now, and quickly. No vulnerable bare feet.

The Stanley knife.

I open the bathroom door sharply. Judy's still standing in the middle of the room. I can see the knife's still there without looking at it directly, which I don't want to do, because maybe she's the crazy one, the really dangerous one, not Johnny, not Floyd.

It would be too shitty to be just. But still. Shit.

I ought to offer her tea or coffee but I don't want to do anything that'll be an excuse for her to stay and I don't want this to drag out. So I don't offer her anything.

If time went any slower it'd be going backwards.

Judy looks down, bites her lip. Some moment has passed. Something she was going to say or do she can't say or do now.

There's the rattle of a key in a lock.

Carly's back.

CARL

So there's Jazz and this woman just standing there staring at each other like my room's a shop display and they're the dummies. She glances at me, looks back at Jazz. She's doing all the right things, but she's not quite pretty.

She hasn't got *innocence*, you know? She's got like a sadness, but it's a bitter sadness and she knows it. *Major loser*, Molly'd say. But I can't be that hard. I put down my Marks & Spencer foodhall carrier bags. Still silence.

Unable to bear a vacuum I say, 'I got us some coffee. Anyone like a cup? S'mocha.' Vacuous in a vacuum. Even more silence.

'Carl, this is Judy,' Jazz says finally. 'Judy, this is Carlton.'

I guessed it was her. Another unhappy cast-off, come for some sort of, I dunno. *Something*, you know? I could leave, wait outside, but I can tell Jazz doesn't want me to go. I want to go and put my arms round his waist but I don't, I go through to the kitchen, pull out two foil packets of mocha and put them on a shelf, making sure to keep the living-room in full view all the time I'm doing this.

Judy doesn't look at me coming and going, just takes in Jazz's eyes, the way they look at her when he talks, the way they look at me. She doesn't even know he stole a horse for me. But she knows the rest and she's afraid: she can tell from his eyes that he's *my* dark knight and she's been fooling herself. That it was all pointless. That she could never have won. Oh, and I've been there, girlfriend, I've sung torch-songs for the straight boys who captured something in me. Fences have two sides, you know?

'It's wrong what you're doing,' she says out of nowhere. 'It says in the Bible. It's against God.'

'Men wrote the Bible. Not God.' Jazz's voice is level, intense.

'It was His will,' she replies flatly.

'Like the Koran was Allah's will?' She shrugs. 'They can't both be God's will because they contradict each other.' No reaction. 'Millions of people believe in the Bible. Millions of people believe in the Koran, right? And one lot's got to be wrong, right? Maybe both.'

'You just don't believe in nothing.' Her voice is sullen. It's all too weird for a bubblehead like me.

'I just don't have the brass to say I know what God thinks,' Jazz says, not letting her get away with anything. 'I don't know why I'd believe that someone else does.'

'It ain't natural,' she says, getting in every tired line every tired bigot ever trotted out. But she's not really engaged. Her eyes have slipped out of gear with her face.

'That process ain't natural, Judy. That plastic handbag ain't natural, but you use it. A Walkman ain't natural. Anaesthetic's not natural. So what? You're going to refuse it if you need it?'

But she's not listening. She turns to me, a weird look on

her face, so weird I ask, 'Are you okay, girl?' before I've even thought about it.

'He don't never shut up, man,' she says. 'You noticed that?' I don't say anything. The conversation, well it's never really been a conversation, but now it's just lines snatched out of the air. I look over at Jazz but she drags my eyes back onto hers.

'You like it then,' she asks me. 'Bending over for a killer?'

I don't get it. She reads my blankness. 'Sucking a murderer's cock? Ain't he told you, then?' She looks at Jazz. I look at him too. I can't read his eyes. 'You ain't told your new *boyfriend*, man?' she says to him, but it's to me really.

Jazz raise a hand to slap her but stops himself. His eyes are cold. His face is like a mask with a stranger underneath it.

'You should of been more honest, Jazz,' she says.

JAZZ

'You should of been more honest, Jazz,' she says, and I know it's the one line she planned on saying before she came here.

The crazy one the really dangerous one.

Carly's face is turbulent. His eyes dart from me to Judy, Judy to me. I want to take him in my arms but I can't. Not because she's here, but because I can't reach across the rent she's torn between us.

I've torn myself.

You should of been more honest.

I can feel tears sliding out of my right eye, the emotional undisciplined side of my brain. Shit I could say to Judy flashes past so fast, so razor-sharp and thin it's not even thoughts, nowhere near words.

The bag falling through the night exploding red Carly knows.

Carly turns and runs.

Judy pins me like a Medusa. My breathing starts to hyperventilate. Tears from her staring eyes run down her cheeks. She knuckles them away harshly. Her eyelids flutter.

'I'm sorry,' she mutters. 'I'm sorry you and me couldn't – I'm sorry you couldn't – shit, man.' She looks down. 'Shit. Look, later, alright, man?' She glances at me as she stumbles over to the door.

'I'm sorry, Jazz.'

Then they're both gone.

CARL

I jump on the back of a 36 at a red light even though I haven't got a pass or money or anything cos I just have to get somewhere I can think, you know?

Fortunately the conductor's a rastafarian with so much attitude that stuff like checking passes and dishing out tickets is completely beneath him. Which is good for me but unfortunate for a bunch of German tourists trying to get to the Trocadero.

I head across Kensington Gardens to the bridge where Jazz took me on the horse that night.

Shit, girlfriend, you think I *don't* want him to find me? Snap snap *snap*. But he's got to find me by looking into his own self, you know what I'm saying?

But even if he does, girl, what then?

JAZZ

As I'm pulling on my leather parka my mind starts churning over: *What if he's lost it and in some desperate moment done something stupid, something irreversible?* I cringe at the thought: the terror, the void. And my own arrogance – someone doing that over me? And face it, man, you've got to be tough just to be Black in this time and place, to be Black and homosexual doubly so. Being disappointed in love won't make you go jump off the nearest bridge, even if you might go there for the drama of it, for the view.

We're survivors, man. We aren't that frail.

The image of bridges makes me think where Carly might go. For a Technicolor moment.

I hail for a cab. A racist eyes me up and turns his fucking light out. Twenty feet past me a red light pulls him up. I'm so wired I want to scream so I go up there and scream through his open window, *DON'T YOU STOP FOR NIGGERS YOU*

FILTHY MOTHERFUCKER! He's so freaked he pulls out through the red light and wavers across the junction getting blasted by the oncoming traffic.

'Racist mother*fucker*!' I yell, throwing an orange-crate after the cab onto the road. It splits and gets run over by a Bedford van. People are looking at me in a disinterested way. My anger punctures, deflates.

Get the fucking bus, man, I think to myself. *Or try another cab. They aren't* all *racists, yeah. And there's enough brothers out there working in Babylon. Let them catch your fare, nuh, man?*

CARL

In the day it's not magical, it's just some park with straights ambling about, people walking dogs, kids, mothers, nannies, tourists etcetera. The air's cool on my bare arms. A cloud covers the sun, turning off the colours. My mind's not working, my thoughts are just whirring like a hoverfly's wings, iridescent, so fast they're slow. It's like time just slowly stops. The air goes solid like perspex.

The bag.

What's in there? I ask.

Bad memories, Jazz says.

Sound starts up again. I turn round cos I hear something in the fallen leaves. Jazz is standing there, watching me.

He found me.

He's so beautiful, girl. I breathe out, swallow. The sun comes out from behind the clouds, making the leaves glitter white gold behind him. He holds out a hand with gold on it. I'm as nervous as I was the first time we were here but somehow now I'm not afraid – of *him*.

But still I can't just take his hand. You know?

'So tell me, Jazz,' I say, keeping my hands at my sides.

His beautiful brown eyes are full of fear.

'I could tell you easier if you'd just hold my hand, man,' he says, his voice bleak but under it begging. And maybe it's wrong, and maybe I'm not shrewd or nothing, but I know he's not going to hurt me. So I do hold his hand.

He literally gasps with relief, almost the sound of someone who's going to throw up. His grip is almost painful it's so tight, his need is the sort of terrible need that makes you want to pull away. Unless you love the person fi true. For Real.

I don't pull away.

We walk hand-in-hand and slow as lovers idling away a sunny afternoon. But we're not idle, we're out there fighting for it all, you know?

'What was it like?' I ask him.

'It was easy,' he says, staring out into the endless sky. 'It was like I was in a movie, you know? Like a kid playing cops and robbers. Like, you've got a gun, you get caught in a tight corner and you use it because that's what it's there for. You know? Just like being on TV. And even the geezer going down was just like special effects. He was like an extra. So it was easy. It wasn't real. Until afterwards.'

JAZZ

Yeah, but at the time it was panic, guy. Tell him that.

'I shouldn't've brought the gun, man. I know that. But I did. And when I used it, it was all like, so sudden, I just *used* it.'

Yeah, that's how little it meant, how little it revealed, no God-like revelation, no insight into the mind of a murderer or even just human nature. And I know I should say killing's wrong. That I did a wrong thing, and I did, but I don't regret it, except abstractly. Because I'm here with him. Because the battle lines are clear.

'Was it like someone you knew?' Carly asks.

'No, it was a policeman.'

'How?'

'We were burglarising a place for funds.'

'You, Johnny, Errol and Floyd, yeah?' Carly says.

I nod. *My posse*, I think. *Yeah. Four lives saved from being fucked up. I can't regret it.*

'Look,' I say, and I can hardly choke the words out. 'You can't do nothing about the past, right? If I could resurrect the guy and make it all not have happened I'd do that because I don't have the right, no-one has the right, to say who ought to live or who ought to die. Or to carry out what they say, yeah?

But I can't, so – maybe I don't care that much. Maybe I don't care enough. Maybe I wish I did but I don't. Like taking out an enemy soldier, right? You don't know them, you don't wish them any harm or nothing personally, but they're the enemy and you've got to survive, right? *Survive.'*

I look at Carly out of the corner of my eye but his mask of make-up is blank. All I can gauge is the pulse of his blood against my finger-tips, the tightness of his grip, but all they tell me is that he hasn't let go.

'All I can do is – ' I sigh. 'All *I* can do is try to do what matters, you know? Do the right thing. And if there is such a thing as atonement, find it that way.'

I've got nothing else to say so I stop. We walk on in silence for a while.

'Could you do it again?' Carly asks abruptly. His voice floats on the still air. Everything's sucked into this pin-point. I hear the sound of children playing, footballers shouting, car-horns.

'Yeah,' I say. My voice is firm now. 'If someone tried to fuck with you, yeah I would do it again. And it would be completely different, I couldn't pretend I wasn't doing what I was doing. It would be *terrifying,* yeah, but you're my star, man. My star and my lover. And I won't let *anyone* fuck up someone I love. And if that's too much of a macho trip for you, just think of it as like mother love, yeah?'

I grip Carly's shoulders, turn him to me and kiss him. He doesn't fight me. I feel his lips answering mine. I know he thinks I'm crazy but I know he doesn't care. Finally I let him breathe. His eyes are full and they take my breath away, they're so beautiful and terrifying. He looks down at my chest. When he speaks, there's a tremor in his voice.

'Let's go home,' he says.

CARL

Shot someone.

It's so strange, you know? A soldier. And not. And I can accept it, and not. Accept what he says about it. Maybe. Maybe that's not for me to do anyway. Maybe what helps me is that he did it for the others too, that there was this thing of sacrifice about it.

Maybe I'm just projecting, girl. Squeezing diamonds out of dirt.

But why *shouldn't* he be noble with it? Just cos we're what we are and where we are doesn't take all that away from us, doesn't, shouldn't steal all that from us, all the better stuff, you know? All the higher stuff. Just cos we're queers and niggers and of the gutter. Jazz right: it *is* a war. Because one way or the other, they don't want us to exist.

And Jazz has killed in that war. But I'm still not afraid of him. Because he killed to protect. Because *he's* afraid. Because he's carrying the weight of it and he's mixed up about it. And maybe I have to help him with a little of that weight. As much as a dainty little firestarter like me can manage, that is. Like, as a duty of war.

We come to the edge of the park, to Queensgate. His hand's strong and warm in mine and it's giving me strength so I don't let go of it.

I don't believe in living in the past, you know? Specially not somebody else's past. What happened then happened to him. What's happening now is happening to *us*. And I don't want *us* to become another victim of it, you know?

If it hadn't been for the gun we'd never have met. Well, connected, anyway. And that's a weight. A dead weight, you know? But that's only one side of the balance.

What we've got to do, me and Jazz, is tip the scales towards life. By what we do. Who we are. How we live.

And we will, girl. *Believe* me.

JAZZ

I thought he would drop my hand the moment we left the park because it was as if we were leaving this other place outside reality where judgement could be suspended and crossing the threshold, stepping back onto the harsh, bright streets where you have to deal with all of it, always, all of the time. With eyes wide open and pupils like pinpricks in the glare. But you can't stand outside reality, not even for a moment, and he doesn't let go of my hand: his fingers even tighten around mine as we stand waiting for the lights to change at the top of Queensway.

Red.

It was only when I told Carly about the shooting that I realised, really realised for the first time, that there was something to deal with, some wrong act.

Unarmed.

Panic. Fear.

To strive to be noble. To live as far as possible without regret. Yeah, so I'm conflicted. And maybe there's a lifetime knotted into that conflict. That's *my* problem.

Amber.

But a life can't be consumed with just that, with just what's past and gone. Not just with the dead, the discontinuous. Not my life, anyway. There's life demanding life: messy, bloody, violent, chaotic, dark and rich and tangled with love and hate and ecstasy, all of us defying death with every heartbeat, with every thrust.

Green.

In the rising elevator Carly and I hold each other close in the close, static air, hot flesh against hot flesh, blood answering blood, life thundering demanding, unrepentant against our eardrums.

Pressure reach.

CARL

Okay, so I got hitched to a crazy-ass motherfucker and not a well-heeled city gent like Auntie wanted, but she got to like him in the end, you know? (Maybe cos the first time Jazz met her he brought two pounds of Belgian chocolates as a gift, as suggested by me.) Anyway, she was happy enough to come to this picnic we organised for his birthday, his twenty-eighth birthday, which was in June. June 13th. The sun was hot and, girl, so was the company! The whole posse was there, sipping Dom Perignon and nibbling on smoked salmon sandwiches. Some illicit substances were imbibed, but not by me or Jazz (the new puritans!).

Caroline drove us out of town in her very upholstered

Daihatsu Fourtrak (with mobile phone and hands-free), Johnny following in his beat-up BMW (also with phone, making it like Jazz was Jackie Kennedy).

She takes us south to this crumbly old lichen-covered stone mansion at the top of a deep valley with a little stream and ponds called Lennard's Lee. You can't go in the house cos it's full of lords and ladies and whatnot, but you can go in the valley. It's long and deep and full of like amazing rhododendron bushes, well more like trees, with twisty, dark, shiny branches, all covered in big flowers, all great bursts of blue, white, purple, pink and red. And I'm no naturist or nothing, but it's like nature's the real fashion show today, you know what I'm saying?

We stroll down one of the little winding paths with our cooler-boxes and hampers, startling silver-haired old grannies from the home counties. But the place is so beautiful there's no ugliness coming from them: it's like we all just come to see the flowers, you know?

Right down in the valley the air is still and the scent of the rhododendrons floats all around us. We go and find a grassy bit by a pond. Big, chrome-green dragonflies dart about, sometimes landing on the round, flat leaves floating on the still surface of the water.

Auntie speads out a oriental rug for us to recline on. Auntie's looking fine in figure-hugging black leather salopettes, bike-boots, a peaked leather cap at an angle on his shaved head, and Raybans. There's a diamond in his ear and a string of pearls round his neck, a chain round his waist. He pops a bottle while I start putting out the food.

Johnny's brought Cockspur rum so we have that and beers as well as champagne. Caroline's not drinking except maybe a tiny bit of champagne, and no amount of drink seems to make any difference to Johnny's driving anyway.

Christopher and Kerry start pulling foil off the cold eats they've brought. Chris is the cute shaven-headed black guy who come to the first Neville L meeting, Kerry's his pretty blonde-braids white girlfriend. They didn't stop to talk or anything then, and we didn't even find out their names. But they showed up at the next one and asked if they could help do stuff and we said yeah of course and he's a advertising graphics guy so our publicity snapped up-market directly. Plus we all liked them which is why they're here on Jazz's birthday.

Did I say Caroline had the baby? Yeah, a little blonde baby boy with hazel eyes called Felix. He's just six weeks old. At the moment he's being rocked by Rafe, Caroline's new boyfriend, a cute biracial black guy with shoulder-length braids and a easy-going manner. They met just about a month after she dumped creepy Rupert, at the Royal College of Art where she started doing this MA. For part of her stuff she's been doing like photos of me! And Jazz. And me *and* Jazz, you know?

Which has been like a bit of light relief cos in the meantime me and Jazz and Johnny and Errol and Chris and Kerry have been busy fighting the good fight. Specially since Neville got off and the pigs who did what they did didn't get the sack or anything, so we're doing letters and petitions and stuff cos they ought to go down for it, you know? And other Justice League stuff like that, like with this racist murder that happened in May. And doing like a lot of marches and meetings and stuff also. Raising our profile as a group that supports other groups. And is also like, solidly pro-gay, and will address and promote those issues, which has already pissed off more than a few people, as you can imagine. But we turn up and get stuff done, so how much can they slag us down, you know?

Errol's even been getting down at Pressure Zone, he's so hip to things queer, even come to Heaven with me and Jazz to see RuPaul, you know? He hasn't got no girlfriend or nothing at present, but whoever does catch him in the end, she'll have one piece of luck, girl. Cos his mind and his heart are open. And that's not a common state, you know?

Johnny's brought a tough flygirl with him, who finds it funny that he hangs out with a bunch of faggots and a blonde princess. Shi name Sapphire ('It's what I was christened, man. Fi true!) and after we drunk a little champagne we get to swapping make-up tips and laughing a lot over Men so I guess she's okay.

Yeah, I know, I can't help being just a little tough on straight people even though they're just people too, I know.

Jazz is wearing a black lycra one-piece with a neon-yellow strip down the front and black Converse hi-tops over thick white socks, a black-and-white baseball cap with 'No Racism' on it in Rasta colours. Round his neck a Afrika medallion on a leather strip, and a black-edge pink triangle on a gold chain. Me, I'm wearing a black vest with a pink triangle on it, a punk black leather kilt and yellow Timberlands. I've got on just a whisper of foundation, a little plum lip-gloss. There's a revolver in my right ear and I've cut my hair in a Mohican, dyed it blond. Which freaked Jazz out when I did it, but he knows better'n to pull any of that self-hate crap on *me*. Anyway, like I didn't hesitate to tell him, all the best blondes are dyed anyway – Monroe, Madonna etcetera etcetera, and now me. He doesn't never tell me what to wear, or what not to wear. The nearest he gets to it is for meetings and stuff:

'What're you thinking of wearing?'

'This or that,' I say. 'Why?'

'Just so I know what to expect. So I can deal with it,' he says.

See, we love each other, right? But it's not a easy thing. It's not a pipe-and-slippers-and-Sunday-papers type of thing, that isn't going to work, not with the tribe of warriors and outlaws we run with, you know? What it is, it's a tough love.

A fierce love.

– THE END –

Also by John R. Gordon

Skin Deep

Two young and talented black men, photographer Ray and struggling actor Chris, are best friends. But Ray is only attracted to white men, while Chris is into heavy sexual masochism.

UK £9.95 (when ordering quote SKI 372)

Skin Deep was widely acclaimed, as well as winning the author a London Arts Literary award:

"Explores how racism and homophobia complicate our most intimate relationships." The Evening Standard

"Gordon knows how to weave an involving, character-driven story thick with both incident and debate." Lambda Book Report

"Skin Deep is thought-provoking and funny, subtly erotic and in-your-face by turns." Larry Duplechan

Black Butterflies

Wesley and Floyd were teenage tearaways in South London, best mates with a strong erotic charge sparking just below the surface. Floyd's tragic death brings Wesley together with Sharon, Floyd's girlfriend, in a marriage based on self-deceit.

UK £6.95 (when ordering quote BLA 996)